BEST SERVED COLD

BEST SERVED COLD

A Jack Dantzler Mystery

TOM WALLACE

Copyright © 2023 by Tom Wallace

All rights reserved.

No part of this book may be reproduced in any form or by any electronic or mechanical means, including information storage and retrieval systems, without written permission from the author, except for the use of brief quotations in a book review.

ISBN: 978-1-958414-30-9

Enigma House Press

Goshen, Kentucky 40026

www.enigmahousepress.com

For Marilyn: Your absence is profound.
"I am a cage, in search of a bird."

Kafka

The Jack Dantzler Mystery Series

Pit of Vipers (2022)

88 (2020)

The Journal (2019)

Heroes For Ghosts (2018)

Murder by Suicide (2017)

The Poker Game (2015)

The Fire of Heaven (2014)

The List (2013)

Gnosis (2011)

The Devil's Racket (2007)

What Matters Blood (2004)

Other Novels

O'Toole's Pub (2023)

Divine Rebel (2020)

Bloody Sundae (2020)

Heirs of Cain (2010)

Sports-Related Books

The University of Kentucky Basketball Encyclopedia

So, You Think You Are a University of Kentucky Basketball Fan

Golden Glory: The History of Central City Basketball

Inside/Outside: A Behind the Scenes Look at Kentucky Basketball

Chapter One

A lengthy prison sentence tends to impact a man's body in one of three ways: he sits on his ass, eats too much, gets soft, flabby and fat; he detests prison food, loses weight and gets thin; or, and this depends on how much time he spends lifting weights (or the extent of his steroid use), he beefs up, becomes muscle-bound and stronger than Samson. Few prisoners remain at the weight they had on the day they were incarcerated.

Tommy Doyle was the exception. He tipped the scales at one-ninety on day one, and now, thirty years into a life-with-out-parole sentence, his weight had never fluctuated more than five pounds north or south of what he weighed on that day when his cell door slams shut. He had managed this miracle by watching what he ate, which meant staying away from the shitty, fat-inducing prison chow. Rather than eat that nasty stuff, early on he came up with a different dietary approach. He'd only eat what he thought best for him. To do this he enlisted the help of his wife Connie. Each

Saturday when she came to visit, she supplied the food. Connie brought enough to get Tommy through the week, provided he was careful and rationed the portions properly. His plan wasn't perfect; on occasion he ran out of food before her next visit, thus forcing him to eat—nibble, more precisely—prison food. But his system, combined with daily walks around the prison yard, proved successful in helping him maintain his normal weight.

Connie came every Saturday for the first three years. She stayed about an hour, handed him his weekly rations, they talked, then she left. Connie was a blessing. No wife could have been more loyal. Until she wasn't. The end came suddenly. One Saturday she showed up as usual with Tommy's food. Along with divorce papers she wanted him to sign. She met someone, she said, they had fallen in love and planned to marry. Tommy wasn't surprised; he didn't figure Connie would remain married to a man destined to spend his life in a prison cell. He couldn't blame Connie for wanting her freedom. What healthy, red-blooded woman wouldn't? She had desires, urges that needed to be satisfied. So, he quickly agreed to sign the papers. On one condition. Connie had to swear she would never change their daughter Nikki's last name. Under no circumstances, regardless of who Connie married, or how many times she might get married in the future. Tommy demanded his now six-year-old daughter would always be a Doyle. Connie agreed, Tommy signed the papers, and beginning next Saturday his brother Ray visited and brought the food.

For the next seven years Ray showed up alone. Always with a smile, food in hand and no shortage of tall tales to tell. Tommy enjoyed those visits, loved hearing Ray's stories, most of which were outright lies or half-truths at best. Then on a cold Saturday in January, Ray arrived as usual. Only this time he wasn't alone. He was accompanied by a young girl. She was tall for her age, had dark hair, blue eyes and strong facial features. Tommy took one look at her and knew instinctively this was Nikki, the daughter he had not laid eyes on since the day he left for prison. She was three at the time, and he made Connie swear to never let Nikki see him behind bars. It was a promise Connie kept.

Now here she was in the flesh, a pretty, tom-boyish thirteen-year-old who gave every indication she would one day blossom into a beautiful woman. In truth, Tommy thought, she was already beautiful, braces and all. He had a hard time believing he could have fathered such a lovely creature.

Tommy's emotions were splintered, however. He was pleased to see his daughter, while at the same time he was disappointed a long-held promise had been broken. This was unacceptable. Ray knew the rules, yet he chose to disobey.

"Why is she here, Ray?" Tommy asked, once they were all seated. He made no attempt to conceal the anger in his voice. "This is not what I wanted. You knew that."

"Look, Tommy, I . . ."

"Why are you asking him?" Nikki interrupted, her voice strong and confident. "Shouldn't you be talking to me, Dad?"

Dad. The first time Tommy had heard that word in ten years. A one-word poem. A sonnet. His anger—and his heart—melted away faster than a snow cone in sunshine. Under these circumstances, how could he be angry at anyone? He couldn't. It wasn't possible.

"Damn, Nikki, I can't get over how you've grown up," Tommy said, tears in his eyes. "How absolutely beautiful you are. You're . . . gorgeous. Do you have any idea how much I've missed you?"

"Well, that's on you, Dad. I begged Mom to let me come with her when she visited you, but she always refused. Said you prohibited me from seeing you. So did Ray. Until I eventually wore him down. Right, Ray?"

"She's a stubborn, strong-willed kid, Tommy," Ray conceded. "Virtually identical to you when you were that age."

"Like it or not, I'm going to visit you every Saturday, Dad," Nikki stated. "Ray can bring me until I'm old enough to drive. Then I'll come alone. Consider me your new source for nutrition."

"Come on, Nikki, you have your own life to live. Making the long drive to a crappy prison once a week shouldn't be part of it," Tommy protested.

"Don't waste your breath arguing, Dad. I will be here every week. Count on it."

And Nikki was true to her word. For the next seventeen years she never failed to show up. Like clockwork, ten o'clock, every Saturday, regardless of the weather conditions. Tommy watched her evolve into a confident teen, then mature into a strikingly beautiful young woman. During those years, Nikki graduated high school, earned a master's degree in Public Relations, started her own firm and became highly successful. One aspect missing from Nikki's life did trouble Tommy; she had no husband or family. When he pressed her, she usually responded with, "dated several guys but Mr. Right turned out to be Mr. Wrong." Tommy made her promise to keep looking. He wanted her to have kids, even though he knew he'd likely never see them if she did. He was a prisoner for life. No chance for parole.

Or so he thought.

That line of thinking changed when he got word a fellow prisoner, another lifer named Carl Hunter, had just been granted a compassionate release. Seems Carl, now seventy-six, had been diagnosed with pancreatic cancer. Terminal. The doctor gave him no more than two months to live.

Hearing this kicked Tommy's thoughts into overdrive. If pancreatic cancer was Carl's ticket out, Tommy saw no reason why it wouldn't work for him. It didn't take Tommy long to conclude that with good planning he could get his ass out of this fucking concrete-and-wire hellhole. Maybe not as exciting as a prison break, but that didn't trouble him in the least. The end result was all that mattered. To put this place in the rear-view mirror.

For the plan to succeed, Tommy had to accomplish two goals, neither of which would be easy. First, he had to bring the prison doctor on-board. Unless that happened, phase two was a dead end. Landing the doctor in his camp would be a challenge but it was possible. After all, the doctor wasn't sin free. He had a little side business in the works, supplying steroids and opioids to certain prisoners, all for a price, of course. Very few prisoners were aware of the Doc's enterprise; Tommy was. This provided him with a pair of options in which to enlist the doctor's help—blackmail or a bribe. Perhaps both.

Tommy approached the doctor, informed him of his plan, then offered twenty-five-thousand bucks for his assistance. Blackmail, his second choice, was waiting on the sidelines in case the doctor refused the money. But the doctor was laughing so hard he couldn't answer.

"That's insane, Tommy," the doctor finally managed to

say. "You couldn't pull that off in a million years. Nobody could. Hell, only a fool would dare try. Forget it. That's my advice."

"Why couldn't I pull it off?" Tommy inquired.

"For starters, you don't look like someone with terminal cancer."

"Give me three months and I will."

"I'm not about to ask how you plan to accomplish that. But let's say you succeed. How am I supposed to prove you have cancer?"

"You still have access to Carl Hunter's X-rays?"

"Yeah."

"We'll use them as proof."

"Impossible. They have his name and the date on them."

"You have scissors, don't you? Trim those details off. Then you tell anyone who inquires that those are my X-rays."

"I'd be risking my career, Tommy, not to mention prison time. You do realize that, don't you?"

"Tell you what, Doc," Tommy said. "You help me get out of here and I'll up the money to fifty grand."

The doctor shook his head, said, "That's a lot of dough. How can I be sure you can get your hands on that kind of cash?"

"Trust me, Doc, money won't be a problem. So, are we good to go?" When the doctor nodded, Tommy said, "See you in three months."

Phase two required transforming his body into one resembling that of a dying man. This meant a massive weight loss. He currently weighed one eighty-nine; he set his goal at one-forty. He had heard Carl Hunter weighed one twenty-one when he was released. Tommy knew he could never get that thin, but he felt one-forty should work for him. If it didn't, he'd go even lower.

Nikki was the only person he told about his plan. She was skeptical at first, but agreed to help. He ordered her to only bring loaves of bread when she visited and to hide diet pills in each slice. She suggested bringing an energy/nutritional supplement, maybe Ensure or Boost, to help him maintain his strength. He agreed.

In the end, it all came down to math—burn off more calories than you take in. A simple numbers game. Tommy set his limit at seven-hundred calories per week. Tough, but he could manage it. He took walks more frequently, and he also did two-hundred sit-ups each day in his cell.

The plan showed immediate results. After a month his weight dipped to one sixty-six. Then he hit a wall. Over the next three weeks he only lost nine pounds. This forced him to cut his calories to six-hundred a week and to take even longer walks. He also threw in a few more sit-ups. The changes worked. Eight pounds melted away in the next six days. He now weighed one forty-nine. His goal—one-forty—was clearly within reach.

Hiding his weight loss was never a problem. It was mid-February and very cold, which worked to his advantage by allowing him to bury his thinning body beneath several layers of winter clothes. Heavy shirts, sweatshirts, hoods and coats. Rather than shower with fellow inmates, he chose to wash off in his cell. No one was aware of the transformation taking place beneath all those outer garments.

That is, until one day when a couple of inmates saw him shirtless in his cell. Both men remarked that Tommy had lost a lot of weight. One of them asked if Tommy was feeling all right. Tommy lied, said no, he'd recently been experiencing severe pain in his upper abdominal area, close to his ribs. They suggested he should get checked out by the doctor. Tommy agreed, saying that sounded like a good idea.

At that moment, Tommy realized phase two had been successful.

The doctor was stunned when Tommy showed up and removed his clothes. Tommy was, the doctor concluded, absolutely emaciated. A walking skeleton. The doctor couldn't believe what he was seeing. More than anyone else, he had been keeping an eye on Tommy. But like everyone else, he had also been fooled by all the clothing Tommy wore during those winter months. Seeing him now, skin stretched tight, bones protruding everywhere, the doctor had to give Tommy credit. His achievement was impressive.

The doctor lived up to his part of the bargain, diagnosing Tommy with pancreatic cancer. Terminal, the doc added in his official report. Three months to live, tops. His concerns about the X-rays proved to be unwarranted. No one checked them. Apparently, the doctor's word was good enough.

Nikki had her attorney apply for Tommy's release. A tedious process that wound its way through the bureaucratic red tape, taking two weeks longer than Carl Hunter's application took. Tommy began to have doubts his request would be granted. Maybe they let Carl out because of his age, he reckoned. After all, Carl was more than two decades older than Tommy. Maybe they felt Tommy was too young and that he should die in prison. But after five weeks word finally came down that Tommy's compassionate release had been approved.

Tommy Doyle's audacious plan had worked. He would soon be leaving prison behind.

On a warm April morning, Tommy breathed in fresh air as a free man for the first time in thirty years. Walking slowly, aided by a cane, he left the prison. The cane was no prop used by an actor in the final stages of his role. He needed it. The sudden, dramatic weight loss had not been kind to his body, leaving him weak and unsteady on his feet. His balance was precarious. Nikki met him halfway between the prison gate and her Lexus, assisting him the rest of the way. Weak as he was, he did manage to give her a hug, an extended one that had been thirty years in the making. Once they were both inside the car and buckled up, Nikki started the engine, pulled away and headed out of town. Next stop: Her condo in Lexington.

Three days earlier, during their final meeting, the doctor asked, "Why did you do this, Tommy? Why submit your body to such extreme torture?"

Tommy shrugged, said, "Let's just say this place had worn out its welcome. It was time to leave."

"No, Tommy, I'm not buying that. Not for a second. There had to be a deeper, more profound reason. What was it?"

"Revenge."

"Revenge? Against who?"

"Jack Dantzler."

Chapter Two

The past six weeks had not been good ones for Jack Dantzler. He felt lost, adrift, deeply saddened. It was as though his entire being was enveloped in a black, gloomy fog. Never in his life had he experienced such a feeling of darkness. It weighed on him like a heavy boulder. Virtually smothered him. The reason for those feelings of darkness was no mystery. They came as no great shock. He suspected from the beginning that some hard days lay ahead, but he never anticipated this level of sadness.

Ending a three-year relationship with a woman he truly loved was bound to have a profound impact. He knew this the moment Erin informed him of her desire to accept a job offer in New York. And yet, despite the pain coming his way, he strongly supported her decision to relocate. In fact, he encouraged her to finalize that decision by helping her overcome an initial reluctance to take the job.

"You do realize this will mean the end of our relationship, don't you, Jack?" Erin asked, tears leaking out of her eyes. "I'm not sure that's what I want."

"That's the wrong way to look at it," Dantzler said. "If you turn down such a prestigious, meaningful job you'll spend the rest of your life regretting it. You'll always ask yourself, did I do the right thing? Or did I blow my big opportunity? You might even come to resent me, come to view me as the obstacle that stood between you and your dream job. You don't want that. And I don't want it for you. Erin, you have to take the job. Way I see it, declining would be a major mistake."

"That's noble, but do you really mean it?"

"Of course, I mean it."

"What about us? Sure, we could try a long-distance relationship. But we both know those never work out. Can you live with us ending what we have?"

"I can live with it much easier than I could live with us staying together and you being miserable."

"I don't have to let them know until Friday. I should give it more thought before I decide."

"No, Erin, you should make the call right now. There is no reason to put it off. Deep down, you want this job. You'd be insane not to. We're talking about the top of the legal food chain, Erin. They don't get any bigger than those folks. If they think that highly of you, if you have impressed them that much, you have no choice but to join them. Make the call now. Tell them you'll take the job."

Even now, six weeks later, his heart still an open wound, he had no second thoughts about encouraging her to accept the position. After all, what ambitious attorney wouldn't kill to work for The United States District Court for the Southern

District of New York? More commonly referred to as S.D.N.Y., it is arguably the most-powerful, most-influential federal court in the United States. No doubt, much of that prestige stems from the fact that Manhattan is included in its jurisdiction. And as everyone knows, Manhattan has been the site for many famous, high-profile investigations and prosecutions.

Since its founding in 1789, S.D.N.Y. has been home to an unlimited number of celebrated judges, attorneys, investigators and various other prominent legal figures. Several of those judges went on to serve on the Supreme Court. Its list of notable cases range from the Rosenberg trial to the investigation and sentencing of Trump attorney Michael Cohen. Because of its age and influence, S.D.N.Y. is sometimes referred to as "Sovereign District of New York." No one wanted to get caught in their judicial net.

And now Erin's name had joined their roster. After only four years as Kentucky's

Assistant Attorney General, where her work clearly made a strong impression on someone important, she was waltzing with the legal giants.

Dantzler hated to see their relationship end, and yet, despite his wounded heart, he could live with it. Erin Collins was exactly where she should be.

Bravo for her.

IN THE MIDST of all this darkness, Dantzler did stumble upon a ray of light. Rather, that ray of light stumbled upon him, materializing like a spirit out of the night. It came in the form of an ancient Black man who referred to himself as Brother Sunshine. Dantzler would later learn the man's name was Isaiah Monroe. He claimed to be eighty-five, but Dantzler was certain that was on the conservative side. He fixed the man's age at closer to ninety-five. Maybe even one-hundred.

Brother Sunshine was a wisp of a man, standing maybe five-four and weighing no more than one thirty-five. He had snow white hair, rheumy eyes and a full set of perfect white teeth. *("The original enamel, just like the Good Lord gave me.")* His wardrobe consisted of a cheap black suit, white shirt, red suspenders, no belt and a pair of dusty, well-worn leather shoes. His voice boomed like thunder, and he carried a beaten-up old umbrella, which also served as a walking stick.

He showed up late one afternoon at the Tennis Center, which Dantzler owned along with David Bloom, the psychiatrist and his old college tennis teammate, and Sean Montgomery, a former homicide detective and now a defense attorney. Brother Sunshine asked if there were any odd jobs that needed to be taken care of. He volunteered to do whatever was required. Carpentry, painting, dusting, taking out the trash, sweeping the tennis courts, cleaning the exercise room . . . anything, no matter how insignificant or menial the task might be. Dantzler took an instant liking to the man, and although there really wasn't much work to be done, he told Brother Sunshine to come back tomorrow and he would find a few odd jobs for him to tackle.

"Wait a second," Dantzler said, after Brother Sunshine thanked him and started to leave. "We haven't discussed wages. What do you think is fair?"

"The wages of sin are never fair," Brother Sunshine stated. "Now, if you're talking about money, well, whatever you offer is what I consider fair."

"Will twelve bucks an hour work for you?"

"Only if that's what you consider fair."

Dantzler nodded, said, "Deal. See you tomorrow."

For the next few weeks, Brother Sunshine spent hours in the Tennis Center while doing very little work. This didn't bother Dantzler in the least. There really wasn't much to be done, but having Brother Sunshine around lifted Dantzler's spirits, an effective palliative that helped offset the end of his relationship with Erin. Equally important, though, was the fact that Brother Sunshine possessed a gift Dantzler genuinely appreciated; he was a natural storyteller. Like all good storytellers, Brother Sunshine had that knack for skillfully blending fact with fiction. Where one ended and the other began was anyone's guess. Perhaps that distinction was best left to the listener.

Dantzler listened but never challenged the veracity of any given tale, even when he knew it couldn't possibly be true. Like the one where Brother Sunshine claimed to have whipped Joe Louis in a fist fight in a Detroit bar. *"Because of a lady we both took a shine to."* Or the one in which Brother Sunshine said he made love to Lena Horne and Rita Hayworth on the same day. *"Skin color never mattered to me."* Though Dantzler conceded those stories were too far-fetched to be believable, he appreciated how Brother Sunshine relayed them with the sincerity of a sinner testifying before the heavenly tribunal.

Sifting through those stories, and after discarding the lies and tall tales, Dantzler had to acknowledge Brother Sunshine had lived a wild and somewhat tragic life. As a book, it would be a masterpiece of marvelous fiction. If the book were made into a film, it would be nothing less than an epic tearjerker.

Brother Sunshine was born in a small Alabama town,

"sometime around nineteen twenty-five." His father, a sharecropper, deserted the family when Brother Sunshine was seven, leaving his mother to raise him and his two younger sisters, which she managed to do by laboring as a cleaning woman for several wealthy white families. Managing to put food on the table turned out to be easier than managing her only son. By his own admission, Brother Sunshine had a penchant for getting involved in activities that hovered somewhere between mischievous and illegal. Also, at times, dangerous. He quit school when he was eleven despite being considered a very bright student. From the age of eleven until he was nineteen, and despite working at a series of low-paying jobs, he always gave half of his paltry salary to his mother and sisters to help pay the bills and to buy food.

In nineteen forty-seven, his life took a dramatic wrong turn, one that altered his future forever. A murder conviction stemming from an altercation with the son of one of the town's most-prominent white citizens. The scuffle was started by the rich kid, who claimed Brother Sunshine had made advances toward a white girl. This constituted a serious offense in the Deep South in those days. A hanging offense if the perpetrator happened to be Black. Brother Sunshine denied the charge, but his denial was rejected. A fight ensued, the white kid pulled a knife and went in for the kill. However, as they struggled, the attacker fell on his knife, stabbing himself in the heart. He died instantly. Though several witnesses, almost all white, backed up Brother Sunshine's version of what had transpired before, during and after the fight, he was arrested, tried, convicted of manslaughter and sentenced to twenty-five years in prison.

"Convicted by a jury of my peers," he told Dantzler.

"Peers? All I saw were a dozen old white men sitting in that jury box staring at me with pure hate in their eyes. There wasn't a single Black person in the courthouse, 'cept for my mother. No one ever informed me that my so-called peers were all crackers. Didn't make a lick of difference, though. The Twelve Apostles would've convicted me in that town."

He was finally released after spending every day of those twenty-five years behind bars. Now a free man, he headed up north, eventually landing in Detroit, where he lived with one of his sisters and her husband. The next few years proved to be prosperous and trouble free. He landed a job as janitor and all-around handyman at the Ford plant. The pay was decent, the work satisfying. He also began to read extensively, especially the Bible. He memorized long passages, which he would recite with little or no prompting. He became particularly intrigued with the Gospel of Mark, the first of the gospels to be written, the one where demons share top billing with Jesus.

Then, he said, two days prior to his sixty-fifth birthday, "God tapped me on the shoulder. When I answered, *'Here I am, Lord'*, he directed me to go forth and spread the Good Word. So, I became a wandering preacher, just like Jesus. I ventured among the heathen and the unbelievers, pleading with them to change their evil ways before the Day of Judgment arrives and it's too late to repent."

Discussions pertaining to religion were of particular interest to Dantzler. After all, he only lacked completing his dissertation for a doctorate in Philosophy, which he always considered a close relative to religion. During their talks, it immediately became apparent that Brother Sunshine was obsessed by one of the Bible's lead characters—Lucifer, whom he referred to as, "Lying Bastard

Lucifer", "Sick Scumbag Satan", or "the Motherfucking Devil."

According to Brother Sunshine, Lucifer is forever tempting each of us. It's a relentless assault that, in Brother Sunshine's words, "takes place while we are awake or asleep."

"If a person has the moral strength to deny Lucifer today, he'll keep attacking until your resolve weakens and you do his bidding," Brother Sunshine warned. "Sooner or later he'll snare all of us in his wicked net. It's only a matter of time. Only Jesus could resist Lucifer's challenge. And ain't none of us Jesus."

"I don't believe in the Devil," Dantzler said during a recent conversation. "If I commit an evil act, it's because I chose to, not because an invisible entity forced me to do it. Each individual is responsible for his or her actions. The way I see it, the Devil is a fictional character employed by religions to scare people and keep them in line."

"Then you're a damn fool, Partner," Brother Sunshine said, shaking his head. "You're blind to the truth."

"Brother Sunshine, I've arrested countless men and women who committed homicides for all different kinds of reasons. Hate, greed, jealousy, money, anger, sheer stupidity . . . you name it, I've seen it up close. And not a single one of those murderers placed the blame on Lucifer."

Technically, this wasn't accurate. One of Dantzler's first cases involved a man named Victor Sammael. But Sammael claimed to *be* Lucifer, not simply influenced by him.

"Partner, you need to understand that Lucifer's special gift is his ability to entice you to commit a sin without you realizing he's the one pulling the strings. You aren't aware of the dark forces propelling you in a certain direction. Those murderers you spoke of didn't understand they were only doing what Lucifer tricked them into doing. You'd better be vigilant, Partner, 'cause one of these days Lucifer's gonna come after your soul. You wait and see. It's only a matter of time until it happens."

"What do you suppose Lucifer will make me do?" Dantzler asked, feigning seriousness.

"Could be he won't make you do anything," Brother Sunshine replied. "Could be he'll politely ask you do do him a favor. Something simple, safe, maybe even charitable. You'll agree, and it will land you in a tub of scalding water."

"What's he look like, Lucifer? How will I recognize him?"

"Who says Lucifer will be a he? Lucifer has many disguises, hides behind different masks. Might be Lucifer shows up as a female. Who better than a beautiful woman to tempt a man down the wrong path?"

A knock on the office door interrupted Dantzler before he could respond. He looked up to see a familiar figure standing in the doorway, a big grin on his face. The surprise visitor was Milt Brewer, a former member of Lexington's homicide unit and one of Dantzler's oldest friends. He had not seen Milt in more than two years.

"Come in, Milt, we were just talking about you," Dantzler said, motioning for Milt to enter. Then he turned to Brother Sunshine. "How about it, Brother Sunshine? Any chance Lucifer would dare disguise himself with this mutt's mug?"

For once, the loquacious old preacher was at a loss for words.

Milt said, "Been called many things in the past, but

never Lucifer. Don't know if that's a good omen or a bad one."

"Milt, this is Brother Sunshine," Dantzler said, as Milt took a seat. "Brother Sunshine, this is Milt Brewer. Milt was a homicide detective when I joined the unit. He and his old partner Dan Matthews taught me everything I needed to know about catching murderers."

"Don't believe a word he's saying," Milt said to Brother Sunshine. "This guy was a better detective his first day on the job than me and Dan were after twenty years. And how old were you when you joined us, Ace? Twenty-four?"

"Twenty-three."

"That's why he was known as the boy wonder."

"How have you been, Milt?" Dantzler asked. "And why has it been so long since we saw each other? Your health okay?"

"Much better than a seventy-seven-year-old probably deserves."

Brother Sunshine snickered, said, "Seventy-seven? Partner, you ain't no more than a pup compared to me. I'm older than Father Time hisself."

"So, where have you been keeping yourself, Milt?" Dantzler said.

"Gulf Shores. Got a nice condo near the beach. Came up to visit my daughter, spend some time with the grandkids before they get too old to give a damn about me. Figured since I was in town, I ought to come by and say hello."

"I would never have forgiven you if you hadn't. It's great seeing you."

"And to bring you a bit of interesting news I recently heard."

"Good or bad news?"

"You remember Tommy Doyle?"

"How could I forget him? It was my first homicide case."

"You worked it with Dan, didn't you?"

"Only for the first couple of days. Then there was another murder and Dan got pulled off to work that one. If I remember correctly, you were in the hospital at the time."

"Yeah, I had appendicitis."

"Why are you bringing up Tommy Doyle's name?" Dantzler inquired.

"Because he's out. Released a couple of weeks ago," Milt said.

"Released? How did that happen? He was in for life, no chance for parole."

"Compassionate release. He has terminal pancreatic cancer."

"Huh. How did you find out?"

"Through a network of prison spies who keep me apprised of inmates we dealt with who are being set free. When I heard about Tommy I felt it was only right you should know. I was in the courtroom the day he was sentenced and I clearly recall him turning, looking at you and whispering that he would one day come after you."

"That was thirty years ago, Milt. If he was gonna get revenge against me, don't you think he would've tried it by now? Maybe paid someone to do it since he was locked up and couldn't perform the task himself?"

"I can't know what he would or would not have done, Ace. All I'm telling you is he's out now. You should keep on the lookout until you see his obituary in the newspaper. I would if I were in your shoes."

"Is he in Lexington?"

"Can't say for sure but his daughter lives here. I'd have to believe a dying man would want to be close to his only kid."

"That is, if he's really dying."

"I'd say that part is true. Hard to fake out prison officials."

"You'd think so."

"Here's what I never understood, Ace. Something you never shared with me or Dan. What reason did Tommy Doyle have to threaten you? That was an open-and-shut case, wasn't it?"

Dantzler nodded, said, "Pretty much, yeah. Tommy was married at the time—Connie was his wife's name—but he also had a girlfriend on the side. Stacy Rollins. Anyway, Tommy heard a guy named Wayne Donovan was hitting on Stacy. Tommy goes to Wayne's apartment, they argue, a struggle ensues and Tommy stabs Wayne to death. Stabbed him more than twenty times. One of Wayne's neighbors got a glimpse of Tommy leaving the apartment building around the time of the murder. That's how we got onto Tommy. I brought him in, interviewed him and knew right off the bat he was guilty. But Tommy claimed to have a solid alibi; he was with Stacy at the time Wayne was killed. I brought Stacy in and interviewed her. Two days later I arrested Tommy for the murder. He believed Stacy had given him up, but he never blamed her. That's because he was convinced she had done so only because I either threatened her or forced her in some way to refute his alibi. But Tommy got it all wrong. Stacy played along, stuck with Tommy's lie. Want to guess who did give Tommy up?"

"Tommy's wife."

"Bingo. She knew about the affair and she'd had

enough. They had a young daughter at the time and I'm sure she factored into her decision. Tommy came home right after killing Wayne. His shirt was drenched in blood. He ordered Connie to burn it, but she had the good sense to hold onto it. When she heard about the murder, she had no doubt Tommy was the killer. She contacted me, came down to the office and showed me the shirt. That sealed it for Tommy."

"And Tommy never knew?" Milt asked.

"Well, he certainly didn't know at the time of sentencing or else he wouldn't have promised revenge against me. If he suspected his wife, his revenge would've been directed at her."

"He gets life with no parole. Hard to believe he's still hitched to her."

"Don't know, don't care, Milt."

"I repeat, Ace. Keep your eyes open. Thirty years is a long time to keep hate buried inside you. It's only a matter of time until it erupts."

"That's the same advice Brother Sunshine gives me regarding Lucifer," Dantzler said. "What's the word you use, Brother Sunshine?"

"Vigilant."

"I don't know from Lucifer," Milt said, standing. "I know about men and women who commit murder. Lucifer is your enemy to battle, Brother Sunshine. The enemies Ace and me squared off against were more terrestrial."

When Milt was gone, Dantzler said, "You just met a righteous man, Brother Sunshine. There's nothing I wouldn't do for him."

"*'Surely he shall not be moved forever. The righteous man shall be in everlasting remembrance.'* Psalm One-Twelve, in case you're interested."

Those were the last words Dantzler heard Brother Sunshine speak. He was gone the next morning, departing as mysteriously as he had arrived. But he did leave a note on Dantzler's desk. It was handwritten, the penmanship perfect.

Time to wander again, Partner. Just like Jesus. Our country is filled with sinners who need to be comforted and strengthened by hearing the Good Word, which I intend to give them. Thank you for your kindness and for being a friend. And don't dismiss my warning. Lucifer is forever on the hunt for new souls to claim. Make sure yours isn't among them.

Your friend, Brother Sunshine.

Chapter Three

Sound nutrition and plenty of exercise were the key elements required for Tommy Doyle to put on weight and regain his strength. Unless he transformed his body back to what it had once been, he had no chance of succeeding in his upcoming mission. But Tommy wanted something else as well—to feel the ocean breeze kiss his face. Throw in that third ingredient and his recovery process would prove to be faster and more successful. He had to head south.

Fortunately for Tommy, Nikki had a good friend who lived in Melbourne, Florida. Her name was Jenna Shadwell. Jenna owned a small two-bedroom apartment less than two miles from the Atlantic Ocean. She agreed to let Tommy stay with her and her two cats. It was the perfect setup for Tommy. He couldn't have imagined a more ideal situation. Three days later he packed a suitcase and moved to Melbourne. Settled in, he purchased a bicycle, which he peddled to the beach twice a day, once in the morning, then again later in the afternoon. Upon arriving at the beach, he secured the bike, then walked in the sand for a solid hour. This was his standard routine with each visit. It wasn't long before walking turned into jogging, then all-out running. His exercise, combined with a healthy diet, enabled him to not only add weight but muscle as well. He figured another month and he'd be in a better position to fulfill his dream. The dream that had consumed his every thought for the past thirty years.

To kill Jack Dantzler.

Since his release from prison, Tommy had come to the conclusion time moves differently for those locked up behind bars than it does for people on the outside. In prison, time drags. The hands of the clock seem to barely be moving. An hour can feel like a day. Conversely, for those fortunate individuals living outside prison walls, time roars by with the speed of a jet plane. Tommy had been free for five weeks, yet it seemed like he'd been released only a couple of days ago. He had forgotten how fleeting time can be.

This realization filled Tommy with a sense of urgency. Dantzler had to die and his death needed to happen sooner rather than later. And yet, Tommy also knew he had to be thoughtful, not rash. Careful, proper planning was essential if he hoped to succeed. He had to be smart, cautious, attentive and meticulous. Nothing could be overlooked, not even the smallest detail. Lack of proper preparation meant failure. And failure would almost certainly land him back behind those cold, steel prison bars.

Despite his dream of getting revenge against Dantzler, it wasn't lost on Tommy that he had never really formulated a plan for how to complete the mission. He blamed this oversight on his belief he would never be released from prison, and, therefore, would never have the opportunity to extract his revenge. Now that he was a free man, Tommy cursed himself for failing to anticipate his possible release, however improbable that seemed on any given day.

Tommy only told one person about his plan to kill Dantzler—Nikki. He trusted her and felt she should know. He didn't ask for her help—he wasn't about to put her in a position to possibly land in prison—but she surprised him by offering to assist in any way she could. He didn't immediately agree to her offer, but he also didn't outright dismiss the possibility. She did ask him why he harbored enough hated for Dantzler to want to kill him. That's when Tommy decided to come clean and tell Nikki the complete truth.

He told his story, certain Nikki was hearing it for the first time. He was wrong. She'd heard most of it from her mother when she was thirteen. Most, but not all. There was one key component of the story Connie never shared with anyone.

"I loved your mom, Nikki, but I was involved with another woman from the time we married until I was sent away to prison," Tommy admitted. "Her name was Stacy Rollins. We'd known each other since we were kids. Our relationship began when we were fifteen and it continued until I got arrested. Thankfully, your mom never knew about Stacy and me. For that, I . . ."

"She did know, Dad," Nikki said. "She knew about it from the very beginning."

"How do you know this?"

"She told me."

"It makes no sense. If she knew what was going on, why didn't she ever confront me about it?"

"Because of me. She was certain a confrontation would

place you in a situation that meant choosing between her and Stacy. She feared you would choose Stacy. If you did, it put me in the middle of what would likely be an ugly family squabble. It could even mean a lengthy custody battle. Or shared custody. Mom didn't want any of that to happen. So, for the sake of peace, and to keep our family together, she stayed quiet and looked the other way."

"But she continued to visit me every week for the first three years I was locked up. Why would she do that if she knew I had been unfaithful?"

"I asked her that very question; she never gave me an answer. Loyalty would be my guess. Perhaps a sense of duty or obligation. God knows I wouldn't have done it if I'd been in her shoes." Nikki opened her water bottle and took a sip. "Did Stacy ever visit you?"

"No, I ordered her not to. Same as I made your mom promise to not bring you when she visited. I never wanted you to see me in prison."

Tommy was surprised by the revelation that Connie was aware of his extra-martial shenanigans. But it really didn't matter now. He hadn't seen or heard from Connie in twenty-seven years. She was remarried and no longer part of his life. Neither was Stacy, a fact that did matter to him. Still in love with her, he had tried to get in touch on the day he was released from prison. But his efforts proved fruitless. He did get word from a mutual acquaintance that Stacy had married and moved to California or New Mexico more than twenty years ago. He had to acknowledge she was a lost cause.

During her recent visit to Melbourne, Nikki asked Tommy why he was so hell-bent on getting revenge against Jack Dantzler. They were walking on the beach at the time.

What Nikki had no way of knowing was Tommy's version of what had happened thirty years ago wasn't accurate. Like her father, Nikki had never been told the complete truth by Connie. Neither one was aware of the one secret Connie kept to herself. She was the one who ratted out her husband.

"The incident that sent me to prison revolved around Stacy," Tommy said. "The murder, me being arrested . . . it all came back to her. When I was brought in and questioned by Dantzler, I provided an alibi. I told him I was with Stacy when the murder went down. Which wasn't true; I went straight home after I killed Wayne Donovan. Well, after I disposed of the knife I'd used. My shirt was soaked with blood, so I gave it to your mom and ordered her to burn it. I had already spoken to Stacy, set up my alibi. I instructed her to tell the cops we were together at the time of the killing. She agreed to lie for me. The next day Dantzler hauls Stacy down to the police station and begins grilling her. He must've threatened her or tricked her in some way, because she eventually broke down and told him I wasn't with her. That's when Dantzler came and arrested me. I never blamed Stacy for what happened. If Dantzler hadn't pulled his bad-cop routine she never would have caved in. She was a tough cookie. But, he wore her down with his threats. He broke her spirit, shattered her resolve and forced her to give me up. No, Dantzler is the one I blame."

"Did Dantzler question Mom?"

"He didn't need to. Once he cracked my alibi I was a goner. Your mom never factored into any of it."

They stopped walking and watched as the waves came rolling in. It was getting late, night was closing in. The beach was more crowded than usual for this time of day. Mostly older folks out for a stroll.

Looking out at the ocean, Nikki said, "Have you put together a plan yet?"

"I've formulated several possible scenarios, played out each one in my mind, but not one has me excited," Tommy said. "But I'll keep working on it. Right now, my top priority is to get fully rejuvenated. Two, maybe three more weeks and I'll be there. That's when I'll shift my full attention to coming up with the best way to take out Dantzler."

"You need to plan for what happens after it's done. Killing a cop means the full weight of law enforcement will be hunting for his assassin with a vengeance. They'll be relentless."

"Dantzler's not a detective anymore. Works as a private investigator these days. But it wouldn't make a nickel's worth of difference if he was still a cop. I'd get my revenge."

"It's been thirty years, Dad. Why didn't you pay someone to kill him? You had to know people who would be willing if the price was right."

"Eyeball to eyeball, Nikki. I want Dantzler to look into my eyes and know who was ending his life. Can't have it any other way. Wouldn't be satisfying."

"You will let me help you, right?"

"Are you positive that's what you want to do?"

"Dantzler was responsible for taking my father away from me virtually my whole life. You bet I want to help. You aren't the only one seeking revenge."

"If things go sideways, *you* could end up where I was . . . in prison."

"Then let's make sure things don't go sideways."

Chapter Four

Amy Countzler wiped down the counter in the Tennis Center lounge area. It was early Saturday morning. The place wasn't busy. A couple of ladies were playing tennis, and a lone male was working out in the exercise room. Basically, a typical weekend morning. Finished with the counter, she turned her attention to the nearest table and began attacking it with Clorox and a rag. Thanks to COVID and its variants, this was a task that demanded her full attention.

Amy had come to work for the Tennis Center early in her freshman year at the University of Kentucky. She was now in the final stages of grad school, well on her way to a master's in psychology. With graduation looming, her days at the Tennis Center were numbered. No one wanted to see her leave. To Dantzler, Bloom and Sean, Amy was family.

She showed surprise when Dantzler strolled into the lounge. Straightening up, she said, "Don't normally see you here this early on a Saturday morning. Leads me to suspect you have a tennis lesson to give. Am I right?"

"Kenny Drake."

"Is he any good?"

"I've worked with worse." Dantzler opened the cooler, grabbed a bottle of water, placed two dollars on the counter and sat at one of the tables Amy had yet to attack. "How much longer until you complete work on your degree?"

"One more semester."

"You should stick around, get your doctorate."

"Dr. Bloom tells me that all the time. Like I told him, I will get it eventually. But I need a break from school. Get a job, see what the real world is like."

"Forget the real world and stay with us."

"Pay me what I'll make as a psychologist and I will stay. You know I love it here."

Dantzler chuckled, said, "I'd be more than happy to, but I doubt Bloom or Sean would go along with it."

"Then I suggest you'd better start looking for my replacement," Amy said, smiling.

"Not sure you can be replaced, Amy." Dantzler stood and held up the water bottle. "You saw me pay for this, didn't you? So, we're squared away, right?"

"Yes, we're square. Unlike Sean, you always pay. Sean's a borderline criminal, you know. He never pays."

"He swears to me he always settles up with you at the end of each month."

"Only because I confront him about it. You think he's ever gonna volunteer to pay? No chance. He should be banned from the place."

"Hard to ban one of the owners, Amy. Besides, we both know you'd miss him like crazy if he didn't come around."

"Hate to admit it, but you're right. Sean is a shyster, but he's a lovable shyster."

"Sean is your battle to fight, Amy. I'll stick to being Switzerland."

"Coward."

Dantzler laughed, went into his office and settled in behind his desk. He had been there less than ten minutes when Amy tapped on the door.

"There's a man here to see you," she said.

Dantzler checked the time on his cell phone, and said, "I have that tennis lesson in forty-five minutes. Ask him to come back in a couple of hours. I'll see him then."

"I think you'll want to meet with him now."

"Who is he?"

"You'll know when you see him."

"Okay, show him in."

Amy was right . . . Dantzler instantly recognized the man. Mike Conley. A successful Lexington businessman whose name and face had been in the newspaper and on local TV screens every day for the past few weeks. And not for a particularly good reason.

A handsome man with dark hair and green eyes, Mike Conley wore a blue suit, white shirt open at the collar and shiny black shoes. He was in his early forties, almost as tall as Dantzler (six-three), had a solid build and a chiseled face. He had that movie star look about him.

"Thanks for meeting with me, Detective Dantzler," Mike said, moving quickly into the office, but not offering to shake hands. "I really appreciate it."

"It's not Detective these days." Dantzler motioned for his visitor to take the chair across from his desk. "Jack will do. Would you care for something to drink? Water, soft drink?"

"No, I'm good. Thanks."

"What is it you wish to talk about, Mike?"

"So, you do know who I am?"

"Virtually impossible not to. You've been quite the media sensation these past several weeks. Like a famous celebrity followed by the paparazzi."

"*Infamous* celebrity would be more accurate. Trust me, Jack, that kind of notoriety was not something I went looking for."

"I can believe that. Back to my original question—what do you want to talk about?"

"How much of my story are you familiar with?"

Dantzler wasn't fond of people who answered a question with a question. "The basics. Your wife was murdered, you were arrested and charged with the crime, you were tried and found not guilty. That's the extent of what I know."

"Have you spoken to any of your cop friends about the case?"

"No, I haven't," Dantzler said, slightly annoyed by the question. "Tell me, Mike, why are you here?"

"I want to hire you."

"For what purpose?"

"To find my wife's killer. I'm innocent, Jack. I'll swear to that on my beloved mother's grave. I did not kill Laura." Mike leaned forward, a look of desperation on his face. "What I've learned since the verdict was announced is there's a vast gulf between the public's perception of not guilty and innocent. People know the jury acquitted me, found me not guilty, yet hardly anyone actually believes I'm innocent. When people look at me, all they see is a guilty man. Or, it's what they believe. They are convinced I committed the murder. Friends have deserted me, family members shun me, three staff members at work recently resigned. Everyone is certain of my guilt."

"Not everyone. The jury believed you," Dantzler pointed out.

"I have serious doubts about that, despite their verdict. What you aren't aware of is their original vote was nine for guilty and three for not guilty. The foreperson said the only reason those nine came around was because the murder weapon was never found. That one detail was all that stood between me and life behind prison bars. Even so, after the trial concluded, my attorney queried all twelve jurors. He came away convinced that deep down they all thought I did it."

"What they think is irrelevant. It's their vote that counts. Their not guilty verdict gets you off the hook for good. You can't be tried a second time for your wife's murder."

"Not in criminal court, anyway. But Laura's family is in the process of filing a civil suit against me. Word is, they plan to seek sixty-million in damages. You know how civil trials work, Jack. All that's required for them to prevail is a preponderance of evidence. If they succeed, and I'm betting they will, I'll be wiped out financially. I'll lose everything. House, cars, my business. I'll be ruined, bankrupt. My only path out of this hellish nightmare is to find Laura's killer. That's where you come in. Will you help me?"

"Who were the lead detectives on the case?" Dantzler asked.

"Jake Thomas and Vee Jefferson."

"Excellent investigators."

"I'm sure they are. But this is one time they arrested the wrong man," Mike stated.

Dantzler checked the time again, then said, "Mike, I'm scheduled to give a tennis lesson in about eight minutes. So, for now, give me the condensed version of what happened the night your wife was murdered."

Mike took a deep breath before responding. "We were at home, having just finished eating dinner. We watched TV for a while, then around nine-thirty I went back to the office. There were a half-dozen unfinished invoices that had to be completed and ready to be mailed the next morning. My CFO was off sick that day. So was his secretary. In their absence, I didn't have time to prepare them. That's why I returned to the office. I got back home a few minutes past eleven. That's when I found Laura's body. It was obvious she'd been shot. I could tell she was dead."

"Did you see a gun?"

"No."

"Did you look for one?"

"Not really, no. That wasn't a priority at the time."

"You didn't find a gun and get rid of it?"

"What kind of a question is that? No, Jack, I did not see a gun, and I damn sure wouldn't have gotten rid of it if I had."

"Why were you certain the cause of death was a gunshot?"

"I'm a hunter. I'm familiar with what a gunshot looks like."

"Did you touch her body?"

"Yes. I shook her, praying I was wrong, that she might still be alive. But I knew she was gone."

"What did you do next?"

"Phoned the police. Then waited for them outside in the yard."

"How long before the police arrived?"

"A patrol car was there within ten minutes. The two detectives arrived about an hour later."

"Did you have your wife's blood on you?"

"Yes, from when I shook her."

Dantzler stood. "I need to get down to the tennis court. What's the best way to reach you?"

Mike removed a business card from his shirt pocket, turned it over, scribbled something on the back and handed it to Dantzler.

"That's all the information you need to contact me," he said. "The number I wrote on the back is my attorney's. His name is Karl Miller."

Taking the card, Dantzler said, "I'll contact you first thing Monday morning."

"Does this mean you are taking the case?"

"Yes, I will look into it for you. No promises, though."

"Bless you, Jack. You're the one person I know who can get me out from under this black cloud that follows me every step I take. I have complete faith you will uncover the truth."

Yeah, but where will that truth eventually lead me, Dantzler silently wondered as he left the office and headed down to the tennis courts.

TENNIS LESSON COMPLETED, Dantzler showered, dressed and made his way up to his office. He had only one thing on his mind—to begin mapping out a strategy for how to proceed with the investigation he had just agreed to undertake. Doubts about accepting the case were swirling around in his head, but he managed to push them aside. For now, at least.

Sitting at his desk, he realized there were three people he needed to speak with before getting back with Mike Conley; Jake Thomas, Vee Jefferson and Karl Miller. Hopefully, information gleaned from that trio would shed light on the situation, thus giving him a better understanding of where he stood and how best to move forward.

There was also much information yet to be gathered from Mike. More questions to be answered. Things like the state of his marriage to Laura, their financial situation, any enemies either one may have had; routine questions any investigator would ask. Dantzler figured most of his questions could be answered by Jake or Vee. Being superb detectives, they would have posed those questions during the first few minutes of their initial interview with Mike Conley. Despite his eagerness to get the ball rolling, Dantzler decided to hold off until tomorrow before contacting Jake and Vee.

LATER THAT NIGHT, Dantzler and Sean Montgomery were drinking Guinness in McCarthy's, their favorite Irish pub. They were seated at the table by the front window, several feet away from the ever-growing crowd. In an hour or so the place would be packed and what little privacy they currently enjoyed would be history.

"How well do you know Mike Conley?" Dantzler asked.

"Never met him or his wife," Sean replied. "All I know

about the guy is he owns a very successful business. Graphics, if I heard correctly. Rakes in some big bucks."

"Strange, neither of us familiar with him."

"Ah, he's probably a golfer. And neither one of us spends any time on the links."

"Could be, but . . . still."

"How did he come across to you?"

"Desperate."

"He's damn lucky, if you want my opinion. I can't believe the jury acquitted him. Weren't they paying attention during the trial? Based on their verdict, I'm not sure they were. Mike's lawyer pulled a miracle out his ass with that not guilty verdict."

"Why? Do you think Mike is guilty?"

"As sin."

"Mike would say welcome to the club. According to him, everyone is certain he killed his wife, including members of his own family."

"Which tells me they're more perceptive than members of the jury were," Sean stated. "I can't believe you don't agree he's guilty. It's clear as day."

"You might be right, Sean. Who knows? I could be setting out on a fool's errand." Dantzler caught the bartender's eye and held up his empty glass, indicating it was time for a refill. "I can't quite explain it, but I have a gut feeling about this. That Mike just might be innocent."

"Yeah, right, and I might get a date with Margot Robbie. Come on, Jack. Mike Conley murdered his wife."

"Why are you so certain of his guilt?"

Sean waited until Dantzler went to the bar, got the two pints of Guinness and returned to his seat before answering.

"Who else could it have been, Jack? Ask yourself that question. An intruder? No way. Mike's your killer."

"What about the matter of the missing murder weapon?" Dantzler inquired. "That fact doesn't trouble you?"

"No, not at all. Why would it? We both know what happened to that damn gun—Mike disposed of it. He probably tossed it in the lake, or down a sewer, or in a Dumpster behind some convenient store. He murdered his wife, then left the house to ditch the gun. That's why he was gone for almost two hours. He didn't go back to the office for the purpose of working. That was a lie, and not a particularly clever lie. It lacked imagination."

"Lack of a murder weapon caused enough reasonable doubt to get him acquitted."

"Good old reasonable doubt. A defense attorney's best friend. It's been the ticket to freedom for more guilty defendants than we can count."

"Says a successful defense attorney."

""You play the cards you're dealt, Jack. You know that. But like I said, Mike Conley is one lucky guy," Sean repeated.

"Not so sure about that. His wife's family is planning to hit him with a civil suit. They are seeking sixty-million in damages."

"Ouch. That would definitely impact the old bank account."

Dantzler said, "What can you tell me about Mike's attorney? Karl Miller?"

"Works out of Atlanta. Earned a big-time rep after successfully handling several high-profile cases. Doesn't come cheap. I'm sure Mike Conley paid a small fortune for Miller's services. Why are you asking about him?"

"I'll need to speak with him at some point."

"Good luck with that."

"What's that mean?"

"Word is he's an arrogant prick. That assessment comes from Daniel Hoffman, a certified arrogant prick himself. When Miller agreed to handle Mike's case, he asked if he could set up shop in Daniel's office. Daniel said sure, be happy to help. But according to Daniel, Miller showed up with an investigator, a legal assistant and a secretary. He pretty much commandeered the entire office. Daniel came to loathe the man. Said he'd never met anyone more arrogant in his life. That's rich, coming from a genuine asshole like Daniel."

"Got breaking news for you, Sean. All attorneys are arrogant pricks, present company excluded, of course."

"Mass condemnation is beneath your dignity, Jack. And you're dead wrong. Believe it or not, there are a few good ones out there."

"I know, Sean. I'm just ragging you."

"All I can say is good luck with your investigation. I have a strong suspicion luck is what you're gonna need."

"What we need is another Guinness."

"Now, that we can agree on," Sean said, holding up his empty glass.

DOWN IN MELBOURNE, Tommy Doyle's road to recovery had run into a roadblock. Just when he was beginning to feel like his old self the COVID virus paid him a visit. The Delta variant, more specifically. Fortunately, he'd received two shots while still in prison—he had yet to get the booster—and those vaccinations played a key role in limiting the extent of damage to his body. Nikki suggested he get to a hospital, but that was out of the question. He reminded her that a hospital stay would likely reveal his lie concerning pancreatic cancer. But he was sick enough to be confined to bed for more than a week. Both he and Jenna Shadwell had to be quarantined. Nikki wanted to come down for a visit, but that was out of the question until the quarantine was lifted.

Before contracting COVID, Tommy's weight had gone from one forty-five to one sixty-eight. Along with the weight gain, his strength was also getting closer to normal. If he could push the scales up another five to ten pounds, he would be ready to leave Melbourne and return to Lexington. He was anxious to depart. And he wasn't alone with that sentiment. Jenna was equally anxious to see him go.

Tommy was well aware time was a factor in his desire for the revenge he'd been waiting thirty years to exact. He realized if he was still alive four or five months down the road, and if certain folks found out, they were bound to wonder why. After all, he'd been granted release from prison based on his impending death from pancreatic cancer. If he outlived the prison doctor's prognosis by too many months, there were bound to be questions. Perhaps even an investigation. Given this possibility, he had no time to waste. He'd have to commit his act, then disappear.

The recent setback had definitely stymied his forward progress, yet there was nothing he could do about it. It was just an unlucky break at an inopportune time. Shit happens, which he knew all too well. All he could do was deal with it, then move on.

His immediate focus was to regain the strength lost due to COVID. To get completely well. And, of equal importance, to continue putting together his plan. Once he declared himself fit, and once his plan was in place, he would head back to Lexington. With only one goal in mind.

Kill Jack Dantzler.

Chapter Five

Lexington's Homicide Unit had Dantzler's fingerprints all over it. The squad was superb when he signed on thirty-one years ago, and it was far superior when he retired. His lasting legacy—aside from a perfect solve rate—had to do with three key figures who were hired because of his strong recommendations. Eric Gamble, now the police chief, became the first Black homicide detective almost twenty years ago. Next came Jake Thomas nine years ago, followed by Victoria Jefferson three years later. All three had more than lived up to the potential Dantzler recognized in each one.

    Hiring Vee had caused a great deal of controversy within the department. It also created a rift between Dantzler and several veterans, all of whom felt better qualified to fill the position. Their complaints were loud and out in the open. They said Vee was too young, too inexperienced, not ready to tackle the demands required to investigate homicides. They also pointed out that she and Eric were cousins.

Dantzler heard the bitching and moaning, but he didn't give a damn. He recognized in Vee the requirements necessary to become a solid homicide investigator. She was intelligent, detail oriented, tenacious, inquisitive and fearless. Vee was not afraid to stand her ground, even when others disagreed with her conclusions. Dantzler lobbied hard to get her assigned to Homicide, and in her four years on the job, she had easily surpassed the lofty expectations he set for her.

But hooking up with Vee on Sunday was next to impossible. Perhaps if she was working a case he might have a chance. Otherwise, no way. Sunday mornings were dedicated to church, then afternoons and evenings spent with family. Dantzler would bet money Vee was with her grandmother, mother, two sisters and a legion of cousins, nieces and nephews. In all probability, Dantzler guessed, Eric was there with them. Eric knew where good home-cooked food could be found.

Jake Thomas was Dantzler's best chance for gathering information on a Sunday. Jake, a war hero with the medals to prove it, was likely watching a sporting event on the tube, if he was home. Dantzler hadn't seen Jake in several weeks, nor did he know if Jake and Amy Countzler were still dating. Amy hadn't mentioned Jake's name in recent days, and Dantzler wasn't inclined to inquired about the status of their relationship.

Dantzler punched in Jake's cell number. Jake answered after a couple of rings.

"Man, I was starting to wonder if you were still among the living," Jake said. "It's been, what, a year since we last saw each other?"

"More like a month," Dantzler corrected. "Too long,

that's for sure. How have you been, Jake? Catching any killers?"

"Caught one several months back, but the jury let him off."

"Mike Conley?"

"Yep, that's the guy. Couldn't be more guilty, yet he got acquitted. Damn miscarriage of justice, you want my humble opinion. But that's the way it goes sometimes, right?"

"All you can do is your job. What happens after is not something you can control."

"Frustrating, though, watching a wife killer walk out of that courthouse not wearing shackles. Vee feels the same way."

"Are you busy at the moment?" Dantzler asked. "Got any plans for the next hour or two? If you're free, I'd like to meet and chat."

"Free as a bird, and if I weren't, I'd make time to meet with you," Jake responded. "What is it you want to talk about?"

"Mike Conley."

Jake paused, then said, "Are you serious? Or are you yanking my chain?"

"Serious, I'm afraid. Mike swears he's innocent. He's hired me to find his wife's killer."

"Tell him to look in the mirror. If he does, her killer will be looking right back at him."

"If he's the killer, Jake, I'll prove it."

"What good would that do? Double jeopardy, right?"

"He's about to face a civil suit with millions of dollars at stake. If he's found to be responsible for his wife's death he stands to lose everything he has. That's the main reason why he wants me to look into it for him. If I find out he's the killer, well, tough luck for him. So, what about it? You willing to meet with me?"

"Yeah, sure. If you need anything from me, you'll always get it. Can't say no to my mentor. Where do you want to meet?"

"You still have the condo in the Patchen Village area?" Dantzler said.

"Haven't moved an inch," Jake replied.

"How about Shamrock?"

"Right around the corner from me. I'll be waiting when you get there."

DANTZLER ARRIVED FORTY MINUTES LATER, spotted Jake in a booth next to the wall, and quickly worked his way through a gauntlet of tables and chairs. It was early, not yet one-thirty, but the place was doing a surprisingly robust business for a Sunday afternoon. Shamrock Bar & Grille was noted for it burgers. Dantzler had eaten his share over the years and he'd never had a bad one.

Jake was smiling when Dantzler scooted in across from him. Two glasses of what appeared to be soft drinks were on the table, along with a basket of onion rings.

Jake pointed at one of the glasses. "I know you're a Pepsi freak, so I went ahead and ordered one for you. Me, I go for Dr. Pepper."

"A clairvoyant as well as a superb detective," Dantzler said, removing the straw from his glass. "You look good, Jake. And it has been too long since we saw each other.

Life's too short to miss spending time with those you truly care about."

"Amen to that. What about Bloom, Sean? They doing okay?"

"That pair is like fine wine, Jake. They only get better with age." Dantzler was hesitant to pose his next question, but he went ahead and asked it anyway. "Are you and Amy still seeing each other?"

"No, unfortunately, that sort of fizzled out. Even though Amy has yet to earn her master's she's had several job offers, none of which are in Lexington. We both realize distance would eventually be an issue, so we decided to call it quits. Shame, too, because we got on really well."

"Sorry to hear that. You guys made a great couple."

"So, moving on to Mike Conley. You're really working for him, huh?"

"Yeah, I agreed to look into it for him."

"Jack, you are by far the best homicide detective I've ever seen. That *any* of us have ever seen. If you really dig into this case, and I know you will, what you're gonna find out is Mike Conley is guilty of murdering his wife."

"If that's what I find, that's what I'll report," Dantzler stated. "Working this case as a private investigator is no different for me than when I was on the homicide squad. I'm only after one thing—the truth. Nothing else matters to me."

"I know," Jake said, after taking a drink. "Okay, how much do you know about the case?"

"Nothing more than what I saw on TV or read in the paper. Laura was found dead, Mike was arrested, charged with the crime, tried, found not guilty. And the murder occurred while he was at his office."

"*Allegedly* at his office."

"All right, allegedly," Dantzler conceded. "Where was she killed?"

"In the den. She was sitting on the sofa, her body bent slightly forward. One shot, close up to the back of her head. She never knew what hit her. It was the classic execution killing."

"What did that say to you and Vee?"

"She knew her killer and trusted him enough to not be worried when he was behind her," Jake said. "Like her husband."

"What caliber weapon?"

"Thirty-eight."

"Which was never found, right?"

"Right. Mike tossed it, that's my thinking."

Dantzler smiled, said, "Any prints found in the house, other than Mike's or his wife's?"

"Several, mostly belonging to Laura's sister and father. None that drew suspicion."

"What about their neighbors? Did you speak with them?"

"Yeah, none of them heard a gunshot or saw anything suspicious."

"Mike said he returned to the office for the purpose of getting several invoices ready to be mailed the next morning. Did you or Vee check to see if those invoices had been prepared?"

"Of course, we did," Jake said. "And yes, there were invoices in the Out box on his secretary's desk. But that hardly proves he prepared them that night. They could've been ready when he left for home at five o'clock that afternoon."

"Possible. But it's equally possible he's telling the truth."

"Consider for a second what you're saying, Jack. For that to be true, it means Laura felt comfortable enough to allow someone into her home, walk behind her and put a bullet in her brain. All this took place in the ninety-minute window when Mike claims he was at his office. How did the killer know Mike would be gone? Or how soon he might return? He couldn't know either of those things."

"Unless he was watching the house. Or Laura told him when Mike left."

"What? She invites a friend over and he kills her? There's no way you believe that."

"I don't believe anything at this point, Jake. Just gathering information."

"If you want to look at the murder book, I'll make it available. As you know better than anyone, that's against department protocol. To be safe, I'll run it past Eric, but given who you are, I don't think he'll object."

"Thanks, Jake. That would be helpful."

"Anything else you want to ask me?"

"Not now. Maybe later I'll get back with you."

"Hate to say it, Jack, but I think you're wasting time on this one. You're working for a guilty client."

"That's what I intend to find out, Jake." Dantzler put a twenty on the table and stood. "Let me know how Eric rules. If he gives the green light, I'll swing by the station and pay you a visit. If not, don't be a stranger. We need to stay in touch."

"Couldn't agree more."

DRIVING HOME, Dantzler was satisfied his chat with Jake went well. He was especially pleased with Jake's willingness to share the murder book. Still, there were issues he didn't address with Jake. He'd bring those up during tomorrow's talk with Mike Conley.

Next on his agenda was a call to Karl Miller, Mike's notoriously arrogant prick attorney. But the call could also wait until tomorrow. For now, Dantzler wanted to get home, dress down, fix a Jameson and Diet Coke, kick back, relax and try not to think about how much he missed Erin. Up to this point it was a battle he wasn't winning.

He missed her like crazy.

Where was Brother Sunshine's ray of light when it was really needed?

Chapter Six

An authentic Southern accent wasn't enough for Dantzler to overcome his instant dislike for Karl Miller's receptionist. She identified herself as Millie, asked Dantzler his name, then hurriedly wanted to know what business he had with the firm, all the while showing a complete lack of interest in what he had to say. When she went silent he inquired if he could speak with Karl Miller.

"Mr. Dancer, Karl is . . ."

"It's Dantzler, Millie," Dantzler said. He then spelled out his name for her. "However, if it's easier for you, just call me Jack."

"What I was about to say Mr. *Dantzler* is Karl can't speak with you at the moment. He is currently on an important conference call. Tell me the nature of your business with him and I'll pass it along. If he finds it worthwhile, I'm sure he'll contact you."

"The nature of my business is between Karl and me."

"Well, you're certainly a rude man, sir. You must be

from the north. In my experience, there aren't many good manners to be found in that part of the country. I don't believe Karl will have any interest in speaking with you. Now, I'm very busy, so . . ."

"Mike Conley."

"What about Mike Conley?" Millie asked.

"He's who I want to talk about with Karl. Pass that information along to your boss. I'll wait for his reply."

Millie put Dantzler on hold, then came back a moment later, and said, "When I hang up, you'll have Karl on the line."

"Okay, Mr. Danton, what's . . ." Karl blurted out.

"The name is Dantzler. But for convenience sake, just call me Jack."

"All right, Jack. Mike Conley is old news. Yesterday's story. What's your interest in him, and why are you bringing up his name to me?"

Two things immediately struck Dantzler: Karl Miller was no Southern boy. New York or New Jersey, Dantzler guessed. Also, Karl was as rude as Millie had been. This confirmed a fact Dantzler learned long ago. Rudeness knows no geographical boundary.

"Mike claims he's innocent," Dantzler stated. "I've been hired to find the actual killer."

Karl laughed, said, "So, Mike is taking a page out of O.J.'s playbook, that's what you're telling me. Swears he'll spend every waking moment looking for the real killer while spending all his time on the golf course. Beautiful. You have to admire his *chutzpah*."

"Karl, I was a homicide detective for almost thirty years. And a damn good one, I might add. My only goal is to find the truth. Which I will. You can take that to the bank."

"Along with Mike's money, right?"

"The money is incidental."

"Rather than hire you, Mike's best play would be to let it go. Accept the jury's verdict and get on with his life. That's my advice to him, free of charge. Hell, the guy beat some long odds."

"Sounds like you think Mike was guilty," Dantzler said.

"Jury said otherwise. What I think counts for *bupkes*," Karl said.

"What do you think? Off the record, of course."

"I think I was handed a win when I didn't really deserve one."

"If he was guilty, as you clearly believe, how did you manage to get him acquitted?"

"Easy. By continually hammering away at one point throughout the trial—the absence of a murder weapon. Truthfully, that's the only nail I could hang my hat on. All the evidence leaned heavily in favor of his guilt. Last person to see his wife alive, a weak alibi for the time of the murder, her blood on his clothes . . . it all pointed the finger of guilt straight at Mike. But I kept reminding the jury about the missing thirty-eight. I can only assume that created enough reasonable doubt among the jurors for them to acquit Mike. Like I said, a lucky win."

"Mike said you spoke to each juror after the trial and came away believing they were convinced of his guilt. Is that correct?"

"Correct."

"Mike is about to face a civil suit brought on by his wife's family," Dantzler said. "They are seeking sixty-million in damages. Which adds to his desire to find the real killer."

"I'm sure it does," Karl replied. "But that's of no

interest to me. I won't be representing Mike in that trial."

"Just suppose for a moment Mike is innocent. Can you think of anyone who might have wanted to murder Laura Conley? You did have an investigator working for you, right?"

"I did. He didn't come up with a single legitimate candidate."

"How deep did he dig?"

"Pretty deep."

"Mind giving me his name? I'd like to see if he'd be willing to share his notes with me."

"*My* notes, not his. He works for me. And no, you can't see his notes."

"Had to ask."

"Can't blame you. I'd do the same if I were wearing your shoes. Are we about done here? We've talked long enough that I'm now running behind schedule."

"Can you point out anything that might help with my investigation?"

Karl was silent for a moment, then said, "Have you asked Mike about his relationship with Laura? And her relationship with him?"

"Not yet, but I plan to," Dantzler said.

"There's your starting point. Now, if you don't mind, I really have to go."

Karl ended the call without saying another word. Or with Dantzler having learned anything of consequence during their talk. As for Karl's advice to ask Mike about his martial status, that was already on Dantzler's list of things to do. He'd only held off this long until he could collect more information. All in all, Dantzler concluded, his call with Karl had been a bust.

What he had learned, however, was being rude must be a requirement for employment in Karl's law office.

DANTZLER HAD no issues with Mike Conley's receptionist; there wasn't one. Mike's graphics business occupied the lower half of a two-story building he owned located on East Short Street. The top floor was split between an insurance agency and an interior decorator.

When Dantzler entered Mike's place there was no receptionist sitting at the desk. Nor was there a nameplate, leading Dantzler to suspect no one currently filled the position. His meeting with Mike was set for three, but as usual Dantzler was a few minutes early. The door to Mike's office was closed, but Dantzler could tell a conversation was taking place inside. He glanced around, saw several chairs, then decided to sit in the one behind the receptionist's desk. Might as well go for comfort while waiting, he reasoned.

Dantzler had been seated no more than five minutes when the door to Mike's office opened. An attractive twenty-something Black female emerged first, followed by Mike. He led her to the door, opened it, thanked her for coming in and told her he would let her know one way or the other within the next two days. She thanked him profusely before departing.

After closing the door, Mike turned, and said, "You look perfectly at home behind that desk, Jack. Like you belong there. How would you like to be my receptionist?"

"Is that why she was here?" Dantzler asked. "To interview for the position?"

"Fourth one today, two more tomorrow, then it's decision time. Be a tough call, too. They're all very impressive. However, unless one of those two tomorrow blows me out of the water, I'll probably go with the lady who just left. I liked her a lot."

"What happened to your receptionist?"

"What do you think? She didn't want to work for a wife killer. Left without giving her notice. Been with me for seven years. Kind of a crappy thing to do, you ask me. That made her the fourth employee to quit. The other three were very important cogs in the machine. However, I can get by without them. But the receptionist? She's vital to my business."

"First impressions, right?"

"You got it. And you don't get a do-over." Mike motioned toward his office. "Let's talk in there. We'll be a lot more comfortable."

Mike's office could best be described as modest. There was his small desk with a computer on it, a round table with four chairs, three cabinets, a bookcase and a wall covered with posters from various movies and television shows. Mike sat behind his desk, Dantzler took the seat across from him.

Pointing at the posters, Dantzler said, "I was aware you did computer graphics, but I had no idea you were in the film and television business."

"Films, television, video games, yeah, we work with all of them. Most of the special effects you see are the products of CGI. Computer-generated imagery. That's what we provide. Pays very well, trust me."

"How did you get into the entertainment business?"

"By accident, really. Started when a friend of a friend ask me to help him with a low budget film he was producing. I did, he liked my work, so he used me on his next project. It sort of mushroomed from there. My name started making the rounds. Pretty soon, the company was in demand. I went out and hired a half-dozen young kids who were all computer mavens and off we went. What these kids today know about computers is beyond amazing."

"Sadly, computers, phones, technology . . . that's the extent of what most kids today do know. Not sure that's a good thing."

"You're probably right, Jack, but . . . discussing young kids and technology is not why you're here," Mike said. "You want more information from me, which I'm fully prepared to give. But could I ask you a question first? Have you spoken to anyone yet?"

"Karl Miller," Dantzler said, opting to keep his talk with Jake Thomas to himself. "We talked for a few minutes this morning."

"I'm sure he had plenty to say about himself, if nothing else. Karl Miller loves Karl Miller. The guy couldn't get in front of a TV camera fast enough after the trial ended. Ran around looking for them. Wanted everyone to believe he was Clarence Darrow reincarnated. Fame at my expense, while at the same time I'm quickly becoming infamous."

"To be honest, he didn't say anything very helpful." Dantzler took out his notepad and pen. "I'm hoping you can give me information that will be helpful."

"Sure, ask me anything," Mike said.

"The obvious first question . . . did you or Laura have any enemies? An individual who hated her—or you— enough to commit murder? Someone seeking revenge? Or who held a grudge?"

"Laura certainly didn't have any enemies. I'm sure I've pissed off a few people along the way. It's impossible to be in a cut-throat business like mine and not ruffle a few feathers. But not to the extent they would commit murder. And besides, if someone was angry with me, why kill my wife?"

"Easier target, to frame you, put you out of business. Those are just a few of the reasons I can come up with."

"Doesn't compute for me."

"Laura worked as a realtor, right?"

"Yes."

"Did she ever mention having any issues with a disgruntled client?"

"If she did, she kept it to herself."

"What about life insurance? Were you both insured?"

"Yes, for a million each," Mike said. "I was her beneficiary, she was mine. Standard policies."

"Would you say your financial situation is sound?" Dantzler asked.

"For now, yes. But it won't be if I lose a sixty-million-dollar civil suit. Neither I nor my business can survive that."

"Have you communicated with Laura's family since the trial?"

"They will have nothing to do with me. I would imagine their attorney has advised them to steer clear of me."

"Let's move on to your marriage. How were things between you and your wife?"

"Honestly, our marriage had something of a roller-coaster aspect to it," Mike said, a hint of sadness in his voice. "I suppose all marriages have their ups and downs. Ours certainly did."

"How so?"

"The first ten years were . . . blissful, almost. Or very close to blissful. Then things began to change. I didn't know why at first, but I later found out Laura was having an affair.

It had been going on for more than a year when I learned about it. Naturally, I was deeply hurt, disappointed, angry. But rather than do the mature thing and confront Laura, I chose to take a different route. I began my own affair. Not exactly a wise move on my part. But my dalliance lasted less than three months. Then I ended it. I thought it was tawdry, dangerous and just plain wrong. It put innocent people in a position to be hurt, and God knows I didn't want that. Finally, I confronted Laura and demanded that she make a decision . . . him or me. That's when she informed me the affair was over, that she had broken it off. Sounded good at the time, but I later found out he was the one who ended it. We went through a few rocky months, as you would expect. But we worked through it, regained each other's trust, kind of fell in love all over again. The past year had been a good one. We even discussed possibly having a child. Then she, well, you know how the story ends."

"I'll need those two names," Dantzler said.

"His, I don't mind giving you, Jack. Mine is trickier. She's married."

"Was she married when you were having the affair?"

"Yes."

"What about Laura's partner? Was he married?"

"At the time, yes. Not anymore. For the record, his name is Robert Hilton," Mike said.

"I know Robert," Dantzler said. "He used to be a member at the Tennis Center I own. And you're right. He recently divorced Kelly and moved to St. Louis."

"I don't know where he moved to, nor do I care."

"Are you aware that Robert is a guy capable of committing violence? I once banned him from the Tennis Center for two weeks after he struck a fellow member with his tennis racket. He's not always an easy guy to like. Did Laura ever mention him getting violent with her?"

"We didn't discuss him. But I never noticed any signs she'd been a victim of violence. No bruises, no cuts, no black eyes."

"And the woman you were with?"

"Jack, I'm uncomfortable giving you her name."

"I may not have to speak with her, Mike. However, I need her name in case I do."

"Marianne Lofton."

"Another member of the Tennis Center. Along with her husband Kent. Who just happens to be the guy Robert Hilton got into the altercation with."

"Jesus. Think that was a coincidence?"

"I'm not a big believer in coincidences. What I can tell you is Kent Lofton is not a man to be messed with. Robert attacked while Kent had his back turned. Had others not quickly intervened, Kent would have torn Robert apart."

"Damn, I shudder to think what Kent would have done to me if he found out about my affair with Marianne."

"Maybe Kent did find out."

"And what . . . murdered Laura?"

Dantzler shrugged, said, "Did Laura keep a diary?"

"If she did, I never saw it."

"Do you still have all her things? Primarily, any letters she might have saved? Any correspondence at all?"

"I have all her stuff. You're more than welcome to go through any of it."

"That's my starting point, Mike. I'd like to look through them tomorrow. Is that possible? If you trust me, you don't need to be there when I do."

"You have my complete trust, Jack. Do you know where I live?"

"McMeeken Place."

"Right. I will leave the front door unlocked tomorrow. All I ask is lock up when you leave."

"Of course."

"Her stuff is in my office. You won't have a problem locating it."

"Thanks, Mike. I'll let you know if I find anything of interest."

Dantzler left Mike's office, got in his car and drove away. His thoughts kept drifting back to the altercation between Robert Hilton and Kent Lofton. Had it been a heat-of-the-moment thing or was there an underlying cause for the confrontation? Jealousy? That didn't make any sense. What reason would Robert have to attack Kent? He wouldn't, unless he suspected Kent had a thing for Laura. Or maybe because Robert thought Kent knew about the affair and feared Kent would inform Mike. Another thought crossed Dantzler's mind. What prompted Robert's sudden move to St. Louis? True, he had a job that allowed him to work from home, meaning he could've remained in Lexington, but he left almost like a thief in the night. Had Kent followed up and threatened Robert? Did Kent tell him to vamoose if he knew what was good for his health? Had Robert been run out of town?

Plenty of questions for Dantzler to chew over. All of which had to be answered if he was to uncover the truth about what happened to Laura Conley.

And he would eventually arrive at the truth.

There was no question about that.

Chapter Seven

As promised, the door to Mike Conley's house was unlocked when Dantzler arrived at seven-thirty Tuesday morning. The home was a two-story brick structure with plenty of space. Dantzler estimated the square footage to be at least five-thousand feet. Approximately three times larger than his house.

Before entering, Dantzler studied the two houses flanking Mike's. Both were virtually identical to his, and both were no more than a few yards away. This caused Dantzler to question how no one living in either house heard the gunshot that killed Laura Conley. Of course, there was always the chance the killer used a silencer. Or that no one was home when it happened. But Dantzler thought that to be unlikely. For both houses to be empty between nine-thirty and eleven at night just didn't seem feasible to him.

Dantzler was pleased Mike agreed to let him work alone inside the house. The last thing he needed was Mike hovering like a hawk watching his every move. Working solo allowed the freedom to check out areas other than the office, which Dantzler intended to do. He wanted to make a close inspection of the Conley's bedroom, and in particular, the dresser where Laura kept some of her clothes. And, hopefully, some of her secrets.

Mike's office was easy to find; it was the second room to the right off the main hallway. Dantzler went in, turned on the lights and looked around. The first thing he spotted was a wall safe. It had once been hidden behind a framed poster of the classic movie Citizen Kane, but the poster was now propped up in a chair, leaving the safe exposed. This didn't matter to Dantzler; he had no interest in what might be in the safe. If Laura was keeping secrets from her husband, she certainly wouldn't hide them in a place where Mike could easily find them.

There was one file cabinet, which Dantzler went through first. He found nothing of interest. The information inside each drawer pertained in some way to Mike's graphics business. Mostly, there were copies of old contracts between Mike's company and the folks who hired him. Dantzler did recognize the names of two prominent, high-profile movie producers. This lent credibility to Mike's statement that his company was doing well financially. Those Hollywood types have a reputation for not being shy about spending money. Mike was wisely cashing in on their lack of financial discipline. Can't blame him for that.

Next, Dantzler sat at what he judged to be a standard desk, one that had a middle drawer beneath the desktop, and three vertical drawers to the left and right of the person occupying the chair. Not unlike a million other desks around the world. In fact, it was almost identical to the one Dantzler had in his office at the Tennis Center.

He rummaged through the middle drawer and found nothing helpful to his investigation. Ink pens, a staple remover, index cards, paper clips, a letter opener . . . the usual items found in a desk drawer. Again, not unlike what you'd find in his at the Tennis Center.

The drawers on his left and right were filled with hanging folders. One by one, he removed the contents in each folder and carefully went through every piece of paper. Only the last folder he looked through, in the bottom drawer to his left, contained something that grabbed his attention. In the drawer were two thick stacks of letters, each stack bound by a rubber band, all addressed to Laura Conley. Dantzler's pulse began to quicken. Maybe he'd finally come across material that would advance his investigation.

However, it didn't take long before his pulse returned to normal.

Dantzler opened and read every letter, his disappointment growing with each one he finished. Several related to various aspects of Laura's life. The usual mundane, typical things all adults have to deal with in their day-to-day life. Bills she paid, bank records, credit card statements, old check registries, that sort of thing. There was an appointment book that reminded her of scheduled showings for potential buyers interested in viewing different houses or condos. But the majority of letters had to do with Laura's health. Reminders of scheduled mammograms, Pap smears, eye or dental appointments, or the results of tests that had been performed. Based on the results of those tests, Laura Conley was in perfect health when she was murdered.

In short, nothing the least bit suspicious. Nothing that would lead to her killer. What he'd found was not much different from what he'd expect to find in any normal woman's correspondence. He was, however, surprised to find nothing of a personal nature. Not one letter from a family member or from any friends.

That changed when he went upstairs to the Conley's bedroom. There, in the bottom dresser drawer, buried under several sweaters, was a stack of personal letters addressed to Laura. Dantzler thumbed through the letters, checking to see who had sent them. He was surprised that all the letters were sent by one person. A woman named Leah Wallin, who, according to the return address, lived in Denver. Dantzler took his time and carefully read through each letter, all of which were handwritten. Apparently, theirs was the classic, old-fashioned pen-and-paper correspondence, the kind you rarely see in today's computer age.

Laura and Leah were longtime friends, a fact that was immediately evident. Although Dantzler was only getting one side of their communications, it was clear the two women shared a deep bond. This included sharing highly personal information, such as Laura's affair with Robert Hilton. By reading what Leah was saying, Dantzler could almost discern what Laura had written in her previous letter. It was the logical extension of a normal conversation.

Dantzler learned their friendship went back many years. He uncovered that tidbit in the first letter he read, when Leah mentioned a favorite third-grade teacher they had at Clays Mill Elementary School. This told Dantzler the two women likely attended high school at either Lafayette or Tates Creek. This was something he might check into later on.

It wasn't until Dantzler read the most-recent letter, one dated only four days prior to Laura's death, that he came across a passage that captured his attention with full force. Leah was obviously responding to something Laura had written. Whatever it was Laura had shared in her previous letter, it was enough to greatly concern Leah.

Most of the letter's content dealt with Leah telling Laura it was time to end the affair, that to continue would inevitably lead to heartbreak, anger and resentment. Possibly even to a divorce. But it was a passage in the next-to-last paragraph that was more than a little ominous.

If you continue the affair, you will be putting yourself in a dangerous situation. We both know KL has an explosive temper and is capable of causing great harm. Whatever you decide, please be vigilant. Make safety your number one priority.

Vigilant. That word again.

KL? Kent Lofton? Had to be, Dantzler concluded. But it didn't make sense to him. What would be Kent's motive for murdering Laura Conley? She wasn't involved with Kent. Not at the time of her death, anyway. But what about the past? Could they have been an item before Robert came into the picture? Was that the reason for the altercation between Kent and Robert Hilton? Kent being jealous because Robert took Laura away from him? But that made even less sense. After all, Robert instigated the altercation by attacking Kent. This led Dantzler to believe their fight had to be for a different reason. But what was the reason? And would a fight between the two men have led to Kent killing Laura Conley? If Kent was jealous of Robert, why not take him out rather than Laura, the woman Robert had an affair with? Did Kent have an affair with Laura? There was no evidence he had. Dantzler realized he was going round in circles, getting nowhere fast. He was trying to fit a square peg into a round hole. He also had no idea all these extramarital affairs were happening. Suddenly, he felt like he was living in Peyton Place.

But Leah's warning to Laura did clear up two things for Dantzler: Mike was wrong when he stated Laura's affair with Robert had ended. And he needed to have a long chat with Kent Lofton, who had suddenly risen to the top of his suspect's list.

That was his number-one priority.

A LATE-AFTERNOON SHOWER cut short Tommy Doyle's second walk of the day. Surprisingly, he was thankful for the downpour. He wasn't feeling well. Hadn't all day. He felt fatigued, somewhat short of breath, slightly dizzy. Also, there was the presence of a dull pain in his upper chest that contributed to his discomfort. Nothing that had him overly concerned. No reason for alarm. He simply felt crappy. Just one of those days.

Tommy was sitting at the kitchen table when Nikki came home from work. She laid her purse on the counter, opened the refrigerator, plucked out a bottle of Coors Light and sat across from him.

After opening the bottle and taking a long swig, she said, "You don't look so hot, Dad. Everything okay with you?"

"Just tired," Tommy said. "All this exercise and trying to come up with a plan is wearing me down. It's nothing serious, not anything for you to worry about."

"You could use a break, Dad. We both could. What do you say we pack a couple of suitcases and head down to

Florida for a week or so? Get some sunshine, smell the ocean air? We'll go to Destin. I vacationed there once. It was great. Come on, let's do it."

"Sounds wonderful, Nikki. But I've had enough of Florida for a while."

"Okay, so we don't go there. We'll head in the opposite direction, up the East Coast, all the way to Cape Cod. We'll take the ferry to Martha's Vineyard, spend a night or two there. Maybe see some famous people. Spielberg, Tom Hanks, Carly Simon. They all have homes on the Vineyard. Does that interest you?"

Tommy shook his head, said, "No, not really. I need to stay here, get this thing with Dantzler over and done with. Once that's taken care of, then we can take that trip to Cape Cod."

"Dad, if you're successful, if you kill Dantzler, you'll have to get a lot farther away than Cape Cod. Every cop in this town will be looking for his killer. You'll have to leave the country."

"Not if I do it right, I won't."

"You don't have a plan yet, do you, Dad?"

"No, but I'm working on it."

"What if I told you I had a plan? One I think would work? Care to hear it?"

"I'm all ears."

"Dad, my plan doesn't involve killing Jack Dantzler. Instead, it . . ."

"You can stop right there, Nikki," Tommy interrupted. "Your plan, whatever it is, does not interest me. Sorry."

"Will you at least let me finish before ruling it out? Please?"

"Go ahead."

"Thanks. Look, rather than kill Dantzler, which will bring all kinds of heat, why not damage him in another way? By ruining his reputation? Or possibly getting him sent to prison?"

"And just how do you plan to make that happen?"

"By getting together with him and making myself available. Sexually, I mean. We've never met, he doesn't know me, so he'll have no reason to be suspicious. I'll flirt, come on to him, then suggest the two of us go somewhere and have a drink together. I may not be Hollywood beautiful, but I'm far from unattractive. And I do know how to be seductive. If he agrees to have a drink with me, I'll make it clear to him I'm ready for some action. That we should go somewhere and have sex. That's the best-case scenario. If, however, he doesn't show much interest in going to bed with me, then I'll take a different route. I'll ask him to do me a favor, tell him I've gotten myself into trouble and need him to help me escape the jam I've found myself in. Either way, I will eventually be alone with him. Like I said, if we have sex, that would be ideal. His semen inside me will seal the deal for us. But even if that plan fails, when I'm alone with him, I will find a reason to give him a big hug. You know, just for listening to me talk about my troubles. I'll pull him close enough for the transfer of hair and fiber to take place. Maybe I'll accidentally scratch him, getting his DNA under my fingernails. Once he's gone, I have a friend who has agreed to bang me around, rough me up a bit. You know, give me a couple of hard slaps, a punch or two, squeeze me tight enough to cause bruising on my arms and wrists. He'll take pictures, which will show me looking pretty beat up. That's when I go to the hospital and tell the doctor I was attacked and there had been an attempted rape. In situations like that, the hospital is obligated to contact the police. I inform them my attacker was Jack Dantzler. They'll have no choice but to bring him in for questioning. Meantime, I file criminal charges against him."

Shaking his head, Tommy said, "Your plan has more holes than three golf courses, Nikki. Hole number one . . . once Dantzler learns your last name is Doyle, and that you're my daughter, he'll know he's being bamboozled."

"He won't know. At least, not initially. You're forgetting that my full name is Nicole Leigh Doyle. I'll introduce myself as Nicole Leigh. That's the name I go by at work, so it won't be too much of a stretch."

"And later on, after you've filed charges, you'll have to come clean and tell them you're a Doyle."

"Won't matter by then, Dad. Dantzler will be drowning in a pool of deep shit at that point."

"No one will believe such a cockamamie story, especially not his cop pals. They'll laugh in your face."

"You've been away too long, Dad. Things have changed dramatically since you were locked up. In today's world, an accusation is equal to a guilty charge. Accuse a man of rape or violent sexual assault and that charge sticks with him no matter how loud he pleads his innocence. The truth doesn't necessarily count for much in situations like that. I'll tell my story in front of television cameras and in interviews with newspaper reporters. Just think about it, Dad. Headlines that declare, 'Famous Homicide Detective Accused of Rape.' His picture will be all over the papers and on the tube. Even if Dantzler does get off scot-free people will view him in a different light. They will always wonder, did he get away with sexual assault and attempted rape? Is the legendary Jack Dantzler really a sexual predator? That cloud of suspicion will haunt him forever."

"Nikki, I appreciate you wanting to help. And for being willing to get banged around to make it happen. But I have no interest in killing Dantzler's reputation. I want to kill the man."

"Okay, Dad, have it your way. Just keep in mind that if you fail to come up with a plan that will work, you do have a second option to fall back on."

"I love you, Nikki."

"Back atcha, old man. Now go and get some rest while I cook dinner. You look like you could use it."

"Yeah, think I'll lie down for an hour or so. Rest my eyes. Wake me when dinner is ready."

"Will do," Nikki said, finishing off her beer and opening a new one.

Chapter Eight

Dantzler was having breakfast at the IHOP on Nicholasville Road with Sean Montgomery and David Bloom in what had long been a Wednesday morning ritual. This get-together went back more than twenty years, and barring some tragedy would go on indefinitely. Until recently, there had been four members present for these private social affairs. But that changed when Erin moved to Manhattan. The quartet was now a trio. Sean and Bloom both missed Erin terribly. They had grown very fond of her during the three years she and Dantzler were a couple. Dantzler was certain they missed her almost as much as he did. Almost.

After finishing off his omelet, Dantzler said to Sean, "Weren't you the one who broke up the scuffle between Robert Hilton and Kent Lofton?"

"Yeah, me and Randall Dennis," Sean replied. "Not an easy thing to do, that much I can tell you. Randall grabbed Robert, leaving me to deal with Kent. The dude is athletic, fit and strong as an ox. Holding him back was like trying to stop a freight train. And believe me when I say he had blood in his eyes. I hate to think what would've happened if he got his hands on Robert."

Bloom said, "Honestly, I was shocked when I heard what Robert had done. I had him pegged as meek, not violent."

"He wasn't meek that day," Sean said. "Cowardly, yes, attacking while Kent was turned away. He whacked Kent pretty good with his racket. Right below Kent's ear."

"Was there an argument prior to the attack?" Dantzler asked Sean.

"If there was I didn't hear it. The attack happened a few seconds after me and Randall walked into the locker room. But that's something you should know, isn't it, Jack? When you suspended Robert, didn't you ask him why he went after Kent?"

"No, I didn't think it was important. At the time, all I wanted to do was punish Robert."

"But now you do think it's important, right? Or else, why would you be bringing it up? Okay, Jack, why *are* you bringing it up?"

Bloom chimed in, "Because it has something to do with the investigation he's involved in. Am I right, Jack?"

Dantzler took a drink of orange juice, then said, "Possibly, but damned if I can figure out how. It's all still a muddled mess in my head. What I can tell you is, there's a lot of bedroom activity going on in Lexington and not always between husband and wife."

"And that surprises you?" Sean said, chuckling. "Hell, Jack, that's been happening for ten-thousand years. Since men and women figured out how to do the big nasty. Even a saint like myself has to plead guilty to that charge on a couple of occasions."

"It's a miracle you're still alive, Sean," Bloom said, "given your many nefarious amorous adventures in foreign bedrooms. Hard to believe some angry husband hasn't put a bullet in that callous heart of yours."

"Yeah, Doc, me and you both. Just lucky, I guess."

Dantzler said, "Were either of you aware that Laura Conley was having an affair with Robert Hilton?"

"I thought it was common knowledge," Sean stated. "It wasn't exactly a well-kept secret."

"How about you, Bloom? Did you know?"

"Yeah. But why are you bringing this up now? You aren't thinking it played a role in the altercation between Robert and Kent, are you? I mean, why would it?"

"I don't know, Bloom, maybe it didn't," Dantzler admitted. "Did you guys know Mike Conley was also having an affair?"

"Nope, that one comes as a surprise," Sean said.

"I had no idea," Bloom echoed. "With who?"

"I'd better keep that name in the vault for the time being," Dantzler said. "Anyway, Mike said he ended it after a couple of months."

"Marianne Lofton," Sean announced, sounding like a school kid who was the first to raise his hand and answer a question. "Had to be Marianne. I'm right, aren't I, Jack?"

"What makes you think it was Marianne?"

"Because she and Mike always played doubles together. And they'd usually go for a drink when their match was over. Always real cozy with each other. Bumping shoulders, shaking hands, hugging after every point they won. I can't believe I didn't figure it out long ago."

"Okay, Jack, these folks are swapping bedrooms like kids trading baseball cards," Bloom commented. "But where does Kent Lofton fit in to all this? You still haven't offered a reason why Robert went after Kent."

"At this point, Bloom, I'm not sure where any piece fits in," Dantzler acknowledged. "Could be none of these affairs played any role in Laura Conley's murder. But I can't help finding it all quite intriguing."

Sean said, "Ask Robert why he attacked Kent. Then ask Kent the same question. Go to the source, that's my suggestion."

"Robert moved to St. Louis, didn't he?" Bloom asked. "Not long after Kelly divorced him."

"And not long after he ended the affair with Laura," Dantzler said, adding, "do either of you think it's possible Laura and Kent had an affair? Maybe before Robert got involved with Laura?"

"Trust me, Jack, that never happened," Sean said. "You can forget it."

"You sure, Sean? It would certainly help explain some things. Like why Robert went after Kent. Jealousy is a powerful motivator."

"But you've got it backward, Jack. If Kent was before Robert, and Robert took Laura away, then Kent should have been the jealous one. He would be more likely to initiate an attack, not Robert. You're grasping at air with that scenario, Jack."

"Well, Sean, it has always been my contention that if I grasp at air long enough, I'll eventually grab hold of something solid," Dantzler said, picking up the check. "Who knows? Maybe I'll get lucky this time."

Bloom yanked the check out of Dantzler's hand. "Not today, Jack. It's my turn to pick up the tab."

"Can you believe this, Sean?" Dantzler said. "Maybe

we've been wrong about Bloom all along. Maybe he doesn't have alligator arms."

Sean said, "My brain is telling me my eyes are lying."

"Sean, your brain only works about fifty-percent of the time," Bloom said. "And that's only on good days."

"You'll certainly get no argument from me, Doc," Sean concurred

After the tab had been taken care of and they were outside, Bloom said, "What's your next move, Jack?"

"At some point today I'm going to give Kent Lofton a call and ask him a few questions," Dantzler answered. "I also need to speak with Robert Hilton. Get him to tell me about his affair with Laura. And why he went after Kent. But first, I'm going to make my presence felt at the police station. Jake Thomas has agreed to let me look through the murder book he and Vee put together for the Laura Conley homicide."

"Does Eric know about this?" Sean inquired.

"He gave the okay."

"Why did I bother to ask that question? Of course, Eric gave you the green light. In those hallowed halls, no one would dare reject your request. You are, after all, a prince among princes. Right, Bloom?"

Nodding, Bloom said, "Or in the vernacular of my tribe, Jack is a *mensch* among *mensches*."

"Awe shucks, guys, you're embarrassing me," Dantzler said.

"Right, like being embarrassed is possible for a cocky bastard like you," Sean said.

"Prince, mensch, now cocky bastard. Not many people can claim such a mixed bag of attributes. Kind of makes me special, wouldn't you say?"

"Keep in mind, Jack, that Hitler thought he was special," Bloom said.

"Ouch," Sean said. "That ought to bring you down to earth, Jack. Old Adolph was a bad dude, you know."

"Thanks for the history lesson, Professor Montgomery," Dantzler said, opening his car door. "Catch you two bums later today at the Tennis Center."

HIS VISIT to the Homicide Unit ended up being more about catching up with old friends than gathering information about Laura's Conley's murder. Dantzler spent the first two hours learning what was going on in the lives of former colleagues, including two retired cops who stopped by just to hang out with Dantzler. He was especially pleased to see Vee, and to hear she was engaged and planned to be married in June. Her soon-to-be-hubby was the varsity basketball coach at one of the local high schools. Dantzler didn't know the man, but Eric and Jake gave him their stamp of approval. Their blessing was good enough for Dantzler.

After much of the crowd thinned out, Dantzler was finally able to break free, disappear into one of the interview rooms and study the murder book. He didn't learn much; Laura's murder was, in virtually every way, a very simple crime. The murder book only confirmed what he already knew to be true.

Crime scene photos showed Laura Conley sitting on the sofa, her body bent slightly forward, eyes open as though she was staring at the floor. She was wearing blue PJs, a white housecoat and fuzzy pink slippers. Blood from the wound to the back of her head had dripped down the sofa and onto the wooden floor. The photos showed no signs of an apparent struggle or that the room had been ransacked. There was a half-empty glass of red wine on a table next to the sofa. The TV was on when the murder occurred. There were no fingerprints that couldn't be accounted for, nor were there hairs or fibers belonging to an unknown individual. All very standard details, none of which were helpful.

Next, Dantzler read through the interviews Jake, Vee and two uniformed officers conducted with the Conley's neighbors. No one remembered seeing or hearing anything suspicious that night. Yet another dead end. The autopsy, performed by a medical examiner Dantzler wasn't familiar with, was professional, thorough and, unfortunately, lacking information either surprising or helpful.

A simple gunshot to the base of Laura's skull was the cause of death. The shot, fired from close range, came from a thirty-eight that was never found. Laura's stomach contents revealed the presence of a baked potato, salad, croutons, bread, and, of course, wine. No drugs or hard alcohol were found in her system. According to the ME, Laura had eaten supper approximately three hours prior to being killed. Between six-thirty and eight, Dantzler calculated.

One fact did continue to gnaw at Dantzler—no sign of forced entry. This indicated to him that Laura knew her visitor and had allowed the person into the house. This also meant Laura was comfortable in the presence of her visitor. Comfortable enough, in fact, to let that person walk behind her. Mike Conley definitely checked all those boxes. Perhaps Jake and everyone else was right. Dantzler had been hired by a guilty man.

But he quickly cast that thought aside. It was far too early in the game to consider tossing in the towel and admitting defeat. As a tennis player, he'd been on the edge of losing many times, only to find the strength, the will, to fight back and notch the victory. Several defeated opponents had christened him "Dracula" because of his knack for rising from the dead when a loss appeared to be imminent. This situation was no different. There was too much to be done before giving in to defeat. Still too many questions that demanded answers. Dantzler's reputation was as a fighter, not a quitter. And he wasn't about to quit just yet.

Furthermore, he actually believed Mike Conley was innocent.

AS DARKNESS DESCENDED, Dantzler sat on his back deck, a glass of Pernod and orange juice in his hand. The deck, which overlooked a small lake that backed up to his yard, was one of his favorite places in the world. He loved to come here, relax and catch his breath, especially in the warmer spring and summer months. That's when the chorus of moonlight singers surrounding the lake serenaded in full volume. The birds, frogs and crickets belted out their nightly ballads and love songs. Dantzler never tired of listening to the music they made.

But business came before pleasure. Setting his drink on the floor, he picked up his cell phone and punched in Robert Hilton's number. He only half-expected to connect with Robert and was surprised when the call was answered.

Dantzler quickly identified himself, then informed

Robert he would like to get together for the purpose of asking him a few questions.

"Sure, anytime," Robert said. "Now is fine with me. Go ahead, ask me anything."

"I would prefer to speak face to face, if possible," Dantzler said. "I know you recently moved to St. Louis, but if you're available tomorrow, I can be there by mid-afternoon. Will that work for you?"

"You're in luck, Jack. I happen to be in Lexington at the moment. I'm here to collect some items I left behind when I moved. I want to take them to St. Louis when I go back. I'll be in town until Friday morning."

"Excellent. What about tomorrow?"

"Sure. Where and what time?"

"What about the Tennis Center? Say around one?"

"I'll be there."

Dantzler ended the call, picked up his drink, took a sip and closed his eyes. For the next few minutes, he listened to —and appreciated—what he had come to call his "Midnight Tabernacle Choir." Makers of absolutely perfect music.

He would've been content to stay there and listen forever.

Chapter Nine

"What did you say to Sean?" Amy Countzler asked Dantzler when he came into the lounge area. "I know you said something. What was it?"

"Not sure what you're referring to, Amy," Dantzler responded, clueless to what she was asking about.

"Sean never paying for items he purchases until the end of each month."

"I never talked to him about that, Amy. What makes you think I did?"

"Because the last two times he bought something he paid right on the spot. That's not normal for Sean."

"Maybe he saw the light, turned over a new leaf. Or maybe he didn't want you to keep jumping his case anymore. With Sean, who can ever know what's going on in that brain of his?"

"True. I wouldn't want to psychoanalyze him."

"Who would? That would be like entering an insane asylum," Dantzler said, laughing.

Amy smiled, and said, "I heard you were asking Jake about me."

"Who told you that?"

"Jake. I called him last night. We talked for about an hour. We're getting together Saturday night."

"Really? That's great. But what changed your mind? I thought you guys called it off because of the long-distance factor."

"Thanks to Dr. Bloom, it looks like I'll be working in Lexington," Amy said. "He gave me a great recommendation to the human resources director for the city school system. I had an interview yesterday and it went well. They've hired me part-time until I finish my master's in August. Then, beginning in the fall, I'll be a full-time school counselor."

"Does this mean you're leaving us sooner than you planned?" Dantzler asked.

"No, I'm here until late August. In the meantime, I will juggle my time so I'll be able to continue working here, take classes and do the part-time gig for the school system. It will keep me busy, but I can manage it."

"I'm sure of that, Amy. But set your priorities. Of all you have on your plate, working here is last on the list. If you feel yourself slipping, mentally or physically, stop working here. You have to think long-term. No one will question you should you decide to leave."

"Thanks, Jack. You're the best, you know that?" Then Amy leaned up and kissed Dantzler on the cheek. "I appreciate everything you've done for me. That also goes for Sean and Dr. Bloom. You guys are my heroes."

Walking away, Dantzler said, "Maybe Jake will be your real hero."

"Fingers crossed," Amy said.

ROBERT HILTON SHOWED up at precisely one o'clock. Dantzler was seated at his desk when Amy ushered him in. Dantzler thanked Amy, stood, shook hands with Robert, then motioned for him to take the chair across from the desk.

"Would you care for something to drink?" Dantzler asked. "Pepsi, Sprite, orange juice, water, an energy drink? I'll have Amy get you whatever you want."

"No, thanks, I'm fine," Robert replied.

"How are you adjusting to life in St. Louis?"

"So far, so good."

"Have they brainwashed you into becoming a Cardinals fan?"

"Never gonna happen, Jack. I'll always pull for the Reds. And the Bengals, of course. How about you? Do you follow baseball?"

Nodding, Dantzler said, "Life-long Yankees fan."

"Say it ain't so, Joe. Darn, Jack, I thought you had better taste than that. Yankees? For real? Never would've pegged you as a fan of the pinstripe boys." Robert shook his head, said, "Oh, well, better you than me. Okay, enough talk about baseball. Let's move on to those questions you want to ask me. Just what is it you want to know?"

"Mike Conley hired me to investigate Laura's murder. He swears he's innocent and he wants me to find the real killer. Given the circumstances, it's only logical that I get some answers from you."

"By circumstances, I'm guessing you are alluding to my affair with Laura, right?" Robert said.

"Right."

"Okay, ask your questions. I've got nothing to hide. But if you want my personal opinion, I think Mike murdered Laura."

"In their own home? By gunshot? A husband would have to be pretty dumb to do that, wouldn't he? Mike isn't stupid. He'd know in those situations the surviving spouse is always the prime suspect. Initially, at least. Until he's fully cleared. Killing her at home would only add to that suspicion."

"Well, Mike claimed he wasn't at his house when the murder occurred. Not being there, that was his alibi. That's awfully convenient, isn't it? And terribly weak."

"Why would he kill her?"

"Because of her affair with me."

"Correct me if I'm wrong, but wasn't the affair over when Laura was killed?" Dantzler didn't believe this, but he wanted to get Robert's answer.

"Yes, that's true. It ended about a year earlier."

"I heard you broke it off. Is that accurate?" Dantzler inquired, ignoring the lie.

"Yes, I ended it."

"Why?"

"Because Kelly was going to divorce me, that's why. She'd had enough of me cheating on her, so she decided to call it quits. Actually, at the time, that came as a great relief to me. You see, I truly loved Laura, and a divorce would give me the freedom to marry her. But when I ask Laura to leave Mike and marry me, she made it very plain that that was never going to happen. That she would never leave

Mike. Naturally, I was crushed. Devastated. I was also trapped in no-man's land. I went back to Kelly and promised her I would walk the straight and narrow if she would give me a second chance. She said, no dice, pal, you're all out of chances. She followed through with the divorce. Wasn't long after that, I moved to St. Louis."

Dantzler said, "Did Mike ever confront you about the affair?"

"No. To be honest with you, I wasn't sure he knew about it," Robert said. "Obviously, at some point he did find out. But he never said anything."

"Were you and Mike friends?"

"No, we were not friends."

"Did you know Mike had a brief affair of his own?"

"First I heard of it."

"Taking Mike out of the picture, can you think of anyone who would want to murder Laura Conley?"

Robert paused for a moment before answering, "Well, Kent Lofton would be my first choice."

"Interesting that you bring up Kent. Which leads me to my next question: Why did you attack him that afternoon at the Tennis Center?"

"How well do you know Kent?"

"Not very well," Dantzler said. "I know he plays some tennis, lifts weights regularly, swims. He works as a parole officer. Married to Marianne, has no kids. That's about it."

"You really don't know much, do you?"

"Enlighten me."

"Kent Lofton is a bad guy, Jack. A genuine killer. And that's not hyperbole, that's a fact A few years ago he was employed by one of those private contract outfits that operated in Iraq and Afghanistan. More specifically, he was a hired killer, a mercenary paid by our government to do shit our soldiers weren't allowed to do. And if they did they'd be court-martialed, given a dishonorable discharge and shipped off to Leavenworth. But guys like Kent could act with complete impunity. The folks he worked for played by their own set of rules."

"That's interesting, Robert, but not an answer to my question. Why did you attack Kent?"

"Does it really matter? That's ancient history. Let the past stay in the past."

"Ancient history or not, I need an answer," Dantzler insisted.

"Kent wanted to move in on Laura and get something going between them. He hit on her several times, but she always refused his advances. She thought he was creepy, which I tend to agree with. There was no chance she was ever gonna hook up with him. Anyway, that day in the locker room he made a couple of insensitive remarks about Laura. Said them loud enough for everyone to hear. Then he snickered and made an obscene comment about me. That's when I lost it. I grabbed my tennis racket and hit him, unaware he had his back to me at the time. My plan was to smash him in that filthy mouth of his. Shut the fucker up. That would've been truly satisfying."

"Robert, do you have any idea what would have happened to you if Sean and Randall hadn't intervened? Kent would've ripped you to pieces."

"Maybe, maybe not, Jack. I'm not bad with my fists."

"You'd have to be a lot better than not bad to handle Kent Lofton." Dantzler collected his thoughts before continuing. Finally, he said, "Why was Kent your first choice as Laura's killer?"

"To punish her for rejecting him," Robert said.

"Murder is a harsh punishment, wouldn't you agree? Especially for a rejection."

"For a guy with Kent's background, no, I'd say killing is right up his alley. Keep in mind he already had blood on his hands. And who knows how much blood? But could be I have it all wrong. Maybe he really wanted to punish Mike by taking his wife away permanently. Or perhaps by killing Laura, the woman I loved, that was his way of getting back at me."

"That's a stretch, Robert."

"Doesn't mean I'm wrong."

"The problem with your theory is, the timeline doesn't fit. According to you, your affair with Laura had been over for a year. Also, your dust-up with Kent took place after the affair had ended, right?"

"Yeah, six months or so after I broke it off."

"I don't see a man with Kent's background holding off six months or more before dishing out punishment. He doesn't strike me as the type to wait. And I certainly don't see him taking out his revenge against Laura for something you did."

"If you don't see Mike or Kent as Laura's killer, then I can't be of much help to you, Jack. No one else comes to mind. Sorry."

"There is one other person I can think of."

"Who?"

"You."

"I was wondering how long it would take before you tossed my name into the ring," Robert said. "Kind of surprised it took this long. But you needn't waste your time looking at me as her killer. I'm not your guy. I loved Laura—

still do, in fact—so I'm the last man in the world who would want to harm her. Besides, I had no motive for killing her."

"Sure you did, Robert. Two motives, to be precise. Your love for her, and having that love rejected. Strong motives, I might add. Tell me, where were you when Laura was murdered?"

"Check with your detective friends. My interview with them is in the case file."

"I did go through the murder book. Read every word. And what I read didn't do you any favors. It left the door wide open to you possibly being Laura's killer."

"That's nonsense, Jack. Why would you even think that?"

"In your interview, you claimed to be home alone, which no one could verify. Not exactly an air-tight alibi."

"I don't mean to sound crude, but I don't give a fuck what you or anyone else thinks about my alibi. I was home when it happened. That's the truth."

"Wouldn't expect you to say otherwise, Robert. But regardless of how vociferously you protest, it doesn't change anything. It's still a weak alibi."

"Are we done here?" Robert said, standing. "I have places to be, things I need to take care of. I did not kill Laura. If you have additional questions, I'll be more than happy to answer each one. But only with my attorney present. You have a good day, Jack. Don't bother getting up. I can see my way out."

"Thanks for stopping by, Robert," Dantzler said, seconds before Robert hurried out of the office.

Dantzler hadn't come into the interview thinking Robert might have murdered Laura. That possibility hadn't been on his radar. But now, after speaking with him, he wasn't so sure. There was something off about Robert's demeanor. Dantzler couldn't put a finger on it, but he could feel it deep down in his gut. It had something to do with the vibe Robert gave off. He was too cool, too quick to lay the blame on Kent Lofton, too assured of his own innocence. Certainly more assured than a man with such a lame alibi ought to be. There was also the lie he told about the affair being over for a year. That was yet another big strike against him.

One fact did stand out—Jake and Vee failed to dig deep enough during their interview with Robert. Failed to press for more answers. To make the guy sweat a little. To put that assurance of his to a real test.

This was an oversight Dantzler promised to rectify.

Chapter Ten

Before scheduling an interview with Kent Lofton, Dantzler needed to collect more information about the man. Everything he'd learned about Kent from Robert Hilton came as news to him. He knew nothing about Kent's past prior to his becoming a member at the Tennis Center. Nothing about Kent having served in Iraq or Afghanistan, his working for a private security firm, or his being, what Robert termed, a "mercenary." Mostly, Dantzler wanted to find out if any of what he'd been told was true, or if Robert had concocted a bullshit story for purposes only he could explain.

Dantzler suspected that much of the tale about Kent's past was probably true. It was a little too wild to have been made up, Dantzler concluded. And too easy to verify. Why would Robert falsify Kent's past when it would be so easy to prove him to be a liar?

However, even if every word Robert said about Kent's past was a lie it failed to diminish one fact: Kent was a tough guy, not a man to take lightly. Dantzler had no illusions about Kent. When interviewing him, Dantzler had to be prepared for anything, including violence. A killer, under any circumstances, is always a killer.

Dantzler also realized he knew even less about Marianne Lofton, Kent's wife. She was attractive, in her mid-thirties, very athletic and a better-than-average club tennis player. Somewhere in the back of his memory, he recalled hearing she played Division One basketball for a school in a major conference. You have to be athletic to play at that level. Beyond those few details, Marianne was, like her husband, something of a mystery.

If anyone could fill in some of the blank spaces, it was Bloom. He and Mindy Stafford regularly played doubles against Marianne and Mike Conley. Realizing this, Dantzler grabbed his phone and punched in Bloom's cell number, opting for that rather than his office number. Dantzler knew from past experience if the call went to voicemail, it meant Bloom was with a patient and he would have to leave a message. But for once, he got lucky; Bloom answered.

"A call during office hours," Bloom said. "Must be serious. What's going on?"

"Relax, Bloom, it's nothing to get excited about," Dantzler noted. "I just need to pick your brain and gather some information. When will you be free?"

"I'm free until school lets out. That's around three-thirty. Then I have a session with a sixteen-year-old. Why do you feel the need to pick my brain?"

"If you're free, can you come to the Tennis Center? I'd rather talk in person."

"Sure. I was planning to get some lunch. Want me to bring you something?"

"Not hungry, Bloom. But get yourself something. You can eat at the restaurant or bring it here."

"If you don't eat, neither will I," Bloom said. "I can pick up something once we're finished and take it back to the office. I'll see you in about twenty minutes."

After ending the call, Dantzler went into the lounge area to speak with Amy Countzler. But that talk had to be put on hold while Amy chatted with Denise Mitchell, a nice lady and one of the wealthiest women in town. While waiting, Dantzler bought a Pepsi Max and put two dollars in the cash register.

Once Amy was finally free, Dantzler said, "You're fairly familiar with most of the members here, aren't you, Amy?"

"Yeah, most of them. Why do you ask?"

"What can you tell me about Kent Lofton?"

"That he never speaks. I'm serious . . . the man is a mute. Anytime I say hello or try to engage him in conversation, he practically ignores me. Usually just stares for a second or two, then walks away. When I see him now I don't even bother speaking to him. Just be wasting my valuable time."

"What about his wife?"

"Marianne? The exact opposite of Kent. She talks all the time. I mean, nonstop. But the thing is, it's almost always about her. She is her own favorite subject. And if she does ask about me, it's obvious she couldn't care less what I have to say. That's because she's not really listening. She's pondering what to say about herself."

"So, am I correct in saying the Loftons are not among your favorites?" Dantzler asked.

"They will never receive a Christmas card from me," Amy answered.

BLOOM SHOWED up at a little past one, a milkshake from Dairy Queen in hand. And a grin on his face. Dantzler couldn't let the moment slide without a comment.

"Milkshake for lunch? Not very healthy," he chided.

"Ah, Jack, some sins can be forgiven," Bloom said, after taking a drink. "There are times when you have to let the little kid in you come out. What does Sean always say? 'We may grow old, but we'll never grow up.' I have to agree with him."

"Sean Montgomery? Philosopher? Hard to imagine." Dantzler pointed at the milkshake. "Chocolate, I hope."

"Of course. Now, what was it you wanted to 'pick my brain' about, Jack?"

"Kent Lofton."

"What about him?"

"That's what I'm asking you, Bloom. What can you tell me about the guy?"

"Why are you asking about him?"

"Answering a question with a question. You know I hate that, don't you?"

"I do, yes, but I'm baffled as to why Kent Lofton interests you."

"Is he a patient of yours?"

"No."

"Okay, then you're free to talk about him. Tell me what you know."

Bloom finished the milkshake, tossed the cup into the trash can, then said, "Very little, if you want the truth. Kent is not a friendly, talkative or particularly likable individual. Getting information from him would be like pulling a tooth.

It won't come easy. I can envision him on my couch for fifty minutes and him not uttering a single word. What little I do know about Kent comes from Marianne."

"Okay, what did she tell you?" Dantzler inquired.

"Just the basics, primarily. They got married seven years ago and moved here a year later. He works as a parole officer, she's a stay-at-home wife. They have no kids. He's a stone, she's a chatterbox. That's really all I know."

"Did she ever mentioned anything about him having served in Iraq and Afghanistan?"

"She never said he was in the military. Why? Was he?"

"Not the military proper, no. What I heard was he worked for Titan Services, a private security firm that operated in those countries during the height of the war. Essentially, he was a mercenary funded by our government. And he has blood on his hands."

"I know nothing about that," Bloom stated. "What does Kent Lofton have to do with anything you're working on, Jack?"

"He's a killer. Maybe he's good for Laura Conley's murder."

"What would be his motive?"

"Don't know just yet," Dantzler said. "What can you tell me about Marianne Lofton?"

"Ah, now you're heading in a much more interesting direction."

"How so?"

"Have you ever given any thought to their marriage? How odd it is?"

"No. And what do you mean by odd?"

"For starters, there's the age difference. Kent is, what, fifty, fifty-five? Marianne is thirty-four. He's an average-looking man, she's stunning. He's more silent than a corpse, she seldom shuts up. In the vast majority of marriages with a big age difference between partners, it's usually the young female who marries the rich older dude, right? But that's not the case here. She's very rich, he's not. I'm having a difficult time figuring the attraction."

"Love is blind, Bloom. Isn't that what the poets tell us?"

"Big bucks are a wonderful cure for blindness. That's something the poets neglect to tell us."

"True."

"Oh, forgot to mention it's her second marriage. Seems her first husband died a few years before she married Kent."

"Died? How?"

"According to Marianne, it was an accident," Bloom explained. "He was cleaning his gun when it went off, killing him instantly."

"Way to bury the lede," Dantzler said.

"Apparently, the guy was very wealthy. That's how Marianne got her money."

"How much money are we talking about?"

"No clue."

"Where did this happen?"

"Palm Beach, Miami . . . somewhere in South Florida."

"Did Marianne know Kent at the time?"

"Couldn't tell you."

"I'd love to know more about that."

"Doesn't Sean have a buddy who works as a homicide investigator in the Miami area? I think we met him once. Give him a call, see what he knows."

"What's his name?"

"Let me think. He's got the same name as one of those

old actors. Come on, Jack, you're addicted to Turner Classic Movies. You know all those movie guys. Think."

"Big-time star, character actor . . . what?"

"He has the same last name as a country. England, English, Ireland . . ."

"John Ireland?" Dantzler said.

"Yeah, that's it. John Ireland," Bloom stated. "Give him a call, see what he can tell you."

"Anything else you care to share with me?"

Shaking his head, Bloom said, "What's your interest in the Loftons? How can they possibly connect to the case you're working? You know, finding Laura Conley's killer? Provided you aren't already working for her killer."

"Maybe there is no connection, Bloom. But before I rule out the Loftons I want to know the details surrounding the death of Marianne's first husband. And whether or not she knew Kent when it happened."

"Happy hunting." Bloom stood, said, "I need to get my butt back to work. Let me know if you learn anything interesting."

"I will. And thanks, Bloom."

"Always happy to help, old friend."

Dantzler sat silent for a few minutes, then picked up his phone and put in a call to Sean. While waiting for Sean to answer, Dantzler listened to Springsteen's "I'm on Fire". Good song. Definitely made the wait a lot more pleasant. Finally, Sean answered.

"What's going on, Jack?" Sean asked.

"You stay in contact with John Ireland?"

"Talked to him last Monday. Thinking about going down for a week next month. Why are you asking about Johnny?"

"I need his phone number."

"What could you possibly want to talk to him about?"

"Marianne Lofton's first husband died of a gunshot wound while cleaning his weapon. They were living in the Miami area at the time. It was ruled an accident, but I'd like to know the details. His death provided Marianne with the big bucks she now has. Maybe John can fill in the blanks."

"When did this happen?"

"Not sure."

"Did Marianne know Kent at the time?" Sean said.

"That's the second detail I'd like to know," Dantzler replied.

"Johnny probably doesn't have much information to give you if it happened more than ten years ago. He only began working Homicide in twenty-fourteen."

"Even so, he should be able to put me in touch with the original investigator."

"Give me a couple of minutes, then I'll email his number to you. Will that work?"

"Yeah, there's no great hurry. Thanks, Sean."

Dantzler ended the call, leaned back in his chair and thought about how his investigation was proceeding. For the most part, he was pleased. There was still much work to be done, including interviews with John Ireland and Kent and Marianne Lofton. Also with Leah Wallin, Laura's pen pal from Denver. He acknowledged those interviews with the Loftons might be nothing more than a wild goose chase. There were plenty of reasons to doubt Marianne had anything to do with Laura Conley's death. Not so for Kent, especially if he was the KL mentioned in Leah's letter to Laura. But Dantzler's detective skills, honed razor sharp after twenty-seven years hunting down cold-blooded murderers, was telling him all trails had to be followed.

Maybe not telling him much, but just enough to keep him on this track.

And he would stay on this track until he ran head-first into the truth.

Chapter Eleven

Nikki Doyle spent the afternoon shopping for clothes. Her goal was to find a dress sexy enough to get a man's attention. One that would cause his head to turn and his heart to beat a little faster. To get those pheromones going at full speed. To serve as key props for the plan she was cooking up.

After looking at and trying on more than a dozen possibilities, she finally settled on a dress that met all the requirements she was looking for. It cost a bit more than she wanted to pay, but that didn't matter. If the dress worked the way she thought it would, the price tag was irrelevant. The end result, not the cost, was what counted.

The dress was black, sleeveless, the hem rising an inch or two above her knees, all factors that worked to her advantage. She chose it because black accentuated her skin color, and because it showcased her toned arms and legs. Most important of all, however, the dress was low-cut in the front, which offered a nice view of her cleavage. Normally, one of the first areas to catch a man's eye. Of course, to get the full effect of that attribute would require some work. Her breasts, though firm enough, were on the small side. "Perky" was the term often used to describe breasts like hers. But this was a problem that could be overcome by simply choosing the right bra. Again, she tried on several before finding one that served her purpose. It provided just the right amount of lift to deepen her cleavage, thus giving the illusion her breasts were larger than what Mother Nature had blessed her with. But as most women understood so well, illusion is often more valuable than reality.

Vanity was not the reason Nikki purchased the dress and bra; Jack Dantzler was. She had formulated a plan of her own and those articles of clothing were crucial to its chances for success. Nikki knew her father was still putting together his plan to assassinate Dantzler and she had no intention of interfering with what he was working on. But she did have ideas of her own. As a back-up in case her father failed to come up with a plan, which was starting to look more probable with each passing day. She hadn't inquired about the status of his plan for a week, but with his recent health issues, she doubted he was making much progress. This meant she might soon have to become Dantzler's assassin.

Nikki's plan was to meet Dantzler—her father could not know about this—and get up-close and personal with him. To let the dress—and her cleavage—be the icebreaker. Her invitation card, as it were. No, she wasn't planning on killing Dantzler. Not immediately, anyway. Not unless her father failed. Her goal was to get to know Dantzler and for him to be comfortable in her presence. If that happened, should the time come for her to kill him, the task would be much easier to accomplish.

And who knows? It just might provide a little fun along the way.

WHEN NIKKI GOT HOME AROUND five-thirty her father was lying on the couch, a waste bucket next to his head. His eyes were closed but he wasn't asleep, and his skin color was a sickly gray. He opened his eyes when Nikki came in. Sitting up, he did his best to force a smile.

Nikki pointed at the waste bucket. "Have you been throwing up, Dad?"

"No, it's just a precaution," he said. "Been feeling somewhat nauseous for the past hour. Didn't want to risk not making it to the bathroom should my stomach erupt."

She walked over to him and felt his forehead. "You're burning up with fever. This is becoming serious, Dad. You should be in the hospital."

"That's the last place I need to be. Think about it. They run a few tests, find out I don't have pancreatic cancer, then what? I'm back behind bars before the sun goes down. I'll be fine, Nikki. It's just a bad case of the flu, that's all. I'm taking some over-the-counter stuff that should help. Give it a couple of days and I'll be good as new. You need to stop worrying."

"You hungry, Dad?"

"Not really." Tommy noticed the bags Nikki brought with her. "Judging by the names on those bags, I'm guessing you dropped a few bucks today. What did you buy?"

"A dress and some underwear."

"You planning on going somewhere special?"

Shaking her head, Nikki said, "No, Dad, I'm not going

anywhere, special or otherwise. These items were on sale, I liked them, so I bought them. Simple as that."

Nikki went into the kitchen, opened the refrigerator and took out a bottle of water. Seconds later, Tommy came in and sat at the table.

"Care to hear the plan I've finally settled on?" he asked.

"Yes," Nikki said, pulling back a chair and sitting next to him. "Tell me about it."

"Well, it's not ideal, because I won't be looking Dantzler in his eyes when I kill him. I worked my way through a hundred different angles, but never could come up with one that provided me with a good, clean getaway. So, I'm going to kill him from a distance. With a rifle."

"Have you ever fired a rifle, Dad?"

"When I was young I used a rifle plenty, Nikki. And I was a damn good shot. There weren't many shooters more accurate than me."

"That was a long time ago. You haven't fired a rifle in ages."

"That's where you're wrong. I haven't exactly been sitting on my ass while you're at work. I've spent a lot of time on the land behind Ray's farm, the wooded area, and I've been practicing with a rifle. Become quite accurate with it, I might add."

"Where did you get a rifle?"

"From Ray. He owns several, including one with a scope. It's perfect for what I have in mind."

"Which is what, exactly?"

"Are you aware Dantzler owns the Tennis Center?"

"Yes, I know that."

"There is an abandoned two-story building across the street from the Tennis Center. The second-floor window offers an unobstructed view of the parking area in front of the building. Dantzler goes there everyday. I'll wait by the window; when he shows up I'll shoot him. It'll be easier than shooting birds or squirrels. And here's the best part. There are stairs leading down to a back door, which opens to an alley. That's where my car will be sitting. I can kill Dantzler, get out of the building and be driving away in less than a minute. Well, what do you think?"

"Sounds good if you can pull it off. When is this going to happen?"

"After I shake this flu bug and get in a few more days of practice. Definitely within the next two weeks, though." Tommy waited several seconds, then said, "Do I have your blessing, Nikki?"

"Yes, of course you do, Dad," Nikki said, trying to sound more optimistic than she felt. "Just promise me you won't attempt it until you are feeling better. And I mean, *much* better. Will you make me that promise?"

"Yes, you have my word."

Nikki stood, leaned over and gave her dad a kiss on his cheek. Then she went into her room to change clothes. She wasn't sold on her dad's plan, thinking success was a long shot at best. A rifle? When did that option pop into his head? But he seemed convinced it could work, so she wasn't about to rain on his parade. Who knows? Maybe the old guy could pull it off. Be nice if he could, Nikki thought. His dream fulfilled.

She thought about something else as well. Her Dad's two-week time frame put the rush on her plan to meet Jack Dantzler. She had to make it happen. And soon.

Like tomorrow.

Chapter Twelve

Sean's email with John Ireland's number came through a few minutes later. Dantzler sent a response, letting Sean know the message had been received. Thankfully, Sean was on his way to a meeting, so he didn't have time to pepper Dantzler with more questions about why he needed to speak with John. This suited Dantzler just fine; he wasn't in the mood for a grilling from Sean. Dantzler punched in John's number, waited, then quickly introduced himself when the call was answered.

"Sure, Detective Dantzler, I remember you," John said, sounding surprised by the call. "We met briefly when I visited Sean in Lexington several years ago. But considering how much Sean talks about you, I feel like I know you very well. According to him, you're the best homicide detective in the country."

"We both know Sean doesn't shy away from hyperbole," Dantzler said. "And it's not Detective Dantzler anymore. Strictly Jack these days."

"Yeah, he did mention you had retired. You're a private investigator, right?"

"Right."

"How can I be of help, Jack?"

"A woman's name came up in a case I'm currently working. For several reasons she intrigues me. Not exactly sure why just yet, but she does. I'd like to ask if you know anything about her. And if you don't, perhaps you could point me toward someone who might be of some help."

"Is this a homicide case you're investigating?"

"Yes and no. The man who hired me was charged with murdering his wife. Despite plenty of evidence indicating his guilt, the jury acquitted him. It was not a popular verdict; everyone was convinced he had gotten away with murder. He adamantly maintains his innocence, so he hired me to find the real killer."

"What about you? Do you think he dodged the bullet?"

"Wouldn't bet my pension on it, but, yeah, I do believe he is innocent."

"And this woman you're seeking information about, you see her as the killer?"

"To be perfectly honest, John, I don't have one iota of evidence that leads me to believe she was involved at all. I can't even be certain she knew the victim. What I can tell you is a decade or so ago her first husband died while living in your part of the world. The Miami-Palm Beach area. That's why I've come to you."

"Sounds like a funky situation to me. What's the woman's name?"

"Marianne. Her married name now is Lofton. Don't know what it was back then."

"Blackstone. Her husband's name was Richie."

"So, you do remember the case?"

"One of my first investigations after I joined the Homicide squad," John stated. "Oh yeah, I remember it well. It's seared into my brain."

"From the information I've come across, Richie's death was ruled accidental. Is that correct?" Dantzler said.

"Accident, yeah, right. But let me tell you, Jack. That death had stink all over it."

"You have time to fill in some details for me?"

"Sure. First, a little about Richie Blackstone. The guy's family is filthy rich. And I'm not talking millions; they had billions. Richie grew up privileged in every way. Went to the top prep schools, graduated from Yale, even studied at Oxford for a year. His future had been mapped out for him before he was born. He'd join his father and help run the family business. But Richie soon became disillusioned with the path that had been so carefully laid out for him. He began to see himself as a puppet, a prisoner to the wishes of others. So, he rebelled by joining the Marines. Naturally, his parents were in a state of shock and disbelief. They couldn't understand why their cherished son would want to mingle with the lowly masses. Of course, once Richie enlisted, the old man tried to persuade his son to at least become an officer. Richie declined, said he wanted the infantry. That's what he got. He was sent to Iraq, where he proved to be a courageous and outstanding soldier. Came home with several medals, including the Purple Heart."

"Sounds like my kind of guy. Okay, so when does Marianne make her appearance in this story?"

"When Richie left the Marines he hadn't changed his mind about not working in the family business," John continued. "He was adamant about forging his own future.

So, he took his trust fund fortune and invested some of it in a small start-up tech company run by a friend of his. Anyway, they invented some type of computer chip that earned them multiple-millions of dollars. The rich get richer, right?"

"Wouldn't know," Dantzler said, laughing.

"Around this time Richie met nineteen-year-old Marianne Lewis at a Gentlemen's Club, where she worked as a dancer, hostess and by some accounts, a high-class prostitute. She also did some modeling for several famous photographers, which tells you all you need to know about her looks and body."

"I was told she played college hoops. Any truth to that?"

"Let me finish with her biography. That should answer your question."

"Continue."

"Along with being beautiful, Marianne was vivacious and wild. Richie fell crazy in love with her, wanted to get married right away. His father was apoplectic, sickened by the prospect of having a woman with her past as a family member. He pleaded with Richie to cut her loose. What's Richie response? He flies Marianne to Vegas, where they get hitched. The couple came back to Palm Beach, Richie buys a mansion on Millionaire's Row and they settle in, happy as two kids in an ice cream store. Less than two years later Richie dies from a gunshot to his face."

"That's the accident you aren't so sure about?" Dantzler noted.

"Think about it, Jack. Richie was a Marine, a combat veteran, earned medals, got wounded. He was no stranger to weapons. He knew how to take them apart, clean them, assemble them. Yet he's cleaning a loaded pistol while it's pointing at his face? He would be that careless? There is no way I buy that for a second."

"But you couldn't prove otherwise?"

"I did everything possible to put that gun—it was a thirty-eight—in Marianne's hand, but I never could. His prints were on the gun, and it landed where you would expect it to after he was shot. It was in his lap, between his legs. All the evidence led the medical examiner to classify it as an accident. But I just can't agree."

"You're right about one thing, John: I smell the stink all the way up here."

"Oh, no, that's probably Marianne's money you're smelling," John said. "She walked away with a fortune. She got Richie's life insurance, the money in his trust and whatever his half of the business was worth when she sold it. Oh, yeah, she also unloaded the big Palm Beach mansion for who knows how much money. In all, I'd estimate that tallies to somewhere between thirty and forty mil. Not a bad haul for a less-than-two-year marriage."

"Yeah, that's a healthy return on investment," Dantzler noted. "So, that's a no on Marianne playing college basketball, right?"

"Marianne isn't exactly the academic type, Jack."

"During your investigation, did you ever run across the name Kent Lofton?"

"Not that I recall. Why? Who is he?"

"Marianne's current husband. I'd like to know if he knew her when she was married to Richie? Or before she and Richie got together."

"That name isn't familiar to me. That doesn't mean he didn't know her. Marianne was no angel prior to marrying

Richie. But if her current husband is wealthy, here's my advice to him: Get rid of all weapons."

"He's not wealthy but he does know about weapons," Dantzler said. "He served in Iraq with one of those private security companies that did a lot of the nasty, underhanded stuff we aren't supposed to know about."

"Hell, he doesn't need money," John stated. "Marianne has plenty. What about their marriage? You think it's solid?"

"I doubt it. She's had at least one affair that I know about. Who knows if there have been others? Kent is about twenty-five years older than she is, so maybe she's always on the prowl for a younger, more studly guy. It would be a dangerous undertaking for any man who does get involved with her. Word is, Kent did some killing in Iraq."

"Think maybe he's the killer you are looking for?"

"He definitely ranks near the top on my list of possible suspects," Dantzler said.

"Well, Jack, I hope you have better luck with your case than I had with mine," John said. "In my humble opinion, you have a female killer walking around free as a bird up in your town. A rich bitch named Marianne Blackstone Lofton."

"She's also on my radar. If I learn anything helpful to your case, I'll give you a call. And thanks for talking with me. I appreciate it."

"Happy to do it, Jack. Tell Sean I said hello. And the next time he visits, feel free to join him. You'd love it here."

"I'll give it serious consideration, John. Thanks, again."

ENDING THE CALL, Dantzler sat back and assessed what he'd just learned from John Ireland. He'd certainly been given plenty of information, yet he had to ask himself if any of it was the least bit relevant. Okay, he admitted, what he'd learned about Marianne Lofton was more than intriguing. Knowing about her past and how she had come into her vast wealth were good facts to have. But what to make of the question hanging over her past, the one about whether or not she played a role in Richie Blackstone's death? What was Dantzler to make of that? From what John had relayed, it sounded like she had been involved. But the important question was, how did any of what happened in Palm Beach more than a decade ago figure into the case Dantzler was now working? Did he have any reason whatsoever to suspect Marianne of murdering Laura Conley? His answer. No, he didn't.

And yet . . .

After what he'd learned about the Palm Beach incident, he wasn't ready to dismiss Marianne as a suspect.

Dantzler was suddenly seized by a revolting thought—was a double standard at play regarding the way he was judging Marianne? Was he being sexist? Was he viewing her situation from an unfair perspective? Through twisted lenses?

After all, the mass of evidence against Mike Conley cried out for his guilt, yet Dantzler continued to believe the man was innocent. Conversely, based on what John Ireland told him about the circumstances surrounding Richie Blackstone's death, and the money Marianne walked away with, all indications were that she had murdered her husband. After hearing the tale John told, Dantzler was inclined to agree that she was guilty.

Which effectively meant he was holding Marianne accountable while letting Mike off the hook. Despite virtually similar circumstances in the two cases.

If that wasn't a double standard, nothing was.

This is not the way a true professional behaves, Dantzler said to himself. *Not the way I behave.*

His last thought: *Shame on you, Dantzler.*

Chapter Thirteen

Pinning down a time and place to speak with Kent Lofton wasn't going to be easy. As a parole officer charged with keeping tabs on convicts released from prison, Kent's duties kept him busy and always on the go. Dantzler had no idea how much territory Kent covered, or the number of parolees he was responsible for. But if form held true, Kent, like the majority of civil servants, was terribly overworked and badly underpaid.

Getting with Kent at his house was out of the question. Dantzler had no intention of questioning Kent while Marianne might be around. He planned to get with her in due time. No, any questioning of those two had to be done separately.

There was always the chance of running into Kent at the Tennis Center. He came in on a fairly regular basis, spending virtually all his time in the exercise room lifting weights. But a random meeting at the Tennis Center didn't appeal to Dantzler. Too many prying eyes, too many eager ears tend to result in gossip, innuendo and fabricated stories. Everyone would wonder why Dantzler was questioning Kent. Dantzler didn't need or want that. So, the Tennis Center was ruled out as a meeting place.

Dantzler decided his best option was to phone Kent, ask if he'd be willing to meet, then let Kent pick the time and place for their conversation. This wasn't ideal; aware of how contrary Kent can be, the better option would be to catch him by surprise rather than with a phone call. Not give him time to ratchet up his unpleasant qualities. But best laid plans and all that.

The call went about the way Dantzler expected it to. Kent answered in a gruff voice, and his tone never changed or softened. In fact, Kent's attitude became more harsh once Dantzler identified himself.

"I'm a very busy man, Dantzler, so let's keep this short," Kent growled. "What's your business with me?"

"I'd like to meet with you, ask a few questions," Dantzler told him. "Shouldn't take more than half-an-hour."

"Questions about?"

"It would be better if we could speak in person. I promise not to take up too much of your time. Would that be possible?"

"Better for you, maybe, not me."

"No, Kent, it would be better for both of us."

"Again, I ask . . . questions about what?"

"A case I'm investigating."

"What case? And in what way do you think I'm involved?" Kent asked.

His patience beginning to wear thin, Dantzler said, "Not over the phone, Kent. Pick a time and place to meet. I'll tell you everything then."

Kent was silent long enough for Dantzler to suspect the call had ended. Finally, Kent broke the silence. "Have to be late, say, around eight-thirty. The Grey Goose on Jefferson Street. That's the best offer you get. Take it or leave it."

"Not a problem," Dantzler said. "I'll see you at eight-thirty."

DANTZLER COULDN'T RECALL the last time he'd frequented the Grey Goose. Had to be at least ten years, maybe longer. The restaurant was known for having an excellent menu and for doing good business. More important from Dantzler's perspective, thanks to the dozen or so tables on the large outdoor patio, it was the perfect place to interview Kent Lofton. If Dantzler got lucky enough to secure a table in the back, privacy was no issue. Truthfully, any table outside was preferable to one inside the restaurant. In the end, however, where they spoke came down to the weather. Dantzler had to hope it didn't rain tonight. If it did, the meeting would have to take place inside, meaning all chances for privacy were lost.

Fortunately, Dantzler's wish came true; the predicted rain never came. The meeting could take place outside.

Kent showed up at exactly eight-thirty, ten minutes after Dantzler had arrived. Kent didn't look like a particularly happy camper. Seeing the expression on Kent's face, Dantzler had the feeling that getting information from the guy would be like digging for coal. Difficult, tough, challenging. He braced himself for a disagreeable interview.

Dantzler had already ordered a Jameson and Diet Coke.

Best Served Cold

The waitress brought it just as Kent scooted back a chair and sat down.

"What can I get for you, sir?" she said to Kent.

"Club soda with lime," Kent responded.

Dantzler picked up the menus she had placed on the table, handed them to her, and said, "We won't be needing these."

"If you change your mind, or if you need a refill, just give me a wave," she stated before walking away.

"Thanks for agreeing to meet with me, Kent," Dantzler said. "I appreciate you taking the time."

"Personally, I think this meeting is unnecessary," Kent grumbled. "I don't have time to waste answering bullshit questions. Like I told you, I'm busy as hell. In fact, I'm scheduled to administer a piss test to a guy in an hour. So, let's get this nonsense over and done with, okay?"

"Sure, no problem."

"How about we begin with you telling me why we're meeting in the first place?"

"To discuss Laura Conley's murder."

"What the hell for?"

"Mike swears he's innocent and he has hired me to find the real killer."

"Mike swears he's innocent? Of course, he does." Kent shook his head and chuckled. "Let me share a hard truth with you, Dantzler. Every one of the convicts I'm babysitting swears on a stack of Bibles he or she is innocent, and every one of them is guilty as hell. I know it, you know it, they know it. I'm betting Mike Conley knows he's guilty as well."

"If he is, and if that's where the evidence leads me, I'll

drop it at his doorstep," Dantzler said. "My loyalty is always to the truth, not to any single individual."

"And to what end? Double jeopardy is still in the books, last time I checked," Kent said.

"Mike is about to be hit with a civil suit that could cost him millions. If the evidence proves his guilt, he'll lose that suit for sure. That will bankrupt him."

"I'm not the least bit interested in Mike Conley. What does interest me is why we're having this conversation. To that question, I have my own answer. You're looking at me as Laura's killer."

"No, that's not accurate, Kent," Dantzler lied. "I'm talking to anyone who knew Laura and Mike. Which includes you."

"I don't know shit about Mike, and I only know two things for sure about Laura—she was murdered and she was having an affair with Robert Hilton. But knowing that doesn't make me smarter than anyone else, does it? Hell, everyone knew."

"I can't speak for everyone, Kent," Dantzler said, wondering if *everyone* knew Kent's wife was having an affair with Mike Conley. Did Kent know? Perhaps. But that was a subject for another time and place. "It's my understanding you spent time in Iraq. You were employed by . . . who was it?"

"Not interested in traveling down that well-worn road," Kent said, after the waitress delivered his club soda. "Anything else? When I finish this drink I need to get going. Wouldn't want my parolee to piss his pants before I get there. An empty bladder doesn't yield much evidence."

Digging coal, Dantzler thought. "Other than Mike Conley,

Best Served Cold

can you think of anyone who would want to murder Laura?"

"Robert Hilton."

"What would be his motive? Their affair had ended several months before Laura was killed." Again, a statement Dantzler knew to be false.

"There's your motive staring you in the face. How can you fail to see it? She ends the affair, finds a new lover, Robert gets jealous and offs her. Simple, straightforward, obvious."

"Possible, but a long shot," Dantzler stated.

"Why is it a long shot? We both know he's prone to violent outbursts."

"Speaking of that, I'm curious about Robert's motive for attacking you in the locker room. He claims it was triggered because you were interested in Laura and you made some insensitive remarks about her."

"Interest in Laura, how?" Kent inquired. "Hooking up with her?"

"That's how I interpreted it."

"That's not only preposterous, it's an outright lie. And Robert knows it's a lie."

"What is the truth?"

"Ask that lying bastard."

"I'm surprised you didn't retaliate. We both know you could handle Robert without breaking a sweat. Why didn't you?"

"He came to me the next morning, said he was sorry and pleaded for my forgiveness. I felt bad for the weak-ass hump, so I decided to let it go. Had he not done that, I would've beat the crap out of him, then shoved his damn tennis racket down his throat." Kent drained his glass. "Are we done here? I need to go."

"Yeah, Kent, we're done." Dantzler stood and placed a twenty-dollar bill on the table. "Thanks for speaking with me. Hope the piss test goes well."

"Right, I'm sure you're really interested, Dantzler."

As Dantzler watched Kent walk away, two thoughts collided in his head—asshole and Laura's killer.

One was a definite, the other a distinct possibility.

TWELVE BEER CANS LINED UP, twelve shots fired, ten hits. Not bad, Tommy Doyle acknowledged, but not nearly good enough. Nor would it be until he could hit all twelve three days in a row. He'd been perfect once, but that was eight days ago. Before he got slammed by the flu bug. Until that damn critter departs and allows his body to heal, perfection was likely out of the question. Still . . . he'd keep working at it.

"That's not bad shooting," Ray said, coming up behind Tommy. They were in the wooded area behind Ray's house. "Ten out of twelve. With these sorry old eyes, I probably couldn't do that good."

"It's not good enough, Ray," Tommy said. "Certainly not for what I have in mind. I won't be satisfied until I knock all of them down three days in a row, which I will once I shake this fucking flu."

"I know what you have in mind, Tommy. Why you're doing this. You aim to kill Jack Dantzler, don't you?"

"Nikki tell you?"

Shaking his head, Ray said, "She didn't have to. Doesn't

take a genius to figure out what you are planning. A dangerous undertaking, wouldn't you agree? That's a fairly famous man you're targeting."

"So were John Kennedy and Martin Luther King and John Lennon," Tommy said, adding, "Their fame didn't protect them very well, did it?"

"What about an exit strategy? Given any thought to that?"

"All worked out."

"What's Nikki's role in your plan?"

"She has no role," Tommy stated, startled by the question. "Why would you think she does?"

"Because she comes here every day, shoots for about an hour."

"Since when?"

"Two weeks, at least. She's gotten to be a damn good shot, too. Maybe better than you. You're telling me you didn't know?"

"First I've heard of it. How is it we've never bumped into each other?"

"She always calls to find out if you're here, how long you've been gone and when I expect you to come back," Ray said. "She makes it a point to miss you."

"That damn kid. What's she thinking," Tommy said, more to himself than to Ray.

"She wants to be ready in case you can't do it, would be my guess."

"What does she think is gonna stop me?"

"Your health, Tommy. I know you disagree, but you don't seem to be getting much better."

"You and Nikki need to stop worrying about me. Another couple of days and I'll be back to normal. Then if you want to worry about someone's health, focus on Jack Dantzler. Because his health is going to decline in a hurry. The flu bug that hits him will be a seven-point six-two, thirty-ought-six Springfield bullet. Trust me, he won't suffer long."

Chapter Fourteen

Assessing herself in the full-length mirror, Nikki Doyle approved of the woman staring back at her. Though she didn't consider herself to be particularly vain (no more than any other woman, that is), she wouldn't hesitate to describe her current look as stunning. Purchasing the black dress had been a stroke of genius. The above-the-knee hemline was ideal, providing a good look at her legs, and the dress being sleeveless advertised her toned arms. The bra? Another perfect choice on her part, lifting her breasts, pushing them closer together, creating cleavage impressive enough to cause any man—and some women—to do a double-take.

All things considered, Nikki reasoned, *I've never looked better, sexier or more appealing. There is no way Jack Dantzler won't be impressed. Not unless he suddenly goes blind or dies.* She doubted either of those catastrophes would occur anytime soon.

She had decided to meet Dantzler later tonight. "Bump" into him would be more accurate. But that was only semantics. Bottom line: get face to face with him at some point before the day was over.

She drove by his house on Lakeshore Drive around seven o'clock, didn't see his vehicle, so she made her way to the Tennis Center, arriving just as Dantzler was getting into his car, where he spent a few minutes making a phone call. When he drove away, she waited a minute before leaving, forcing herself to stay at least two vehicles behind his. She couldn't forget he was a former cop and as such might be wary of being followed.

She continued trailing him as he headed toward downtown, made a left onto Main Street, drove for a quarter-mile, then turned right onto Jefferson Street. Nikki suddenly began to feel uneasy; her office was a mere three blocks from Jefferson. Then she quickly reminded herself Dantzler didn't know her or where she worked. She was worrying for no reason.

Dantzler parked across the street from the Grey Goose restaurant. From Nikki's perspective, this was a good location. She had never been to the Grey Goose, nor did she know anyone who had. She also wasn't familiar with any of the employees. This cut the odds of her running into someone she knew. Of course, there was always the possibility someone might recognize her and want to join her for a drink. No big deal if that happened. She could always say she was waiting for a client, and maybe they could have that drink on another occasion. Smile, be nice, act interested, but be firm. There could be no distractions this evening.

One negative thought did cross Nikki's mind: What if Dantzler was there to meet a woman? A date, not a client? That would surely throw a monkey wrench into the heart of her plan. But her worst fears quickly disappeared. Dantzler sat, and after he ordered a drink, another man showed up and joined him at the table.

It's all good, Nikki said to herself. *The plan was still alive. All I have to do now is cool my heels until that meeting breaks up. Then I "accidentally" bump into Dantzler.*

She didn't have a long wait; the meeting ended after maybe fifteen minutes. Then the man got up and walked away, leaving Dantzler alone. He stood, placed some money on the table, started to leave, stopped and sat back down. Putting the money back in his pocket, he caught the waitress's attention and ordered another drink.

Nikki couldn't believe her luck. It was as though Dantzler was following a script she had written. He was sitting there, alone, like he was waiting for her to join him.

Okay, Jack, your waiting is over, she thought.

The time had come to play her part . . . stand up, walk slowly in his direction, smile, and let the dress, her legs and her cleavage do the rest.

Her plan worked, right down to the part where Dantzler did a double-take. *Bless you dress, bless you bra*, Nikki whispered under her breath as she drew closer to Dantzler. She unveiled a big smile. It was time for the fun to begin.

"Hey, I recognize you," Nikki said, her smile firmly in place. "You're a cop, right? A detective? Can't recall your name, but I've read about you, seen your picture in the newspaper dozens of times."

"Jack Dantzler, retired. No longer a detective. And you are?"

"Nicole Leigh. Like Vivian, not Bruce."

"L-E-I-G-H, not L-E-E," Dantzler said, spelling out the two names. "Is that what you're telling me?"

"You know your movies stars. Good for you. Yes, you are correct."

Dantzler stood, slid back a chair, and said, "Care to join me?"

"Would love to." Nikki sat next to him, crossing her legs slowly, provocatively. "Thanks for the invite."

"Looks like you could use a refill. What are you drinking?"

"Rum and Coke."

The waitress, standing two tables away, apparently heard what Nikki said. She looked first at Nikki, then at Dantzler, who held up his glass, indicating he also wanted another drink. The waitress nodded before making her way to the bar.

"Do you come here often, Nicole?" Dantzler asked.

"First time. What about you?" Nikki replied.

"Can't remember the last time I was here. Had to be ten or fifteen years at least."

"Judging by the crowd, this appears to be a popular place."

"The Grey Goose has a good reputation. And this warm weather helps, too. Opens up the patio. Gives folks a nice place to eat or drink."

"Call me crazy, but aren't you a great tennis player? I'm positive I've read about you winning a bunch of big tournaments."

"Great is a notch above my level, but, yeah, I know my way around a tennis court."

"Mind if I ask a personal question?"

"About tennis?"

"No, your old job."

"What would you like to know?"

"Why did you stop being a cop? Run out of bad guys?"

Dantzler laughed, said, "There will never be a shortage of criminals, Nicole. Trust me on that. No, I left the force because it was time for me to go. Time to do something different."

"Are you doing something different?"

Dantzler waited until the waitress served their drinks before responding, "I'm working as a private investigator."

"Isn't that almost like what you were doing as a detective? I mean, you're still working cases, aren't you?"

"Only now I don't take orders from anyone. I call the shots."

"You currently working a case?"

"I am."

"How long were you a detective?"

"Twenty-seven years."

"Wow. How many cases did you investigate during all those years?"

"Oh, I would estimate the number to be close to five-hundred. But not all of them were homicides. We looked at all suspicious deaths. The majority of those ended up being suicide, accidental or natural. Homicides? Probably around one-fifty."

"Do you remember your first case?" Nikki said, after taking a drink.

"No detective on the planet forgets his or her first case. So, yeah, I remember it well."

"Care to tell me about it?"

"Are you really interested in hearing about an event that happened thirty years ago?"

"You kidding? Getting the story first-hand from the detective involved in the case? How exciting."

"Hate to disappoint you, Nicole, but it won't be all that exciting. Turns out, it was an easy case to solve. Oldest motive in the world . . . jealousy. The murderer was married but he also had a mistress. He heard there might be some hanky-panky going on between his mistress and another man. He confronted the guy, they argued, he pulled out a knife and stabbed the guy to death. Stabbed him more than twenty times."

"You remember the killer's name?" Nikki said.

"Tommy Doyle," Dantzler replied. "He got life with no chance for parole. But it's my understanding he was recently granted a compassionate release. Supposedly, he has pancreatic cancer."

How the hell did he know that? "You said the case was easy to solve. How did you solve it?"

"Someone turned him in."

"Let me guess . . . the mistress, right?"

"No, his wife."

Nikki was stunned by this revelation. Her mother was the rat? The reason her father went to prison? She couldn't believe it, couldn't process what she'd just heard. Dantzler had to be lying. But why would he? He had no reason to. She wanted to challenge him, to get further clarification, but doing so was out of the question. Pressing him for more details would be a mistake. He might become suspicious, begin to question why she was so interested in that particular case. Might somehow put two and two together. No, she had to let it go. Processing what she'd learned had to come later.

"Enough about me," Dantzler said. "Tell me about you. Are you from Lexington?"

Collecting her thoughts, Nikki said, "All my life. Only time I left was to attend college."

"What did you study?"

"Public relations."

"Is that what you do for a living?"

"Yes. I have a small firm here in town. Not far from here, actually. Oddly enough, most of the people I represent are from out of town. Folks willing to pay a lot of money to turn the tide of public opinion in a more favorable direction after things have gone bad for them. I've worked with several celebrities and politicians, some of whom you've probably heard of. My job is to turn sinners into saints."

"Unlike my old job . . . putting sinners away." Dantzler dug into his pocket, took out two twenties and placed them on the table. "Hate to be the one who waves the white flag, but I need to leave."

"So soon? It's only nine forty-five," Nikki pointed out. "Still early."

"They close at ten. However, if you're interested, we could get together again at some point. Maybe have dinner at a nice restaurant."

"I would love that. Here, let me give you my number." Nikki wrote her number on a napkin, handed it to him, stood and smoothed her dress. "Call anytime. I'm almost always available."

Dantzler typed her number into his Contacts list, then said, "It was great meeting you, Nicole. I'll give you a call in the next few days."

"I look forward to hearing from you."

NIKKI'S HEAD was spinning as she drove away from the Grey Goose. Her night had been a blessing and a curse. She'd made contact with Dantzler, got him interested in her and that had been priority number one. Mission accomplished. But the news he laid on her, that her own mother had turned against her father was shocking and heartbreaking. She had always believed her mother should have confronted her father about his affair. Most wives would have. Failing to do so was a sign of weakness. But finking on him to the cops? That's what traitors do. Unacceptable.

What to do now? That was the question facing her. The answer was neither clear nor easy. She felt trapped in a dilemma that offered only bad options. Should she tell her father, or let him go on believing his version of what happened thirty years ago? Would he accept this new truth if she did tell him? Could he possibly be made to believe Stacy Ross didn't confess because Dantzler threatened her or got tough with her? That Stacy Ross didn't confess at all. That it was his own wife who gave him up?

Nikki doubted her father could be convinced this new revelation was true. How could he be persuaded to believe otherwise? After all, he'd had thirty years to cement his version of the truth. Breaking through that wall, getting him to hear and digest this new version was likely never going to happen. In his mind, it was solid and impenetrable. For that reason, Nikki decided to keep Dantzler's version of what happened from her father. She wasn't happy with this decision. It made her feel like her father's enemy. But telling him would probably make her even more unhappy.

Clearly, Nikki acknowledged, she was caught on the horns of a no-win situation.

Chapter Fifteen

The police cruiser leaving the parking area in front of Nikki's condo complex wasn't unusual. One of the women living there was dating an officer. He was always visiting her, so Nikki didn't give it a second thought. Nor was she surprised to see Ray's truck parked three spaces down from her designated spot. But the sight of a white van with CORONER on the side did cause her to become alarmed.

She parked, killed the engine, cut the headlights, got out and practically ran up the steps to her condo. When she opened the door and took one look at Ray's face she knew something bad had happened.

"What is it, Ray?" she asked, dreading what he was about to tell her. "Why is the coroner's van parked out front? Has something happened to Dad?"

"Your dad is gone, Nikki," Ray answered, choking back tears. "He passed away about an hour ago. I'm truly sorry."

"Dead? He was getting better. He . . ."

"Tommy wasn't getting better, Nikki. He only said that

to keep you from worrying. I think we both can agree he had been going downhill for several weeks."

"Were you with him?"

Before Ray could respond, the coroner emerged from Tommy's bedroom and introduced himself to Nikki. "Based on what I see, your father died from natural causes," he said. "Obviously, I won't know the actual cause of death until I complete the autopsy and get the results of his blood work. You will be requesting an autopsy, won't you?"

"Yes, of course," Nikki said, still trying to process what had just happened.

Ray said, "Are you sure, Nikki? That could be, well, problematic."

"I'm sure, Ray." Then to the coroner, "How soon can you do it?"

"Barring unforeseen circumstances I can have it done tomorrow. That said, it may take a couple of days before the blood work results come back. If you are ready, my assistant and I can take your father's body and transport it to the hospital."

"Can I have a few minutes alone with him?"

"By all means. Take whatever amount of time you need."

Nikki only stayed with her father for a few minutes. She had no interest in staring at a dead man, even if that person was her father. Anyway, it wasn't really her father lying there. His spirit had departed. Seeing him lifeless, silent as a rock, sleeping the eternal sleep, only a shell of what he had been . . . none of that did anything but add to her sorrow and her sense of grief. She needed to cry but she couldn't. Her father wouldn't have wanted her to shed any tears for him. He would insist she be strong, move on and not look back.

And that's what she planned to do.

She just wasn't in a hurry to do it.

ONCE TOMMY'S body had been removed, Ray said, "Why insist on an autopsy, Nikki? The coroner digs around inside Tommy, he's gonna discover no signs of pancreatic cancer. That won't go over well with the prison officials."

"What are they gonna do, Ray, throw him back in a jail cell? I don't think they'll give a damn what the coroner finds," Nikki replied. "You didn't answer my earlier question: were you with Dad when he died?"

"We were sitting at the kitchen table playing gin rummy. I got up to go pee. When I got back Tommy was sitting there with his eyes closed. For a second I thought he had dozed off. But when I took a closer look I could see he wasn't breathing. I shook him, tried to rouse him, but it was too late. He was already gone. I phoned nine-one-one, a cop came almost immediately, then the coroner. You arrived shortly after he did."

"Do you think Dad suffered?"

"He died peacefully," Ray said, adding, "losing all that weight, that's what did him in. He lost too much too fast. That's not healthy. It probably damaged his organs and affected his immune system. That's why he could never shake the bug he caught. Damn you, Tommy. Why'd you do something so insane?"

"You know why, Ray. To get out of prison and complete a mission."

"To kill Jack Dantzler? Look what that mission accomplished—it killed Tommy, not Dantzler. How's that for terrible irony? But you know what? Maybe it's for the best Tommy's dream died with him."

"Maybe it's not dead," Nikki said.

"Please don't tell me you're seriously thinking about going after Dantzler. That would be a foolish move on your part. Let it go, Nikki."

"Here's a question for you, Ray: Do you know the reason why Dad was arrested for murder?"

"We both know the reason," Ray said. "Stacy Ross turned him in. Under extreme pressure from Dantzler."

"What if I told you that version wasn't true?"

"What other version is there?"

"Stacy Ross didn't squeal on Dad. Someone else did."

"Who?"

"Mom."

"That's bullshit. Never happened. Who fed you that nonsense?"

"Jack Dantzler."

"What? You've gotta be kidding? When did you talk to Dantzler?"

"Tonight. We had drinks at the Grey Goose. That's when he told me."

"And you believe him?"

"What reason would he have to lie? He doesn't know me. I introduced myself as Nicole Leigh. To him, I'm just some chick who owns a PR firm. Anyway, we were talking about his first case as a homicide detective—Dad's—and he told me it was solved because someone informed on Dad. I asked if it was Dad's mistress, he said no, it was his wife. So, yeah, I do believe him."

"Before you go casting stones you need to call your mom and verify if that story is true."

"Ray, I haven't spoken to Mom in twenty years. I'm not going to speak with her now. When she left Lexington she left me for good. I don't give a damn about her or what she did. You raised me, not her. Far as I'm concerned, she died long before Dad did."

"Maybe it's a good thing you found out the truth."

"Good? In what way?"

"Nikki, if you believe your mom turned Tommy in, then you have to concede Dantzler didn't threaten or intimidate Stacy Ross. That she played no role in your dad's arrest. Therefore, you have no cause to go after Dantzler."

"Regardless of who ratted out Dad, the fact remains that Jack Dantzler is the man responsible for taking my father away from me for most of my life. He's guilty of that, and I aim to make him pay."

"Tommy committed the murder, Nikki," Ray stated. "He's responsible, not Dantzler."

"I'm not cutting Dad any slack," Nikki said. "I know he was guilty of committing homicide. But it was Dantzler who took my father from me."

"Dantzler was only doing his job. Surely, you understand that. Please don't let this eat away at you like it did to Tommy. Especially now that you know the real truth. Let it go. Move on. Don't go looking for trouble you don't need."

"I'll think about." Nikki reached out and took hold of Ray's hand. "You know I love you, Ray. I owe you more than I can ever repay. Whatever I am, it's because of you."

"I'm hoping you aren't an assassin," Ray said. "Your dad wouldn't want that."

"I know."

"What about an obituary for the newspaper? How does that usually work? Do you give them the information, then they write it?"

"I need to write this one," Nikki said. "It's critical that my name is listed as Nikki Doyle, not Nicole Leigh Doyle. Dantzler can't find out I'm Tommy Doyle's daughter."

"Nikki, my advice is, stay clear of Dantzler. Nothing good can come from you hanging out with him."

"Maybe I like spending time with him. He is, after all, a damn good-looking man."

"Ah, Jesus, tell me I didn't hear that."

"I could tell he's interested in me, Ray. I got his attention. He'll call, ask me out. Count on it."

Shaking his head, Ray said, "What about funeral arrangements for Tommy? Any thoughts on that?"

"Once the autopsy is completed and Dad's body is released to us, we'll have him cremated," Nikki said. "No need for a service. You okay with that?"

"That's what Tommy wanted."

RAY LEFT a few minutes past midnight. Nikki undressed, exchanging her sexy dress and bra for a pair of gym shorts and a T-shirt, went into the kitchen, poured herself a glass of Merlot, went back into the den and sat on the sofa. All alone. Again. The place felt eerily silent, like she'd suddenly lost her hearing. And part of her soul.

She felt a desire to cry, but the tears wouldn't come. Not now, anyway. Maybe they would come later on, but for now, some invisible dam was holding them back. What was it that kept her from weeping for a father she loved with all her heart? Who she would miss every second for the rest of her life? Deep down, she knew the answer.

Anger.

At Jack Dantzler.

Misplaced? Probably. Unreasonable? No doubt. Ray's words rang loud and clear in her head. Her father was responsible for his own actions, Dantzler was only doing his job, the real blame belonged on her mom's shoulders. Every word Ray spoke made sense. She couldn't deny that.

Still, she wasn't about to forget one undeniable fact—while she was growing up without a father, Jack Dantzler was reaping the benefits of his glory as a homicide detective. Once-a-week-visits to the prison couldn't begin to make up for the absence and loneliness she felt every minute of her life. For not being allowed to touch or hug her father.

Was she being overly emotional? Sounding too much like her father? Yes and yes. But she didn't care. Her father might be gone but his spirit was alive and well inside her. And it always would be.

He had spent thirty years preparing for a single mission. A mission he would never be able to accomplish.

Death closed the door on that dream.

But he lived inside her.

So did his dream.

Chapter Sixteen

Dantzler spent two days attempting to get in touch with Marianne Lofton. He left numerous messages, none of which were returned. He began to wonder if perhaps Kent had alerted his wife to the possibility she might be under investigation, and that the wise thing to do would be for her to avoid being questioned. If that were true, Marianne's reluctance to provide answers was troubling. Did she have something to hide? Was she involved in Laura Conley's death? To Dantzler's way of thinking, dodging questions indicated she might be.

Concluding three sets of tennis, Dantzler showered, dressed and went up to his office. Sean Montgomery was inside talking with Amy Countzler. Dantzler entered and sat at his desk, pleased to finally witness a conversation between Amy and Sean that was cordial, not combative. Fireworks are never a good sign, he thought.

"Jack, Amy just informed me she will be leaving us in

August," Sean stated. "Think this place can survive without her?"

"We'll probably shut down by Christmas," Dantzler said, smiling. "No organization can live without its heart. Amy has been our heart for six years."

"She's also quite a pain in the ass, especially mine."

"Well, Sean, that's because you've always been, shall we say, rather lax when it comes to paying for purchases," Amy said.

"Sean claims he's a changed man, Amy, that he's been paying in a timely fashion," Dantzler said.

"Which only proves even an old dog is trainable," Amy said. "And with that, like a drunk Frenchman once said, I will bid you guys adieu."

Sean settled into the chair across from Dantzler, and said, "That's one special lady. She will be missed."

"Probably more than we know." Dantzler took a sip from his water bottle. "Sean, are you familiar with a lady named Nicole Leigh?"

"Name doesn't ring a bell. Why are you asking?"

"I met her two nights ago at the Grey Goose. She introduced herself right after I finished speaking with Kent Lofton. She's about five-seven, dark hair, expressive eyes, great figure. Really quite beautiful. She owns a PR firm here in town. You being a notorious ladies' man, I thought you might know her."

"Based on your description, she sounds like someone I'd like to know. She must be one of the few that slipped past me."

"I told her I would call and ask her out. But a voice in my head is telling me that might not be a good idea."

"Why? Was something about her suspicious?"

"Yeah, but I can't put my finger on it," Dantzler said. "I got the feeling she sought me out, that her sole purpose was to meet me. A woman who looks like her, I should be flattered, right? But . . . I don't know."

"What would be the problem if she had been seeking you out?" Sean asked. "Women have every right to approach a man. No rule book says otherwise."

"Agreed. But it seemed planned, not accidental. I don't think she saw me, then decided to introduce herself. It's like I was targeted. Another thing—she was way overdressed for the Grey Goose. She looked like a movie star on her way to a fancy, high-class Hollywood party."

"Damn, Jack, she's sounding better all the time. Give me her number if you pass on taking her out."

"Know what she wanted me to talk about? My first case as a homicide detective. That's strange, don't you think? How could that possibly interest her?"

"Maybe she was simply making conversation. She'd just met you, she knew you were a detective, so that was the logical starting point for a conversation. Sounds perfectly normal to me."

Dantzler laughed, said, "I'm reminded of Brother Sunshine's final warning before he left town. That Lucifer could very well be a female. He said female Lucifer might show up one day, intent on claiming my soul."

"Hell, Jack, if Lucifer is a female, I've dated her about ten different times," Sean said.

"Sean, if anyone is Lucifer, it's you. Everybody knows that."

"Keep that secret to yourself, Jack. I have a reputation to live down to."

Just then, Dantzler's cell phone buzzed. The call was

from Milt Brewer. Dantzler answered, said he'd put the call on speaker phone.

"You busy, Ace?" Milt asked.

"Not at all. Just sitting here listening to Sean tell me how great he is."

"Hey, Sean."

"Milt," Sean said.

"Jack, did you happen to read yesterday's newspaper?" Milt asked.

"No."

"Then you missed an interesting bit of news. Tommy Doyle is dead. He died three days ago."

"You said he had pancreatic cancer," Dantzler said. "It killed him. What's so interesting about that?"

"Two reasons. First, the guy who swore revenge against you is no longer a threat. Second, and this is where it gets interesting, according to the warden, Tommy did not have pancreatic cancer. Or any kind of cancer. He died of congestive heart failure."

"What are you saying, Milt? The pancreatic cancer story was a con?"

"That's precisely what I'm saying, Ace."

"How the hell did he pull that off? And who confirmed his cancer diagnosis?"

"According to the warden, Tommy secretly went on an extreme weight loss regimen. He lost forty-five pounds in a matter of weeks. Before going on his crash diet, Tommy made a deal with the prison doctor to support the cancer diagnosis. Tommy promised the doctor fifty grand for his help. Apparently, to make it look legit, the doctor used old X-rays of a prisoner who actually had pancreatic cancer. The plan worked; Tommy was granted a compassionate release. As you might expect, the doctor has been arrested and charged with multiple crimes."

"What you're hinting at is Tommy staged his bullshit con so he could get released from prison and come after me. Is that what you're saying?"

"What other reason would he have to put himself through such an ordeal?" Milt said.

"When was Tommy released?"

"Seven weeks ago."

"Why hasn't he come after me? Seven weeks is plenty enough time to kill someone, if that's your intention."

"He probably had to regain his strength after losing all that weight. And he'd need time to work up a plan. But that's all moot now, Ace. You never have to worry about Tommy Doyle ever again."

"Hate to break it to you, Milt, but I *never* worried about Tommy Doyle. But thanks for the heads-up. Good to know you still have my back."

"Always, Ace. You take care. See you around, Sean."

"Tommy Doyle?" Sean said, after the call ended. "Your first case, right?"

"Yeah."

"So that would be the case your beautiful female Lucifer was asking about, correct?"

"Correct."

"Don't know, Jack. Maybe you should heed Brother Sunshine's warning."

Dantzler wasn't inclined to disagree.

GLASS OF PERNOD and orange juice in hand, Dantzler sat on his deck listening to the nightly music coming from the birds, crickets and frogs that surrounded the lake. He never tired of hearing their comforting sounds. And he doubted he ever would.

On this night, however, their music was being sabotaged by a fierce debate taking place inside his head: should he call Nicole Leigh and ask her out, or was the better option to simply let it pass? Like most debates, the final outcome tends to come down to the last voice you hear. And that held true in this instance. Despite a strong case against making the call he yielded to the voice that whispered, "go for it." He wasn't sure it was the wise voice, but it was the winning voice.

Grabbing his cell phone off the table, punching in the number Nicole had given him, he silently ask himself if Pernod had been the deciding factor in his internal debate. He hoped not. Alcohol . . . surely Lucifer's best ally.

Nikki answered, said, "I had a feeling you would call tonight."

"Almost didn't," Dantzler acknowledged.

"Why the reluctance?"

"Not sure."

"I'm happy you did. I'm sure we can have a good time together. I really believe that."

"Did you know Tommy Doyle?" Dantzler asked, startled by his own question.

"He was your first case as a detective, right?" Nikki quickly answered. "Isn't that what you told me?"

"Yes. But had you heard of him prior to my mentioning his name?"

"No. Why are you bringing him up again?"

"Because I find it curious that you immediately ask about my first case."

"I don't know why I did that, to be honest with you. Maybe because it seemed like a natural question to ask a homicide detective. Would you have felt less curious if I had ask about your second case? Or your third? I certainly didn't mean anything by it, Jack. I was just making small talk, trying to get to know you better. But for the record, I do not know Tommy Doyle. Is this going to be a problem for us possibly moving forward?"

"No, Nicole, it won't be a problem."

"Good. I'm relieved," Nikki said, feeling like she'd successfully dodged a bullet.

"So . . . are you available to have dinner with me tomorrow night?"

"Yes, I would love that. What time did you have in mind?"

"Will seven work for you?"

"Seven is perfect. Here, let me give you my address."

Dantzler scribbled it on a notepad, and said, "I'll pick you up at seven."

"Looking forward to it."

Dantzler ended the call, finished his drink, closed his eyes and listened to the voices continue to do battle inside his head. It was, he suspected, a war that likely wouldn't end anytime soon. And even when it did end, he had to wonder which side would eventually emerge victorious.

Didn't matter . . . he'd already picked a side.

Chapter Seventeen

Dantzler continued to agonize over his decision to ask Nicole on a date. The demon of doubt never ceased its relentless attack. But right or wrong, wise or unwise, his decision had been made. There was no turning back now.

Pushing the demon aside (as best he could), he shifted his attention back to the case he was working—attempting to prove Mike Conley did not murder his wife. Dantzler suddenly realized he had failed to run a thorough background check on Laura Conley. What he knew about her amounted to nothing. Basically what he discerned from those few letters exchanged between Laura and Leah Wallin. He needed much more information about the woman. Hidden somewhere in her past might be the clue that exposed the reason why she was killed. And the why might lead to the who.

Which could very well be Mike Conley, the man Dantzler was attempting to exonerate.

Talk about cruel irony, if that was the ultimate outcome.

"I WAS PLEASED you called so soon," Nikki said, settling into her chair. She set her purse on the chair next to hers, smoothed her skirt (different from the one she wore when they met, but still the same length), reached across the table and touched Dantzler's hand. "Obviously, I am excited about going out with you."

"Have to admit, I was looking forward to it as well, Nicole," Dantzler said, not sure he believed his own words. "Thanks for saying yes."

"Have you been here before?"

They were in Tony's, a pricey steakhouse in downtown Lexington.

"No, my first time. But I have several acquaintances who have eaten here and they all rave about it. In the words of my good friend David Bloom, the steaks are to die for."

"Well, if the steaks don't kill you, the prices will."

Nikki made that assessment just as the waitress arrived. "Would you care for something to drink?" she asked, handing them both a menu, her eyes scanning the dining area. "This is a great place to eat, but no way I can afford to. Not unless Bill Gates tips me. Don't tell anyone I said that, okay?"

"Our lips are sealed," Dantzler said. "Bring us a bottle of Black Stallion Cabernet Sauvignon. Never had it, but it sounds intriguing."

She took the order, thanked Dantzler and briskly walked away.

"Full bottle," Nikki pointed out, her hand still clasped to Dantzler's. "Are you planning to get me drunk, then have your way with me?"

"Trust me, Nicole, that will never happen."

"You're a genuinely good guy, aren't you, Jack?"

"I try to be."

"Mind if I ask you a question?" Nikki waited until the wine arrived and Dantzler poured them each a glass before continuing. "All those tennis tournaments you won. That had to mean you were really good, right?"

"Yeah, I did okay."

"Were you talented enough to play at the professional level?"

"Probably, yes, I was good enough to compete at the highest level," Dantzler acknowledged. "But how well I would have succeeded at that level is another matter. People can't begin to comprehend how good those top-tier players are. Men and women. In any professional sport. I could've competed against Becker or Edberg or Sampras or Agassi, but competing doesn't necessarily translate to winning. Maybe I could've made a decent living, or maybe I would've ended up being a pauper. Who knows?"

"You speak of tennis with such passion. Why didn't you go pro?"

"Initially, that was my plan. But life happened."

After the waitress came and took their orders, Nikki said, "What changed the trajectory of your plans?"

"My father was killed while serving in the Vietnam War. I was six at the time. My mom was murdered eight years later. That event sealed my fate. I knew then that I wanted to be a homicide detective."

"And you made it happen. You should be proud. I'm sure your parents would be."

"I was lucky," Dantzler said, after sipping his wine. "Being exceptionally good in the classroom allowed me to advance several grades during my early years. I graduated from high school when I was barely fifteen. I went to UK, played tennis, earned an undergraduate degree when I was nineteen, my master's and most of my doctorate by the time I was twenty-one. I joined the police force while still in college, briefly worked as an officer before being bumped up to Homicide at twenty-three. I was then, and remain so today, the youngest Lexington cop to be awarded a gold shield."

"Was your mother's murder ever solved?"

"About ten years ago, yes, it was. Ironically, solving her murder also led to finding my father's killer."

"I thought you said your father was killed in Vietnam."

"My father was on a covert mission in Laos to locate and apprehend a renegade CIA agent working for a government company dealing in illegal drugs. He was ambushed and killed. Turned out my father's killer also murdered my mother. Complex, I know, but that's how it was."

"Wow," Nikki said, taking a look at the size of the steak being placed in front of her. "This has to be the single biggest piece of meat I've ever laid eyes on. No question I will be asking for a to-go box when we leave."

"Eat what you can, save the rest," Dantzler said, pouring Heinz 57 on his New York strip. "Okay, you've heard my background story. Tell me about yours."

Taking a bite of her filet mignon, Nikki said, "This is so damn divine." Another bite, then, "Well, my story isn't nearly as exciting as yours. My parents split when I was three, I lived with my mom until I was thirteen, she got remarried, moved to California and whatever relationship we had came to an end. We haven't spoken to each other in close to twenty years. I was raised by my uncle, whom I dearly love. Like you, I was an excellent student, graduated high school, went to college, got my degree in public relations and opened my own firm. Never been married, no kids, no significant other. That just about sums up my life until now."

"What about your father? Is he not in the picture?"

"He passed away a few years ago. But no, we were practically strangers."

The conversation went on hiatus as full attention turned to the food. It didn't take long for Dantzler to agree with Bloom's assessment that Tony's steaks were to die for. He'd had more than his share of steaks in his life, but he couldn't recall one being superior to this one. It was top of the line.

Dantzler polished off his steak, but Nikki's earlier prognostication about requiring a to-go box proved to be accurate. The waitress asked if they wanted desert (neither did), took Dantzler's credit card and hurried back inside.

Dantzler refilled their glasses with wine, set the now-empty bottle on the table, and said, "I have a question for you, Nicole."

"Okay, shoot," Nikki said, taking a sip of wine.

"When we were at the Grey Goose you asked me specifically about my first homicide investigation. I'm curious about why you singled out that case. What interest did it have for you?"

"I thought I had already explained that to you. Why do you keep asking me about that?"

"Like I said, I'm curious."

"To be perfectly blunt, and no disrespect intended, I wasn't the least bit interested. I simply saw it as a way to begin a conversation. That's the extent of it. As for this man you ask if I knew. What was his name?"

"Tommy Doyle."

"Never heard of him. You said he stabbed a guy, right?"

"Multiple times. Like I said, the guy was hitting on Tommy's wife. Or at least that's what Tommy thought."

"Sorry, Jack, I'm not familiar with any murderers, unless one of my more ominous clients has been more naughty than I'm aware of."

Quick thinking, Dantzler thought. *But was it a lie?*

"Where to now?" Nikki asked, standing.

"I'll take you home."

"You will come in, won't you? At least for a short while. Maybe have one more drink."

Dantzler signed the bill and put his credit card away. "No, I'm going to head home. I'm working a case and it's not going well. I need to figure out what I'm doing wrong, and what I need to do to turn things around. So far, this case has me going around in circles."

"A murder case?"

"It revolves around a murder."

"Sounds exciting. Does it get your blood flowing, trying to track down a killer?"

"Not really. When it comes to catching a killer, my mind is more important than my blood flow."

DANTZLER DROVE HER HOME, parked, got out and walked her to the front door. He wasn't sure what to do, so he did nothing. The next move would have to be hers.

Nikki leaned up and kissed Dantzler on the lips. Quick, but not lacking passion. She pulled back, said, "Why don't you come in? We could really get to know each other."

"Tempting, but I'm gonna decline," Dantzler said, fighting the urge to say otherwise. "The timing just isn't good."

"Are you in a relationship?"

"Just coming out of one. Still haven't completely gotten over it. But I'm sure in time I will. We can see what happens then, if you're still interested."

"That sounds fair." Nikki leaned up and gave Dantzler a second kiss, this one on his cheek. "Call me when you think you're ready. Goodnight, Jack."

"Night, Nicole."

DRIVING AWAY, Dantzler tried to figure out what it was about Nicole that troubled him so. Why he believed segments of her story were lies. There was something, but he couldn't pin it down. Maybe he was wrong. Maybe it had nothing to do with lies. Maybe it was because she was coming on too fast. But was that a legitimate reason for his concerns? Okay, so she wants to have sex. Not a hanging offense by any means. Happens everywhere, all the time.

But that demon of doubt continued to nag at him.

And he didn't envision it letting up anytime soon.

Chapter Eighteen

At seven-thirty the next morning, Dantzler was parked a safe distance from Marianne and Kent Lofton's house. Close enough to see without being seen. The ideal spot for surveillance. Kent had already gone, having left a couple of minutes after Dantzler arrived. Marianne had yet to make an appearance. Didn't matter when she left—Dantzler was prepared to wait as long as it took.

He didn't have to wait long.

At eight-fifteen, the garage door opened and a red Porsche backed out into the street, made a right and headed toward New Circle Road. Dantzler couldn't see Marianne's face, but her well-coiffed hairstyle was a dead giveaway. Marianne was one of those women who made a point of always looking like she was on her way to a photo shoot for some glamorous magazine. God forbid she ever looked average.

Dantzler trailed her until she reached her final destination—the Tennis Center. This came as a surprise. He knew she played on a regular basis, but he'd never known her to play this early. She was normally an afternoon or early evening player. He kept at a distance, making sure he wasn't seen. Marianne exited her car, reached back inside and extracted her tennis bag. She was dressed in what Dantzler would call non-traditional attire. A white top that did little to hide her sports bra, shorts that barely covered her butt cheeks and designer sneakers. This was definitely not a conservative look. Dantzler reckoned the verdict inside would be evenly divided. Men would view it with great enthusiasm, the female members, not so much.

Dantzler had been so focused on Marianne he failed to notice the car parked next to her Porsche. Or the man getting out of the car. A man with a very familiar face.

Mike Conley.

What happened next convinced Dantzler this was no accidental meeting. This was not a situation where two people happened to bump into each other. This encounter was planned. Mike stepped forward, gave Marianne a hug and a lingering kiss on the lips while letting his hands wander down her back, eventually stopping at her butt. A quick squeeze, then the embrace broke up. Smiling, they went inside the Tennis Center looking like lovebirds on their way to a Las Vegas wedding chapel.

Those two behaving all huggy-kissy in public wasn't good, Dantzler decided. And it certainly did nothing to support Mike's plea of innocence. His statement that their affair had ended was a lie, pure and simple. And if he lied about that, what else had he lie about? Not killing his wife? Dantzler was left with the sick feeling he was being played. That Sean and Jake Thomas and everyone else (except the jury) was right. Mike Conley was a cold-blooded wife killer.

The continuing affair between Marianne and Mike could mean something else—Kent Lofton was next to die. It had to happen if Marianne and Mike wanted to be together long term. This led to a darker thought: Was it possible both of them had eliminated previous spouses? The odds they had were starting to look better all the time.

Dantzler stayed put until the two lovebirds entered the Tennis Center and had time to make their way to the courts. Only then did he start his engine and pull into the parking area. He waited another five minutes before getting out of his car and making his way toward the front door. He had no desire to speak with Marianne while she was with Mike. His chat with her would have to come later.

AMY COUNTZLER WAS SITTING at one of the lounge tables, text book open, furiously typing notes into her laptop. A half-filled bottle of orange juice rested next to her elbow. She stopped typing when she saw Dantzler.

"Did you see the pair that just showed up?" Amy asked. "How they were acting? Made me want to puke. Get a room, that's what I say. And what about that scandalous outfit Marianne has on? Is there a porno shoot here that I don't know about?"

"Yeah, rather inappropriate," Dantzler agreed. "I need to speak to Marianne within the next day or two. I'll mention that what she has on today is unacceptable."

"Personally, I'd kick her ass out of here for good. She's a world-class bitch, you ask me. I wouldn't miss her for a second. And I'm not the only one who feels that way."

"What surprises me is the risk Mike is taking by going

public with the relationship. The affair, or whatever you want to call it. If Kent gets wind of this, he'll go after Mike with Old Testament vengeance. Mike might be lucky to survive."

"Unless Kent doesn't care."

"Marianne has too much money for Kent *not* to care."

"Money can't be the only reason Kent stays with a tramp like Marianne," Amy said. "There has to be more to it. Maybe he wants to leave but can't. Maybe she has something on Kent and she's blackmailing him with whatever information she has. That's why he stays. He's basically a prisoner. Anyway, that's how I see it."

Dantzler's eyes lit up. "You're right, Amy," he said. "Blackmail. Only you have the roles reversed. Kent is blackmailing Marianne. That's why they are together."

"Hey, Jack, I was kinda just kidding about the blackmail thing."

"Maybe so, but I think you have stumbled upon a hidden truth that's yet to be uncovered."

"What are you talking about?"

"Amy, how do you think Marianne got so rich? Talent, skills, work ethic? No, she has none of that. Did she inherit wealth from her family? No. Did she win the lottery? No. She got rich because her husband of less than three years died from a gunshot to his face? Even though Marianne claimed to be in a different room at the time, the cops suspected her of being the shooter. But they found no evidence that proved her guilt. His death was ruled an accident."

"So, what are you saying, Jack? That Kent knows she was the real killer and that's why he is blackmailing her?"

"Makes perfect sense." Dantzler leaned across the table

and squeezed Amy's hand. "At the very least, Amy, you've given me a fresh avenue to travel."

"That's me, little Miss Nancy Drew. Missed my calling, I guess."

"Thanks, Amy," Dantzler said, getting up and walking toward his office.

BEFORE ENTERING HIS OFFICE, Dantzler made a quick detour, went to a place where he could look down and observe the action taking place on the tennis courts. Marianne and Mike were playing doubles against a couple in their late fifties, Sandra and Gary Richardson. Dantzler could only imagine what each of them thought about Marianne's skimpy outfit. Probably a split decision. Gary appreciative, Sandra appalled.

In his office, Dantzler gave more thought to the incident that occurred in Florida and to the possibility Kent was indeed blackmailing Marianne. A good theory, yes, but one with big holes in it, beginning with a crucial question: Did Kent know Marianne prior to her husband's death? If he didn't know, it lessened the chances he was blackmailing her. He'd have no reason to. Unless she confessed to committing the murder, or he found out about her involvement in some other way.

Another thought occurred: What if Kent killed Marianne's husband? Or they were in it together? No, he immediately ruled out that second possibility. If they were equally guilty, there would be no reason for blackmail. However, if Kent was the killer, maybe he threatened Marianne with a similar fate if she leaves him and goes to the cops. In that case, blackmail was out, intimidation was in.

There was an alternative scenario Dantzler couldn't dismiss: Marianne was blackmailing Kent. Why? Dantzler failed to come up with a quick answer, but it was another avenue worth pursuing. Something strange was definitely going on. Marianne showing no fear of Kent finding out how she and Mike were behaving in public had to mean something. She had to know what Kent had done overseas. That he had killed. And yet, she didn't seem to be fearful of what Kent was capable of doing to her and to Mike if he learned of their open displays of affection. And Mike certainly had to be aware of the risk he was taking. Yet, he also didn't seemed worried.

There were some weird dynamics at play among that trio, Dantzler concluded.

Dantzler's desire to speak with Marianne had reached the critical stage. Now more than ever he had hard questions to ask, and when he did he wasn't going to let her off easy. If she killed her husband, or if Kent had, or if they acted in cahoots, he wouldn't walk away until he uncovered the truth.

And he would uncover it. Of that, the demon of doubt didn't exist.

Chapter Nineteen

Walking from the barn to his house, Ray Doyle stopped when he saw Nikki's car pull into the driveway. She parked behind his truck and got out. Ray checked his watch—twelve-fifteen—and asked himself why she was showing up in the middle of the day. The answer came when he saw what she was wearing—ratty jeans, a denim shirt, hiking boots. He knew exactly why she was there.

And he didn't like it one bit.

"Don't you have a business to run, Nikki?" Ray said, after giving her a hug.

"I'm the boss, Ray," she said. "I delegate. That's the primary reason why I started my own business. So I don't have to take orders from anyone. I call the shots."

"You're here to practice, aren't you?"

"Hence these boxes of cartridges." Nikki reached into her car and retrieved two boxes of ammo. "I plan to be here all day. Or until these boxes are empty."

"What if I said you can't do it?"

"I'd do it anyway. Because I'm on a mission and I know you won't stop me."

"That's one mission you should cancel," Ray stated.

"Not gonna happen, Ray," Nikki countered.

"You're going to end up in prison, Nikki. Or worse—dead."

"If either of those happen, so be it. Just so long as Jack Dantzler is dead."

"Damn, Nikki, you're more obsessed about this than I imagined. When did this happen?"

"When Dad died. He couldn't finish his mission. I'll finish it for him."

"You ready to live with having taken a human life? That's a question you need to ask yourself. It takes a toll on a person, no matter how tough that person thinks he or she is. I speak from experience. I killed six enemy soldiers in Iraq. That was war. I was a Marine, killing was what I was trained to do—*expected*—to do, and I did it well. I get that it was combat. That it was kill or be killed. Yet, not a day goes by that I'm not haunted by what I did, justified or not. Are you certain you can deal with the cost that goes along with killing another human being?"

"I'll worry about that after Dantzler is dead, Ray."

"You have no idea what you're in for."

"I knew you served in Iraq when you were in the Marines," Nikki said. "But you never told me about any of your combat experiences."

"There was no reason for me to dump my horror onto another person, especially someone I love as much as I love you. That's why I kept it from you."

"Did Dad know?"

"Yes. He's the only person I talked to about what went down in Iraq."

"Think Dad felt the same way after killing Wayne Donovan?"

"No, sadly, I don't think he gave it a second thought. But Tommy and I, although brothers, were cut from different cloth."

"Then Dad and I are from the same cloth. He didn't give it a second thought, and neither will I when I kill Dantzler."

"Easy for you to say that now. Let's see how you feel once his body is cold."

"I'll feel exactly the same way Dad felt. Mission accomplished."

"Perhaps you should spend more time with Jack Dantzler," Ray said. "Maybe if you did, you'd find out he's not the monster you've created in your mind."

"I have spent time with him. And he is anything but a monster. He's actually a really nice guy. But that doesn't matter. He's the man who took Dad away from me for thirty years. For that, he has to die."

"I'm gonna say this one last time, Nikki: Your dad committed murder. He stabbed Wayne Donovan to death. That's why he went to prison. And aren't you conveniently forgetting it was the jury, not Jack Dantzler, that found him guilty? And it was the judge, not Dantzler, who handed down the sentence? Dantzler had no role in any of that. Tommy's hate for the man was misplaced, just as yours is."

"Maybe so, but Dad held Dantzler responsible, wanted him dead, and I plan to fulfill his wish. I will not rest until it's done."

"Do you have a plan?"

"Same one Dad outlined for me," Nikki replied.

"Exit strategy?"

"All part of the plan."

"No way I can talk you out of doing this?"

"Nope."

"Then I suppose all I can do is wish you good luck," Ray said, lowering his head as he began walking toward his house.

NIKKI CONTINUED to practice until both boxes of ammunition were empty. It was closing in on six-thirty. Plenty of daylight left, enough in fact that she cursed herself for not bringing one, maybe two more boxes with her. The more practice, the better. Still, though, she was pleased with today's effort. Her goal was to knock down all ten bottles or cans or rocks or whatever she could find three times in succession. She'd actually gone one better, knocking down all ten four times in a row.

I'm almost ready, she whispered out loud. *Jack Dantzler's days are numbered.*

On the drive home she mentally went through her plan a dozen times, breaking it down into each individual segment. She had to give her father credit. His plan, which she would follow to the letter, was foolproof. A sure thing. Fire the shot, collect the spent shell, race down the stairs, out the back door, into the car, drive away. Don't drive too fast, and don't worry about cameras in the alley, because there are none.

She continued to play out the final stages in her head,

referring to herself in the third person as she silently narrated her mental movie.

Make no phone calls until you get home. Cops have ways to trace where calls originate from based on which tower each call pings off of. However, once you're home, immediately make a phone call. Doesn't matter to who. It can be to anybody. You should be home within fifteen minutes after killing Dantzler. That will provide you with a fairly tight alibi. Above all else, never lose your cool.

Only if I fuck up will my plan fail to be successful, she thought, shifting the narrative back to first person. *And I will not fuck up.*

LATER THAT EVENING, after dressing down and eating supper, Nikki poured a glass of wine, then settled on the sofa to read the latest Stephen King novel. She'd read most of King's stuff, and she always looked forward to his latest one. Sitting comfortably, legs tucked beneath her, she tried to get into King's story. But she couldn't concentrate, couldn't focus. Another thought kept getting in the way.

Specifically, Ray's question about whether or not she could handle taking another life.

Only now did she realize she'd never once considered the aftermath of what she was about to do. Sure, she had thought about the consequences of what would happen if she got caught. She would, like Ray said, either end up in prison or dead. Those possible outcomes went with the territory.

But . . . what if I succeed in killing Dantzler and get away with it? What will be the psychic impact on me if that happens? she now asked herself. *Will I be able to live with the knowledge that I took a human life? Will I be able to look at myself in the mirror and not see a heartless assassin staring back at me? Will I be able to go on with my life as though nothing happened? Will I ever again see myself as anything other than a murderer?*

Or will Jack Dantzler's ghost haunt me to my grave?

Nikki finished her wine, closed the King book, stretched out on the sofa, closed her eyes and drifted off to an uneasy sleep.

Chapter Twenty

Dantzler was surprised to look up and see Marianne Lofton entering his office. He could tell from the angry expression on her face and her tense body language she hadn't come to deliver good news. Clearly, she was on fire about something.

"I'm here to lodge an official complaint against the vile young lady who works in the lounge," Marianne barked, stopping at the edge of Dantzler's desk. "Furthermore, I'm suggesting you terminate her immediately. She is a disrespectful woman."

"I'm assuming you are referring to Amy," Dantzler said.

"Yes, she the one. Amy. I want her gone."

"What has Amy done that so offends you, Marianne?"

"She had the audacity to tell me my tennis outfit is cheap and sleazy looking. Those were her very words. Cheap and sleazy looking. Can you believe that? It is none of her business what I wear when I play tennis. Just who does she think she is? The clothing police? More like clothing Nazi, you ask me."

"You're absolutely right, Marianne, Amy shouldn't have commented on what you're wearing. That's my job. But what she said is accurate. The outfit you have on is not appropriate for the Tennis Center. To be perfectly blunt, it borders on vulgar."

"That's a matter of opinion."

"Well, that's my opinion, and mine is the only one that counts around here. I respectfully ask that you not wear it here in the future. I'm sure you can find an outfit a little less revealing. And one more thing, Marianne. The public displays of affection between you and Mike Conley are also not appropriate. Show as much affection as you want, just do it some place other than here."

"Really? What if I disobey your request? Respectfully, of course?"

"You will be immediately escorted from the premises. No suspension for a first offense, but if it happens again, you would be suspended."

"You wouldn't dare."

"Don't put me to the test, Marianne. You won't like the outcome." Dantzler smiled, said, "Have a seat. Relax. You did me a favor coming here today. I've been meaning to speak with you, but you're a difficult lady to track down. I have a few items I'd like to discuss with you. Shouldn't take up too much of your time."

"You gonna suspend me if I refuse?" Marianne said, sarcastically.

Dantzler ignored the snarky remark. "Did you know Kent before you married your first husband? Wasn't his name Richie Blackstone?"

The question caught Marianne by surprise. Taking the chair across from Dantzler, she replied, "Why do you want to know about that? It's hardly any of your business. And yes, my first husband's name was Richie Blackstone."

"That's not an answer. As for it not being my business, that's not entirely accurate. I'm in the process of trying to prove your lover did not kill his wife. If I'm to do that, I have questions that need to be answered. This is your chance to help Mike."

"Mike and I are just friends, nothing more. Whatever relationship we had is in the past."

"Sure, Marianne, and river water flows upstream. Look, I don't give a shit about the status of your relationship with Mike. That's for Kent to deal with. After all, he's your husband. But answer my question: Did you know Kent before you met Richie Blackstone?"

"Yes. I was working as a dancer in a club. Kent came in, bought me a few drinks, and we chatted for a while. Then he left. That's it."

"How much time passed before you met Richie Blackstone?"

"I don't remember, exactly. Not long. Maybe two or three days. No more than a week for sure."

"Okay, you met Richie, obviously there was a mutual attraction, you dated, then you got married. When was the next time you saw Kent?"

"Why the sixty questions about Kent? I thought you were trying to help Mike."

A fair question, Dantzler thought. *One requiring an evergreen response.*

"It all blends together," he stated, fingers crossed that she didn't further pursue the matter. "Every answer you give will be helpful."

"Oh, okay, well, let me think," Marianne said. "It had to

be four or five months after Richie and I got married that I next saw Kent."

"Where did you see him?"

"In a South Beach bar. I was with a girlfriend, he was alone. The three of us got together, spent a couple of hours drinking, talking, dancing, having a good time. He left, went his way and I went home."

"Did Richie ever meet Kent?"

"No, absolutely not."

The forcefulness of her answer led Dantzler to conclude she was lying. Her body language tensed, further indicating his question had triggered a high degree of stress. Marianne was clearly uncomfortable with the direction this conversation was going.

Time to push down hard on the gas pedal.

"Your first husband died from a gunshot wound, didn't he?" Dantzler asked.

"How did you hear about that?" Marianne wanted to know.

"I'm an ex-cop, remember? I have access to all sorts of sources, not that any were required regarding that particular incident. Information can easily be accessed from police records. Or newspaper accounts. It's not exactly a secret."

"Yes, gunshot. A tragic accident."

"I have to tell you, Marianne. An accident? That's a hard one for me to believe. A Marine, a combat veteran, cleaning a loaded weapon while it's pointing at his face. I'm sorry, but that defies all logic."

"Logical or not it's what happened," Marianne stated. "The cops agreed. So did the coroner."

"Maybe so. But I spoke with one of the detectives who

worked the case," Dantzler said. "He didn't agree with the official ruling."

"Let me guess. His theory is I killed Richie."

"Did you?"

"I most certainly did not."

Again, a little too forceful.

"What do you know about Kent's previous employment?" Dantzler asked, shifting directions, hoping to keep Marianne off-balance.

"Not much. He rarely talks about it," Marianne said.

"Are you aware he worked overseas and was involved in several combat situations?"

"Yes, he told me that much. He just didn't go into great detail about what he did."

"Did he tell you he killed in the line of duty?"

"No, he never shared that with me." Marianne was clearly becoming exasperated with the questioning. "Where are you going with all these questions, Jack?"

"Did Kent murder Richie Blackstone?"

"No, no, no. Richie's death was an accident. How many times do I have to say it? And why would you even think Kent had anything to do with Richie's death? That's insane. They didn't know each other."

Her most forceful answer yet. Dantzler knew she was definitely hiding something.

"What's keeping you and Kent together, Marianne? Can't be love. Least-wise, not on your part. It's obvious how you feel about Mike and how he feels about you. You guys are deeply in love. Where does that leave Kent? If he doesn't already know about you and Mike, it won't be long until he does. The way the two of you are behaving in public there's no way he won't eventually get wind of what's going on. And the fact neither of you are showing the least bit of fear that Kent will go ballistic once he does find out? That's what is really puzzling. I can't see Kent accepting his wife's infidelity with a smile on his face. Unless some kind of deal or compromise has been reached, which, if true, opens up a whole world of possibilities. Such as one of you is blackmailing the other one."

"You really should be a fiction writer, Jack, because this is truly one out-there tale you're concocting. Why would there be a need for blackmail?"

"Because either you or Kent murdered Richie Blackstone. And the one who didn't physically pull the trigger is blackmailing the actual killer. Of course, I can't rule out the possibility both of you were in it together. Which eliminates the blackmail angle. However, committing the crime together would serve as the cement that bonds you forever."

Marianne stood. "I've had enough of your insane innuendos. I'm leaving."

"Thank you for speaking with me, Marianne. I appreciate it."

"Trust me, Jack, I will share your beliefs with Kent when I get home. I doubt he'll be pleased to learn you suspect him of murdering Richie Blackstone. You'll likely be hearing from him very soon."

"He knows where to find me. And, oh, by the way, Marianne. That outfit? Never want to see it again in the Tennis Center."

Marianne was steaming when she left Dantzler's office.

Dantzler was smiling.

DAVID BLOOM CHUCKLED when Dantzler told him about Marianne's complaint against Amy and her demand that she be fired. It was typical of Marianne to expect things to be done to suit her. However, Bloom wasn't surprised to learn it had been Amy who pointed out Marianne's outfit was inappropriate. Amy wasn't shy about speaking truth to power, even to someone like Marianne, whose power lie only in her ego. Also, Bloom completely agreed with Amy's assessment.

"Truthfully, I should've said something to Marianne when she showed up in that outfit one day last week," Bloom said. "I chose to hold off because Marianne was with three of her friends. I had no desire to embarrass her in front of those women. My mistake was letting it pass. But hats off to Amy for having the guts to do what I failed to do."

"Amy can't stand Marianne," Dantzler said. "Really detests her."

"She's not the only one in that camp. Marianne has a gift for making everyone she interacts with feel inferior. Of course, that stems from her deep feelings of insecurity. Having plenty of money is her form of security. It's false security, at best. Take away the money, her self-esteem would crumble faster than a child's sandcastle in a windstorm."

"I'm not sure I agree with that. I don't know about her self-esteem, but I see Marianne as clever enough, savvy enough, ambitious enough to utilize her physical attributes to reel in another rich sucker. She wouldn't stay poor very long."

Before Bloom could respond, Kent Lofton barged into

Dantzler's office and immediately said, "We need to talk, Dantzler." Then to Bloom. "Alone."

Bloom stood, said, "Give me a call later this evening, Jack. We'll have dinner at Jeff Ruby's."

After Bloom had left, Kent closed the door, then sat across from Dantzler, leaning forward like a lion ready to pounce. The look on his face was one of pure anger. Dantzler prepared himself for verbal warfare. However, before Kent could begin venting his rage, Dantzler beat him to the punch.

"I anticipated you showing up at some point," he said. "However, I am somewhat surprised you got here so soon. What's on your mind, Kent?"

"You know damn well why I'm here. Because of what you said to Marianne earlier today."

"You mean, about the scandalous outfit I warned her to never wear here again?" Dantzler asked, knowing this would further enrage Kent.

"Not about her goddamn outfit," Kent bellowed. "I don't give a fuck about that shit. No, I'm talking about you claiming I murdered her first husband."

"Did you?"

"No, I did not. I resent you insinuating I did. And what's this nonsense about blackmail? Where the fuck did you come up with that?"

"Kent, I'm going to ask you the same question I posed to Marianne: What keeps the two of you together? Specifically, why do you stay with her? Is it simply because she has so much money? Or because she's your trophy wife? What is the reason? Tell me, I'd really like to know."

"Because I love her. Because we love each other."

"Come on, Kent, we both know your love boat sank

faster than the Edmund Fitzgerald," Dantzler said, referencing the classic Gordon Lightfoot song. "Marianne's has, anyway. You aren't stupid and you aren't blind. You have to know about Marianne's affair with Mike Conley, past and present. And now they are flaunting it in public for the whole world to see. I don't see you as a particularly forgiving or tolerant man. And yet, you don't seem troubled or humiliated by your wife's public behavior. Which causes me to wonder why you are acting as though nothing is going on. Again, I ask, what's keeping you and Marianne together? And the only answer I come up with is blackmail."

"You think I'm blackmailing Marianne? Why would I do that?"

"Because you somehow found out she murdered Richie Blackstone."

"That's outrageous."

"Or maybe both of you were in it together. That's why neither of you can afford to end the marriage, regardless of who carries on with whom, publicly or not."

"Why would I kill him? I didn't even know the man."

"I have my doubts about that, Kent. As for reasons why you would kill Richie, here are two easy ones—to get his wife and his money."

"You need to keep one thing in mind, Dantzler," Kent said. "You're not a cop anymore. You don't enjoy the same protection you once did."

"That sounds ominously like a veiled threat."

"I don't make threats, Dantzler. I—"

"Make promises. Yeah, Kent, I know the cliché. Okay, you want to hear a promise? Listen up: I promise I'm going to find out what really happened to Richie Blackstone. And to Laura Conley. My suspicion is those two deaths are linked somehow. And the only two individuals connected to both homicides are you and Marianne."

"How can you possibly link me to Laura Conley's death?"

"I'll keep that piece of knowledge to myself."

"Fair warning, Dantzler. Don't push too hard. You just might find yourself on the wrong side of a homicide case."

"The veil has officially been lifted from your threat. Or promise, if you prefer. Okay, Kent, fair enough. We both know where we stand. Let the games begin."

Dantzler waited for a glib remark or another threat, but Kent said nothing. Instead, eyes shooting darts at Dantzler, he simply stood and stomped out of the office, leaving Dantzler with a single thought:

Be wary of that guy.

Chapter Twenty-One

Paranoia, a sense of impending doom, almost never factored into Dantzler's thinking. Having been a detective all those years, listening to criminals he apprehended swear vengeance against him, had somehow immunized him against such feelings. He understood the bellowing was a means of calming their fear of what lay ahead. Time spent in prison is no piece of cake. Even the most hardened criminals understood that. With that in mind, Dantzler never took seriously a single threat against him.

Until this morning.

After pulling into the Tennis Center parking area and cutting the motor, he sat for almost ten minutes trying to piece together a solid, legitimate reason for this strange feeling danger was lurking close by. Nothing came to mind. He tried to cast his worries aside, but they lingered like the smell of a rotting corpse.

What should I be worried about? he asked himself. *Can't be*

Tommy Doyle; he's deceased. And Tommy's threat was the loudest. But death silenced that threat.

Running through a list of potential suspects, he kept coming back to Kent Lofton. Depending on what actually transpired in Florida, Kent may or may not have a motive to take him out. However, there could be no denying one fact—Kent had recently issued a not-so-veiled-threat at Dantzler for suspecting him of murdering Marianne's first husband. And he must never forget Kent had the willingness to take a human life. His track record proved it. The man had blood on his hands.

Dantzler mumbled a silent curse, scolding himself for showing weakness. For allowing fantasy to overshadow reality. This was totally out of character for him. He slowly climbed out of his car and began walking toward the front door. Several cars were in the lot, including Amy Countzler's white Mazda.

To his left, not far from his car, he noticed a wadded-up cigarette pack and an empty Ale 8 bottle. Had to be kids, he reasoned, leaving trash without giving it a second thought. This had become a common occurrence during the past few weeks, teens using the parking lot as a meeting place after the Tennis Center closed around one a.m. David Bloom recently suggested installing cameras, an idea Dantzler and Sean had rejected as an unnecessary expense. But perhaps Bloom was right about adding more security. God only knew what went on here in the early morning hours.

Bending over to pick up the trash, Dantzler felt the bullet hit his left arm several seconds before he heard the crack of gunfire. The bullet's impact spun him to his left, knocking him to his knees. Realizing what had just happened, his survival instincts automatically kicked in. He quickly crawled behind his car, using it as a barrier between him and the shooter. Rising up, he briefly glanced at the empty building across the street. He had no doubt that was the shooter's location.

Despite blood streaming down his arm he knew the wound wasn't serious. Primarily a flesh wound, or a "crease" as it was often referred to in those old cowboy movies he loved as a kid. He was lucky the bullet hadn't penetrated and damaged muscle or bone. That could've caused extensive long-term damage. But the real stroke of luck had been when he leaned over to pick up the trash. Had he not done that, the bullet would have hit close to his heart.

Dantzler suddenly realized Amy had stepped outside the Tennis Center and was yelling at him, asking if he was all right. Not getting an immediate answer, she started running in his direction.

"Get back inside, Amy," Dantzler commanded. "Lock the door, then call nine-one-one. Tell them a shot has been fired and the police need to get here quick. Also, call Jake."

"You're bleeding, Jack," Amy said.

"Forget about me. It's not serious. Hurry, make the call."

Within three minutes sirens could be heard coming from several directions. When the first patrol car screeched into the lot, Dantzler stood, certain the shooter was long gone. A second patrol car showed up, followed moments later by an unmarked vehicle with Vee and Jake inside. They both exited the car before it came to a complete stop.

Then to no one's surprise, vans from two local TV stations arrived almost simultaneously. The buzzards had begun circling.

"How bad are you hit, Jack?" Jake asked.

"Looks worse than it is," Dantzler replied. "Basically a flesh wound. Just need to stem the bleeding."

Vee said, "Hold on while I get some bandages from one of the patrol cars."

"Keep the media as far away as possible," Jake yelled to one of the uniform officers. Then to Dantzler: "Any idea where the shot came from?"

"The vacant building across the street."

"Great, the paramedics are here," Vee announced. "They can treat your wound better than I can."

As the female paramedic knelt down and began cleaning and bandaging Dantzler's wound, Vee followed Jake and one of the officers to the building across the street. All three approached with weapons drawn. Though they doubted the shooter was crazy enough to stick around, they were taking no chances.

The crime scene van arrived and two techs exited, stationing themselves safely behind their vehicle. One of the techs asked a uniform officer if it was safe to approach the building. The officer spoke into his shoulder mic, listened, then nodded to the tech in the affirmative. He'd probably radioed either Jake or Vee and had been told the building was cleared and safe to enter. The two techs grabbed their gear and headed across the street.

Dantzler, his wound cleaned and perfectly bandaged, ask the paramedic for a couple of Aleve or Tylenol. The discomfort he felt wasn't intense; it was more of a burning sensation than outright pain. But that would soon change, he knew. At some point, the pain would become more intense. She handed him two Aleve and a bottle of water. He swallowed the pills, then thanked her for the great patch-up job she'd done on his arm.

Just then his cell phone chirped. The call was from Sean. No doubt he'd already heard what had happened. Dantzler smiled. How Sean found out so fast was a mystery. The man did have his network of spies.

"Don't bullshit me, Jack," Sean said. "Are you okay?"

"I'm fine, Sean. The bullet grazed my left arm. Don't even need stitches. One of those butterfly do-hickeys did the trick."

"Anything I can do?"

"Call Bloom, tell him what happened and that I'm fine."

"You got it."

Dantzler looked up to see Eric Gamble, the police chief, strolling in his direction. Several paces behind Eric were Vee and Jake.

"Any idea who did this, Jack?" Eric asked.

"Not a clue, Eric," Dantzler lied. He did have a clue—Kent Lofton. Then to Jake and Vee: "Find anything helpful?"

"Not unless you count empty beer cans, broken whiskey and wine bottles, cigarette butts, used condoms and needles helpful," Jake said. "That place is party central. Lots of dust, which makes for excellent shoe impressions and fingerprints, but sorting through all that will be a challenge. I don't envy the crime scene folks."

"We did find something that might turn out to be helpful," Vee stated. "Below the window where the shooter fired from were several fresh shoe impressions. Might be something, might be nothing. In that petri dish, being able to pinpoint a single individual could be next to impossible. However, if those prints do belong to the shooter, the guy doesn't have big feet. Based on those prints, I would estimate he wears from size seven to size nine."

Eric said, "Jack, we'll work this case twenty-four/seven until we find the shooter. You have my word on that. Obviously, you trained all of us, so any help or advice or direction you can offer will be more than welcome."

"Thanks, Eric, but I'm working a case at the moment," Dantzler said. "My time is pretty much accounted for. This one is all yours."

"Any chance your case ties in with what happened here?" Jake said.

"Don't see how, Jake."

Another lie.

To Jake and Vee, Eric said, "You guys take the lead on this one. Leave no stone unturned. One of ours has been shot. We don't take kindly to that."

"Roger that," Jake said.

"Same here," Vee echoed.

"Twenty-seven years a cop and you dodged every bullet that came your way," Eric said. "Now this. Hard to figure some things out, wouldn't you say? Other than you were lucky."

"I was more than lucky. Had I not bent down to pick up an empty cigarette package I would probably be dead. That bullet was aimed at my heart. I've always considered smoking a bad thing. This is one time I'm happy someone was a smoker."

THE BURNING SENSATION in Dantzer's arm quickly morphed into real pain as the evening progressed. He took two more Aleve, hoping it would help but it didn't. His discomfort only seemed to get worse. David Bloom, a psychiatrist, phoned around nine, and when he heard Dantzler was experiencing pain, he offered to prescribe serious medication. Dantzler declined, preferring to deal with the pain rather than being doped up on some Class A narcotic.

Sean Montgomery stopped by at nine-thirty to give Dantzler an update on information he had received from Jake. According to Sean, Jake had nothing new to say relating to the crime scene, but he did go into greater detail about the shooter's escape plan. Nothing Jake said surprised Dantzler. To him, the shooter's exit strategy was obvious. Take the shot, run down some steps, leave through the back door, hop into a vehicle and drive away. One thing Jake said did interest Dantzler—the shooter took the time to scoop up the spent shell casing before leaving. This told Dantzler the shooter was a pro.

Kent Lofton.

Dantzler was one-hundred percent convinced Kent was the assassin.

Jake also told Sean the crime scene personnel had traced the path of the bullet but had yet to locate it. Jake's theory was, once it grazed Dantzler's arm it smashed into the asphalt, flattened, then continued on its way. He said they would continue looking for it tomorrow morning.

Good luck with that, Dantzler said to himself.

Dantzler had promised to refrain from drinking alcohol after having taken four Aleve, but it was a promise he couldn't keep. He went into the kitchen, mixed a Jameson and Diet Coke and went out onto his deck. Sitting, he took a drink and gazed out at the darkness, his only thought being an obvious one—how best to go after Kent Lofton. He was checking off a list of possible ways when his phone buzzed.

He glanced at the Caller ID—the call was from Nicole Leigh.

"Oh, my God, Jack, I just saw on the news that you were shot," Nicole said, before Dantzler had time to say hello. "How bad is it? Are you all right?"

"I'm fine, Nicole," Dantzler said, taking another drink. "The bullet only grazed my arm. Hurts like hell at the moment, but the pain is bound to ease up at some point. I was lucky, though. I'd likely be dead had I not bent down to pick up some trash. That bullet was heading straight for my heart."

"Sounds like the shooter was a professional."

"That would be my guess."

"Is there anything you need? Anything I can do for you?"

"No, I'm good. But thanks for offering."

"Well, if you need something—*anything*—don't be shy about calling. I'm here for you, Jack."

"I appreciate that."

"Goodnight, Jack."

"Goodnight, Nicole."

Dantzler set his phone on the table next to his chair, picked up his glass and took another drink. The Jameson tasted especially good tonight. Maybe his good fortune to still be alive was the reason why. Whatever it was, he decided to have a second drink. Enough alcohol just might accomplish what the Aleve had thus far failed to do—ease the pain he was feeling.

After going back into the kitchen and fixing another drink, he returned to the deck, sat and once again began charting a path that would lead to Kent Lofton. However, before he began his journey, he had another task he wanted to complete. It involved making a phone call first thing tomorrow morning for the expressed purpose of gathering information.

And for an even more important reason:

To scratch an itch that continued to plague him.

Chapter Twenty-Two

Dantzler rang the prison number, got a male voice, identified himself and requested to speak with Warden Thad Curtis. Dantzler was put on hold for almost a minute before the Warden answered.

"Jack Dantzler, been a long time since we last communicated," Curtis remembered, sounding cheerful and upbeat. "How has life been treating you these past few years? Good, I hope."

"So, you do remember me?" Dantzler asked.

"Sure, I do. You came here to interview Elijah Whitehouse. The Reverend. Must've been, what? Ten, eleven years ago?"

"Sounds about right."

"You proved the man was innocent. That he spent the bulk of his adult life behind bars for a crime he didn't commit. Got him released shortly before he died. That was a wonderful thing you did, Detective Dantzler."

"No longer a detective, Warden. Retired about three years ago. Working as a private investigator these days."

"Probably pays better than being a cop, doesn't it?" Curtis asked.

"Depends on how deep the client's pockets are," Dantzler replied.

"Of course, there's another reason why I remember you. No chance I'll ever forget the sound beating you gave me in the high school state tennis tournament about a hundred years ago."

"Must've been lucky that day."

"Luck, yeah, right. We both know that's not true. You were simply out of my league. But thanks for not bringing it up. It was a slaughter I've tried to forget."

"Like I said, Warden Curtis, I had a good day."

"You weren't good only on that day. You cruised through the tournament without dropping a set." Curtis laughed, said, "Enough about the darkest day of my life. What prompted this call?"

Relieved to end this trip down nostalgia boulevard, Dantzler said, "Tommy Doyle."

"What about Tommy?"

"Anything you care to share with me, Warden Curtis?"

"Why Tommy?"

"He was my first collar after I became a homicide detective. After he was sentenced to life without parole he swore revenge against me. I didn't give his threat a second thought. Happened with a lot of criminals I arrested. Then yesterday someone took a shot at me. I—"

"Jesus, Jack, are you all right?"

"Bullet grazed my arm, so, yes, I'm fine. Lucky, too. Had I not bent over to pick up an empty cigarette pack the bullet would have hit close to my heart. Ironically, something that kills people saved my life."

"Sounds like the shooter was no slouch."

"On that, we agree."

"Well, if the incident happened yesterday Tommy can't be your shooter."

"Yeah, I know. Tommy died a few days prior to the shooting." Dantzler paused, sipped water, then continued. "How well did you get to know Tommy?"

"He'd been here about five years before I took this job," Curtis stated. "But he and I did have a few good conversations. He was an intelligent man, much more so than the average inmate."

"What kind of prisoner was he?"

"Model. Helpful, thoughtful, courteous, good work ethic. A perfect prisoner. If all inmates here were like Tommy Doyle, running this place would be easier than running a senior citizen retirement home." Curtis hesitated, then let out a long sigh. "Model prisoner until he wasn't. Do you know what he did to get released? Have you heard that story?"

"Conned you with a pancreatic cancer diagnosis. Received a compassionate release. How'd he manage to pull that off?"

"Promised to pay our doctor fifty grand, which the doc never received. Can you believe he fell for that? Like, once Tommy was out he was gonna give the doctor money? No way that was gonna happen. And what could the doctor do? Turn Tommy in? No, he couldn't do that. Then he would be admitting his own complicity in the scheme. He fell for the con hardest of all."

"Some people are blinded by the promise of a big payoff."

"Anyway, a few months earlier, another inmate had been released after being diagnosed with pancreatic cancer. Our doctor used that inmate's X-rays and claimed they were Tommy's. That, combined with Tommy losing about fifty pounds in a matter of weeks, was enough to get him his compassionate release. Sad part is, no one here, including yours truly, gave it a closer examination. We all screwed up on that one."

Dantzler said, "I take it you are aware that Tommy's autopsy showed no signs of any cancer?"

"Yes, I'm aware of that," Curtis acknowledged. "He died of congestive heart failure."

"Did Tommy have many visitors?"

"Only three, but they were as reliable as the sunrise. They never let Tommy down. At least one of them was here every Saturday, bad weather or good."

"Are you willing to share information about those three visitors, Warden?"

"Don't see why not. But if you know Tommy wasn't the shooter, what are you hoping to find?"

"Probably won't find a thing. But I'd still like to have a look."

"Hold for a few seconds while I get Tommy's file." The Warden's few seconds turned out to be several minutes. "Sorry that took longer than I anticipated. Had a hard time locating Tommy's file. I do apologize for putting you on hold so long."

"Don't apologize, Warden Curtis. I'm not on a clock."

"Okay, here we go. Tommy's wife visited him regularly for the first three years he was locked up. Her name is

Connie. Obviously, I never met her; she divorced him before I took over here. After they split, his brother Ray Doyle became Tommy's regular visitor. He came alone for several years, then showed up one day accompanied by Tommy's young daughter. She and Ray always came together. That is, until at a certain point, presumably when she was old enough to drive. Then she almost always came by herself. Ray came with her on several visits, but usually she was alone."

"What's the daughter's name?"

"Oh, yeah, forgot to mention that minor detail. Nikki, spelled with two K's. Any of this helpful?"

"Not sure at this stage, but it's definitely possible," Dantzler said, writing down the information he'd just been given. "Do you take photos of visitors?"

"Oh, sure," Curtis said. "I have nice head shots of all visitors, including the three who came to see Tommy. Would it help if I sent them to you? Hell, I'll copy Tommy's file, the pertinent parts anyway and ship it all to you."

"Warden Curtis, you have no idea how helpful that would be."

"Give me your address, I'll get it in the mail first thing in the morning. You should have it in a couple of days."

"Send it COD. Least I can do is pick up the tab."

"Nah, we'll let the government foot the bill. We both know for sure they have deep pockets," Curtis said, chuckling.

"Either way is fine, Warden Curtis. Just know that I'm truly appreciative. If I can ever be of help to you in the future, don't hesitate to call. I owe you big-time."

"Well, unlike Tommy Doyle, I won't be seeking revenge against you on the tennis court."

Wise decision, Dantzler said to himself, ending the call.

DANTZLER REGRETTED NOT SUGGESTING to Warden Curtis that he send Tommy Doyle's file via overnight mail. That way, the file would likely arrive first thing in the morning. Even better would have been sending the information via email. But that would have translated into more work for the Warden, or for whomever he assigned the task of copying the file and preparing it to be emailed. Dantzler didn't blame Warden Curtis for not going that route.

Sitting at the desk in his office, Dantzler thought about Tommy's three visitors. Connie, the ex-wife, wasn't of interest to him. She had been out of the picture for decades. Also, she was the person who turned Tommy in to the police. He had no reason to suspect her of anything having to do with Tommy, or with Dantzler being shot. Ray Doyle was an unknown, but certainly worth a look. Dantzler would check him out, see if he had any past criminal history. However, without question, it was Tommy's daughter who intrigued him the most.

In particular, her name.

Nikki.

Could be short for Nicole.

Getting a look at her mug shot was his primary reason for requesting photos of Tommy's visitors. To find out if the woman Dantzler knew as Nicole Leigh was in fact Tommy Doyle's daughter. If so, she had been lying to Dantzler from the beginning.

The question was . . . why?

Was it possible she was more than simply a liar? Dantzler asked himself. Did she have a nefarious reason for seeking him out at the Grey Goose that evening? Was it possible she planned to get revenge now that her father couldn't?

More questions that begged for answers.

Perhaps, Dantzler thought, *I'm being too hard on her. Silently calling her a liar; where did that come from? What reason do I have to draw that conclusion? None, really. Based on what? She claimed to not know Tommy Doyle? What right do I have to challenge her on that assertion? Again, the answer is none. Tommy was locked up until recently, Nicole lives hundreds of miles from the prison, what are the odds their paths have crossed? No,* Dantzler concluded, *I'm being unfair to her.*

At least, until I know for sure. Until I get a look at that photo.

Still . . . Brother Sunshine's words echoed in his head:

Who says Lucifer can't be a female?

BACK HOME, sitting on his deck, listening to the calming sounds of his nightly chorus, his wounded arm now more sore than hurting or burning, he shifted his attention to the case he was working. Working unsuccessfully, he had to admit. He felt like the villain in one of those old jungle movies, who, while attempting to flee being captured, runs straight into the quicksand. The guy struggles like crazy, trying to free himself, but to no avail. Everyone knows what his fate will be. The more he struggles, the faster he is sucked under. Not many escape quicksand.

Dantzler wondered if perhaps he had been sucked into a different kind of quicksand. A case destined to take him down regardless of how hard he worked to uncover the truth. A harsh reality kept staring him in the face—his chances of solving the case were sinking.

But one fact remained unchanged: He still didn't believe Mike Conley was guilty of murdering his wife. Yet, when he stepped back and evaluated the overall picture, another fact also remained unchanged: All roads lead straight to Mike as the killer. A real conundrum, as David Bloom often points out.

Despite his mixed feelings, Dantzler continued to believe Kent Lofton was Laura Conley's executioner. Unfortunately, evidence backing up his belief was sketchy at best. Only the initials KL in a letter sent to Laura from a friend. But how many people have those same initials? Dantzler asked himself. Had to be in the millions. Once again he worried that he was jumping head first into a pit of quicksand.

Was he also leaping to a wrong conclusion about Kent taking that shot at him? What evidence did he have to support that belief? He had no evidence, only suspicion. Again, just another missing piece of a puzzle.

Another thought: If neither Mike nor Kent killed Laura Conley, then who stood out as possible suspects? Robert Hilton? Couldn't be him—he had an alibi (though not a good one). What about Marianne Lofton? Doubtful, but she couldn't be ruled out. Not until he found out for sure what happened to her first husband in Florida. If she murdered once, who's to say she wouldn't murder a second time? She had to be considered a suspect until or unless she was officially cleared of killing Richie Blackstone.

Dantzler realized he had to widen his net of potential suspects. His mistake, he now admitted, was being too narrowly focused this deep into his investigation. It was lousy detective work and he couldn't afford to be lousy. He had to be at the top of his game. Therefore, expanding his search parameter was necessary if he hoped to have any chance of finding Laura's killer.

And to keep from running straight into the looming quicksand.

Chapter Twenty-Three

Nikki was in her office speaking with an associate when Ray opened the door and stepped inside. Nikki was stunned to see Ray; he had never once set foot in her office. Furthermore, she had no idea he knew where her office was located. His being there was definitely baffling.

"That will be all, Diane," Nikki said, cutting their meeting short. "Write up a statement for me to take a look at. Have it ready by tomorrow afternoon. Hopefully, we can send it out then. The client needs it."

After Diane thanked Nikki and left the office, Nikki motioned for Ray to take a seat. He remained standing, his eyes surveying every inch of the office. To Nikki, he reminded her of a hawk searching for prey.

"Is this room bugged?" Ray asked, eyes still scanning the room.

"Bugged? What are you talking about, Ray?" Nikki said, totally confused.

"Bugged. You know, cameras, recording devices. Any of those here?"

"Are you crazy? This is a public relations firm, not the CIA. We don't spy on people here."

"Is it safe to speak freely? I mean, no one will hear what we say, right?"

"No one will hear us, Ray. You have my word. Now, will you please sit down, relax and explain to me what this is all about?"

Ray sat in the chair just vacated by Diane. "During all your planning did you factor in the possibility of failure? Was that even considered?"

"What are you talking about?" Nikki said, more confused now than ever. "Failure? What failure?"

"You know damn well what I'm talking about. You had your shot, you missed. The man is still alive."

"Jack Dantzler? You're referring to him?"

"Yes. Your big plan to kill him didn't work out so well, did it, Nikki? What's your new plan? Or do you have one?"

"I've got news for you, Ray. I did not take that shot. Somebody else did."

"You really expect me to believe that? You have to be joking. Come on, Nikki, be honest. Who else could it have been?"

"I can't answer that, Ray. All I can say is it wasn't me," Nikki stated. "When I left your place the other day, I didn't feel like I was ready. I needed extra practice, so I bought three boxes of cartridges. I was going to come to your place this Sunday and do more shooting. Once those boxes were empty, I would assess whether or not I was ready. If I felt positive, then I would put my plan in motion. If not, more practice."

"That's a terrific story, but one I find hard to believe," Ray argued. "I saw how eager you were to fulfill your father's mission. Now you want me to believe you changed your mind? I don't."

"Believe it, Ray, because it's the gospel. Here's something else you need to consider. The rifle I've been practicing with, the one I'm going to use, it's still at your place. I don't even have it. You can check that for yourself."

"If you didn't take the shot, who did?"

"Didn't you hear what I just said? How am I suppose to answer that question?"

"Talk about lucky. Dantzler was saved because he bent down to pick up a discarded pack of cigarettes."

"Where did you hear that?"

"One of the TV talking heads mentioned it." Ray stood, said, "I would hope this convinces you to give up the dream of killing Jack Dantzler. After this you really have no other choice."

"Why do you say that?" Nikki asked.

"Because the cops will be relentless in their search for the person who shot one of their own. And don't forget who the victim was. Jack Dantzler. Who just happens to be considered a god in that place. Let it rest, Nikki. It's far too risky to go after Dantzler now."

"My plan is not dead, Ray. It's temporarily on hold for the time being."

Shaking his head, Ray said, "Is killing Jack Dantzler really so important to you, Nikki?"

"As important as breathing. It's the oxygen that keeps me going."

NIKKI POURED A GLASS OF MERLOT, went into the den and plopped down on the sofa. She was angry and she knew why. Because of what Ray had said earlier in her office. Not his contention that she had taken the shot at Dantzler; he had every reason to suspect her. After all, she had been preaching to Ray that her intent was to kill Dantzler, to get revenge for sending her father to prison for thirty years. Ray could be excused for making that statement.

No, the reason for her anger was his assertion she had no choice but to give up her goal of killing Dantzler. She loved Ray, maybe more than she loved her own father, but what right did he have to lecture her about choices? What right did anyone have to lecture her about the choices she chose to make? No one can tell another person, especially an adult, how to live. As someone once said, "If I choose to go to hell, I have every right to do it my way."

Sipping wine, she considered all Ray had said, some of which she knew to be true. Especially the part about the cops being all over this case. Dantzler was, as Ray correctly stated, worshiped within the police department. Even in retirement he was their golden boy. An attempt had been made on his life, and because of that, along with his status within the department, no stone would be left unturned in their hunt to find the shooter.

So she had to give Ray credit . . . he got that part right. But that didn't mean she had no choice but to give up her dream of killing Dantzler. Like she told Ray, it only meant her task would be put on hold until the actual shooter was apprehended, or until the investigation went cold. Once either of those outcomes occurred, she would be free to take her own shot at Dantzler.

As the wine began to kick in (this was her third glass),

her thoughts shifted in a different direction. Who was the actual shooter? Of course, as she said to Ray, there was no way she could answer that question, tantalizing as it was. Having been a cop all those years, Dantzler surely made his share of enemies. Tommy Doyle couldn't have been the only one to swear vengeance against the detective who led the investigation that resulted in jail time. All Nikki could do was give thanks the shooter failed to accomplish his mission. Had Dantzler died her dream would have died along with him.

Thank the Good Lord for the empty cigarette pack Dantzler bent down to pick up. That single act kept him alive. Along with her dream.

How best to proceed at this point? she asked herself. The answer came quickly. Her courage fortified by the wine, she grabbed her cell phone and punched in Dantzler's number. To keep the devil close, she reasoned, you sometimes have to dance with the bastard.

A wise move? Probably not. Careless? Yeah, more than likely. But ending the call? Not gonna happen.

She spoke before Dantzler said hello.

"I realize it's late, Jack, but I was thinking about you, and was wondering how you were doing," Nikki said. "Hope I didn't wake you."

"You didn't wake me," Dantzler said. "To be perfectly honest, I was thinking about you."

"That's encouraging. But how are you feeling? Is your arm still hurting?"

"It's sore, itches like crazy, which, according to the doctor, is a sign the wound is healing."

"That's good news. Saved thanks to an empty cigarette pack. Lucky guy."

"Yeah, lucky guy, right."

"Again, I apologize for calling at such a late hour."

"No need to apologize, Nicole."

"Any idea who the shooter was?"

"No, not really," Dantzler lied.

"Call me if you want to get together again. When you feel up to it, of course. The next round of drinks is on me."

"I'm sure you'll be hearing from me within the next couple of days."

"Looking forward to it, Jack."

DANTZLER WASN'T LYING when he told Nicole he was thinking about her prior to receiving her call. How could he not be thinking about her? He was eager for Tommy Doyle's file to arrive. When it did, he would find out for sure if she was Tommy's daughter. If she was, it changed everything. About her, and possibly about Kent Lofton. If she was Tommy's kid, then Kent might not have been the person who fired that shot.

What Dantzler hadn't anticipated was a late-night phone call from Nicole. And one he judged to be rather strange, particularly the tone of her statements and questions. *I was wondering how you were doing. How are you feeling? Is your arm still hurting? Any idea who the shooter was? Call when you want to get together again.*

All perfectly proper comments, true. But they came across as cold, almost clinical. Like a doctor inquiring about your health. Not one sounded genuinely sincere.

Once again he wondered if he was being too critical of her. She did sound as though she might have been drinking.

Maybe the alcohol affected her tone. Could be she was more sincere than he gave her credit for.

Any concerns he had about her would be answered when Tommy's file arrived. He was hoping it would come tomorrow, but he had his doubts. More than likely, it wouldn't get here until the day after tomorrow.

Didn't matter, really. One look at the photo of Tommy's daughter would tell him all he needed to know.

For good or bad.

Chapter Twenty-Four

The three photos that came with Tommy Doyle's file were much better than Dantzler expected them to be. Color, not black and white, four by seven, not three by five. However, despite the excellent quality they reminded him of typical driver's license photos. No matter how hard an individual tries to look good, the outcome is rarely ever flattering.

Connie Doyle looked exactly the way Dantzler remembered her. Brown hair, green eyes, narrow nose, strong chin, crooked front teeth. Attractive in a certain way, like a pretty Russian peasant woman. Connie appeared to be unhappy in this photo. For good reason, Dantzler imagined. Although he had no idea when the photo was taken, obviously it had been after Tommy was locked up. After she had turned him in to the police. And yet, there she was visiting the man she had betrayed. Who knew what thoughts and emotions were running around inside her head? Little wonder she didn't look happy.

Gary Raymond Doyle was twenty-eight when his photo

was taken, meaning only four years separated Ray and Tommy age-wise. Ray had shoulder-length black hair, a full beard and dark eyes. Judging by his angular face, he was thin and wiry. Dantzler wouldn't swear to it, but he had a feeling he'd seen this man somewhere in the past, perhaps when he'd taken his car in for repairs. But it didn't matter; Ray Doyle was not on Dantzler's radar. Nor would he be unless Dantzler's deep dive into Ray's past revealed a criminal history. In that case, circumstances could change and Ray might become a person of interest.

The third photo was the only one that mattered to Dantzler. It was the picture of a young girl, only fourteen at the time, with brown hair tied back in a ponytail, blue eyes, braces on her teeth and a sullen expression on her face. A defiant look that did little to hide her alert eyes. Or the fact she was on her way to becoming a beautiful woman.

A woman Dantzler had no trouble recognizing.

Nikki Doyle.

Nicole Leigh Doyle.

Mystery solved. The woman who had sought him out at the Grey Goose was indeed Tommy Doyle's daughter. Who had lied to him from the beginning. Lied about not being familiar with Tommy Doyle. Lied that she knew nothing about Tommy committing murder. Lied about everything.

This revelation forced Dantzler to admit he could be wrong to believe Kent Lofton fired that shot at him. Maybe Kent was involved in the murder down in Florida, but was he the person who attempted to assassinate Dantzler? Kent might be off the hook for that crime; maybe the actual shooter was Nikki Doyle.

Dantzler was hit by a second revelation: In his heart of hearts he'd suspected from the start that Nikki was the shooter, and that her story was all lies. What solid evidence did he have to support this conclusion? None, really, except for an observation Nikki made during an earlier conversation, one only the shooter could have known. It was this piece of evidence, flimsy as it might be, that would hang her.

He would point this out to her when they met tonight, then gauge her reaction. Hopefully, it would put her in the precarious position where lying wouldn't serve as her get-out-of-jail-free card. The truth has a way of correcting false testimony. Nikki's immediate reaction would indicate for certain if she was guilty of trying to kill him. And he was betting she was guilty.

Dantzler picked up his cell phone and dialed Nikki's number. She answered immediately.

"What a nice surprise," Nikki said. "I've been hoping you would call."

"Are you free tonight?" Dantzler asked. "Maybe have a couple of drinks somewhere?"

"Yes, anytime after seven-thirty. Where do you want to meet?"

"What about my place? On Lakeshore Drive? Say, around eight? I promise to be a good boy."

"Awe, shucks," she said, laughing. "Yes, your place is fine with me. What's the address?"

Dantzler told her, said goodbye and ended the call. Leaning back in his chair, smiling, he said to himself:

Who says Lucifer can't be a female?

"LET ME GET THIS STRAIGHT. You're going to have a date with the woman might have taken a shot at you?" Sean asked Dantzler. They were sitting in the Tennis Center office. "Is this what you're telling me?"

"Yes, Sean, that's exactly what I'm telling you," Dantzler replied. "Tonight, eight o'clock, my place."

"That's probably the dumbest thing you could possibly do, you know that? Why would you even think of meeting with her? She's already made one attempt on your life. What's to prevent her from making a second attempt?"

"That's the least of my worries."

"Well, I'd certainly be worried. Look, Jack, if you truly believe she was the shooter, take your evidence to Jake and Vee, let them handle it. That's what they get paid to do."

"I need to be one-hundred percent certain she took that shot, which, at this stage, I'm not. But if I'm right, and she was the shooter, I will contact Jake and Vee."

"You're taking a big risk," Sean stated. "You hit her with hard evidence, let her know you suspect her of being the shooter, box her into a corner, she may feel there is only one way out and that's to kill you."

"Whatever she tries, Sean, I'll be one step ahead of her. I've been in dangerous situations before. I know how to take care of myself."

"I still say it's a foolish move on your part. An unnecessary move. What about this? Let me be there as backup. I'll stay hidden. She won't know I'm there."

"Thanks for the offer but this is something I have to do alone. Stop worrying. I'll be fine."

"I hope you're right, because if you're wrong, the alternative ain't good."

NIKKI ARRIVED at Dantzler's house a few minutes before eight. Dantzler invited her in, led her to the kitchen, pulled back a chair at the table (the chair he planned for her to sit in) and motioned for her to take a seat.

"Always the gentleman, aren't you, Jack?" Nikki said. "Ever wonder if you were born in the wrong century?"

Ignoring her question, he asked, "What would you like to drink? I have wine, beer, bourbon."

"What are you having?"

Certain she wouldn't care for Pernod, he said, "Jameson and Diet Coke."

"Then make it two."

Dantzler mixed the drinks, handed Nikki her glass, then took the chair across from her. A folded newspaper lay in the chair next to his. Hidden under the paper was his Glock. Like he told Sean, he would be one step ahead of anything Nikki might try. He was leaving nothing to chance tonight.

Nikki said, "You don't appear to be favoring your left arm. Must mean it's healing okay."

"Good as new," Dantzler said, flexing his left arm.

Dantzler picked up a brown folder lying on the table, opened it, removed the photo of Nikki and placed it in front of her. Any hope he had that she would register surprise or shock immediately flew out the window. She simply offered a strange grin.

"God, what an awful picture. Looks like I was about ready to vomit." Nikki took a drink. "Okay, Jack, now you know the truth. I'm Tommy Doyle's daughter."

"You're also a liar."

"I confess. I did lie to you. But think about it. What other choice did I have?"

"For starters you could have told the truth."

"Oh, really, that's your answer? How much time would you have spent with me if I had told you Tommy Doyle was my father?"

"About ten seconds."

"Exactly." Nikki took another drink, said, "Look, I recognized you that night at the Grey Goose. You're an attractive guy I wanted to meet and get to know, so I introduced myself as Nicole Leigh. I couldn't come right out and tell you who my father was. So, I withheld that bit of information."

"That's bullshit," Dantzler said. "You didn't just *happen* to be in the Grey Goose that night. You followed me there. Our meeting was no accident. It was planned."

"What reason would I have to follow you?"

"To monitor my movements."

"For what purpose? I didn't know you prior to that night."

"What purpose? Isn't it obvious? To do what your father couldn't do."

"I'm trying really hard to keep up, Jack, but you're losing me. How does my Dad fit into this?"

"Nikki, your dad conned his way out of prison for one reason—to get revenge against me. He died before he had the chance to exact his revenge. So, his loyal daughter takes it upon herself to fulfill her father's big dream of killing me. Which she tries. Lucky for me, she failed."

"Wait a minute. Are you accusing me of shooting you? Is that what you're saying?"

"That's exactly what I'm saying," Dantzler stated.

"Well, I'm sorry to burst your bubble, but you are dead wrong," Nikki said, emphatically. "I did not take that shot at you."

"Had to be you, Nikki."

"Why did it have to be me?"

"Because you knew a detail only the shooter could know."

"What detail are you referring to?"

"That I bent down to pick up an empty cigarette pack. How did you know that?"

"I'm not sure. Probably heard it from one of the TV announcers."

"You didn't hear it from anybody. That particular detail was never released to the public. All the police said was I leaned over to pick up some trash. The cigarette pack and the Ale 8 bottle were never mentioned. You knew the truth. Which means you took the shot."

Nikki picked up her purse, dug around inside, then took out a pen. Grabbing the photo in front of her, she flipped it over and began writing on the back. When she finished, she handed the photo to Dantzler.

"For your information, I was nowhere near Lexington the evening you were shot," she said. "I was meeting with a client in Cincinnati. Diane Warren, my assistant, went with me. We left Lexington around six, got to the client's house at seven-thirty, stayed until a little past nine, then drove home, arriving around ten-thirty. I dropped Diane off at the office so she could get her car. Then I went straight home, dressed down, turned on the TV and saw you had been shot. That's when I phoned you to see if you were okay. What I just gave you is the client's name, address and cell phone number. Give him a call. He'll confirm that Diane and I were there.

If you require further proof, there are cameras all around his property, inside and outside. He's rather famous—you've probably heard of him—so he's big on security. Hate to disappoint you, Jack, but I'm not your shooter. And I have an airtight alibi to prove it."

Dantzler did recognize the name. An NFL player currently under investigation for domestic abuse. No doubt in need of Nikki's PR bullshit to help facilitate his image rehabilitation tour.

Nikki stood, picked up her purse, and said, "I know this is crazy, but after you've checked my alibi, after you're satisfied I didn't try to kill you, what are the chances we could continue to see each other?"

"Zero chance. After tonight, we're done."

"Too bad, Jack, I really like you." She pointed at the photo. "Keep it. My gift to you. As a souvenir."

When she was gone, Dantzler ripped the photo to shreds, still unsure she had told the truth. *How did she know about the cigarette pack*? If she wasn't the shooter, as she claimed, then she had to know who the shooter was. How else could she have known that particular detail? That single question kept buzzing around inside his head.

Female Lucifer or not, he'd had enough of Nikki Doyle and her lies.

For tonight, anyway.

RAY DOYLE AWOKE to sounds coming from his kitchen. Glancing at the clock, he noted the time was twelve-twenty. Easing out of bed, he opened a dresser drawer and took out his forty-five. Wearing only his boxer shorts and a T-shirt, he quietly moved to the door and peered into the kitchen. Where he saw Nikki pacing like an agitated tiger.

Lowering his weapon, he went into the kitchen, and said, "A person could get shot sneaking into someone's home at midnight. Been nice if you'd given me a heads-up you were coming."

"You're lucky I don't have that pistol right now, Ray," Nikki snapped, pointing at the weapon in his hand. "I'm so fucking angry at you I just might blow a hole in your heart."

"What did I do to piss you off?"

"You know very fucking well what you did. Goddammit, Ray, I can't believe you did it."

"Did what, Nikki?"

"Shot Jack Dantzler."

"What are you talking about? I didn't shoot the guy."

"Stop it, Ray, we're way beyond your lies. I happen to know for a fact it was you who took that shot."

"Whose facts have you been listening to, Nikki?"

"I just left Jack Dantzler's house. He accused me of being the shooter. Know why? Because I had told him he was lucky to have bent over to pick up an empty cigarette pack. He asked me how I knew that. I repeated your line, Ray, said I heard it from a TV announcer."

"Well, that is where I heard it."

"No, you didn't." Nikki countered. "That particular detail was never released to the media or to the public. What they were told was Dantzler bent down to pick up *trash*. Like Dantzler said, Ray. Only the actual shooter could know that detail."

"Okay, you got me. It's true, Nikki. I took the shot at Dantzler."

"Why? It was on me to fulfill Dad's dream of killing Dantzler. You played no part in it."

"I did it for you, Nikki. I didn't want you living the rest of your life knowing you had killed a fellow human being. That's too much weight for you to carry. For anyone to carry."

"You have no right to make decisions for me, Ray. It's my life to live. If I kill Jack Dantzler and it haunts me forever, so be it. I'll carry that weight you're so worried about. Just as long as Dad's revenge is complete and Dantzler is dead."

"*If I kill Jack Dantzler*. You aren't still thinking about going through with it, are you?"

"Now more than ever."

"Jesus, Nikki, that's insane. It's also impossible now."

"I'm in no hurry, Ray. I know how to be patient. Once the heat dies down, and it will, then I'll kill Dantzler. And I will do it the way Dad originally planned. Up close, face to face, eyeball to eyeball. I want my face to be the last thing Dantzler sees before his lights go out."

Chapter Twenty-Five

Nikki's alibi did turn out to be someone Dantzler was vaguely familiar with. Duffy Bryant, an all-pro NFL linebacker currently under investigation for committing physical violence against a female companion. Contrary to what Dantzler heard on the news, the battered woman was Duffy's mistress, not his wife. Duffy pleaded not guilty, claiming, as bullies normally do, that it was all a misunderstanding. However, the evidence proved otherwise. Seemed Duffy made the mistake of committing the violent act outside a bar that just happened to have six security cameras in place. Making matters worse for Duffy, several people witnessed the altercation. Given those circumstances, Dantzler doubted Nikki's PR onslaught could do much to rehabilitate Duffy's image. Or to keep him out of a courtroom.

Dantzler's phone call to Duffy was akin to dealing with the Marx Brothers. Or the Three Stooges. Sheer chaos. The call was initially answered by a man claiming to be Duffy's personal assistant. He was loud and gruff, but Dantzler persuaded him to let Duffy know about the call. The next person Dantzler spoke with said he was Duffy's manager. He came across as more gruff and louder than the first guy. Next came Duffy's attorney, who relented (reluctantly) before putting his client on the phone. At least the attorney spoke in a civil tone.

"You're a difficult man to get in touch with, Duffy," Dantzler said, adding, "Well-protected by your own front line."

"Have to be," Duffy stated. "Plenty of barracudas out there want a piece of me. You're not a barracuda, are you?"

"Nope, just a private investigator."

Hearing that, Duffy held the phone away from his mouth, then directed a loud string of profanities at his attorney for failing to find out Dantzler was an investigator. Dantzler was certain Duffy would slam down his phone and was surprised when he didn't.

"Okay, barracuda, who are you working for?" Duffy asked.

"No one, Duffy. I just have a couple of questions for you. Answer them, you'll never hear from me again."

"Ask your questions."

"Do you know Nicole Leigh Doyle?"

I know a Nicole Leigh. But no one named Doyle."

"How do you know Nicole Leigh?"

"She's handling public relations for me. Trying to save my ass from the mess I'm in."

"When was the last time you saw her?"

"Let me think about that. It was one night last week. Yeah, that's right. She and another woman were here. They brought a script for me to follow when I spoke to the media.

Pure fiction, naturally, but what choice did I have other than to follow it word for word?"

"What time did they arrive? And when did they leave?"

"Come on, dude, what's with all the questions? I feel like I'm back in school."

"Need those answers, Duffy."

"They got here around seven-thirty, stayed a little more than an hour, then left."

"If I needed proof to back up your story could you provide it?" Dantzler asked.

"Sure, from the security tapes. I never erase anything. But, dude, if you do want to see them I'll have to check with my lawyer. He might say you need a warrant or a court order."

"I don't think that will be necessary, Duffy. I'll take your word for it. Thanks for speaking with me. You've been very helpful."

"No prob, dude," Duffy said, ending the call.

DANTZLER LEFT his office and went into the lounge area where Amy and Sean were sitting at a table. He grabbed a bottle of water from the refrigerator, put two ones in the cash drawer, then sat between them.

Sean said, "Did Duffy the quarterback slayer verify Nikki's alibi?"

"Duffy the quarterback slayer? Where did that come from?"

"That's the guy's nickname. You know, from the TV series, Buffy the Vampire Slayer."

"Yeah, the quarterback slayer verified Nikki's alibi,"

Dantzler said, taking a drink of water. "She didn't take that shot."

But she knows who did.

"Who do you suspect?" Sean inquired.

"Still can't answer that, Sean. But here's something that might surprise you. I like Kent Lofton for killing Laura Conley."

"Really? What's his motive?"

"He wanted to start an affair with Laura Conley, she rejected him, he gets pissed, takes her out. Anger, jealousy, being rejected . . . those are strong motives for murder."

"That simply doesn't track for me," Sean said. "What evidence do you have to support that theory?"

"When I was going through Laura's things, I came across some letters sent to her by a friend," Dantzler said. "Leah Wallin. She lives in Denver. Anyway, in the last letter Leah sent, she warned Laura to end the affair with Robert because KL could be dangerous. I've racked my brain trying to come up with someone other than Kent Lofton with those initials and I can't."

"I can," Amy said.

"Who? Dantzler asked.

"Kelly Hilton."

"Kelly? You sure about that, Amy?"

"Yes, I'm sure. Remember when her mom came to visit? This was about a month ago. You met her, Jack, when she came to play tennis with Kelly. She only referred to Kelly as Kelly Lynn. There's another KL for you."

"*That* does track for me, Jack," Sean stated. "She had much more of a motive to kill Laura than Kent did. To get rid of the woman her husband was having an affair with. With Laura out of the way, Kelly saves her marriage."

"But she didn't save it. She filed for divorce. According to Robert, he begged her to forgive him and take him back. She refused."

"That's his story. Who knows if it's true?" Sean paused, then said, "You read through the murder book, Jack. Was Kelly ever considered a suspect? Was she questioned by the detectives?"

Dantzler was silent for a moment before answering. "Kelly was questioned by Vee," he remembered. "She provided an alibi, but I can't recall what it was."

Dantzler picked up his cell phone and dialed Vee's number. He put the phone on speaker.

"Hey, Boss, what a nice surprise," Vee said. "How's the wounded wing coming along?"

"Almost completely healed," Dantzler stated. "Have a quick question for you, Vee. About the Laura Conley murder."

"Fire away."

"At any time during your investigation, did you and Jake consider Kelly Hilton as a potential suspect for Laura's homicide?"

"Initially, yes, of course, we considered her. I mean, how could we not? Her husband was having an affair with the murder victim. That's maybe the oldest reason in the books for committing homicide. We had no choice but to look at her as the possible shooter. But we ruled her out fairly soon. She had a solid alibi."

"Which was . . . what?"

"Give me a second, it'll come to me. Oh, yeah, she made a couple of phone calls around the time of the murder. One to Robert at about nine-fifteen. Lasted less than a minute. Then she made a second call to her mother at nine-forty. They talked for about five minutes. Both calls were made from her house. Based on the time of those calls, and when the murder occurred, we cleared her."

"Thanks, Vee, that's all I needed to know," Dantzler said.

"Why are you inquiring about Kelly Hilton?" Vee asked. "Do you know something we don't?"

"Just tying up some loose ends, Vee."

"Happy to help, Boss. Don't be a stranger, okay?"

"Never a stranger to you and Jake." Dantzler ended the call, laid his phone on the table, looked at Sean, and said, "You thinking what I'm thinking?"

"Yeah, Kelly's alibi ain't all that damn solid," Sean said. "The Hiltons live, what, fifteen minutes from the Conleys? Twenty minutes, tops? Laura was killed sometime between nine-thirty and eleven, right? Plenty of time for Kelly to end a conversation with her mother at nine-forty, drive to the Conley house and kill Laura. She purposefully left her phone at home. That way it couldn't be traced to the Conley's location."

"But how could Kelly possibly know Laura was alone?" Amy asked.

"That was the purpose of her earlier call to Robert," Dantzler explained. "To find out where he was. She must have assumed he was with Laura, probably at her house. After hanging up with her mother, Kelly drove to the Conley house intent on killing Laura *and* Robert. It's the perfect setup for her; she kills them both, then makes it look like a murder/suicide. Robert killed Laura because she wanted to end the affair, then he kills himself. It's perfect."

Shaking her head, Amy said, "But what if Kelly showed up and Mike was home?"

"Same thing, only this time Kelly kills Laura and Mike. That scenario works even better for her. Mike kills Laura because she is having an affair with Robert, then he kills himself. Kelly Hilton went to the Conley house that night prepared to murder anyone who was inside."

"Laura would never let Kelly in the house," Amy argued.

"She would if she had a gun pointing at her," Sean countered. Then to Dantzler: "Here's my problem with your murder/suicide scenario, Jack. I can buy Kelly as the shooter. But you're making her out to be a very sophisticated killer. She goes to the Conley house unsure who is inside, yet she's already planning to stage a murder/suicide scene if either Robert or Mike is there with Laura? You don't seriously believe Kelly is that calculating, do you?"

"You're probably right, Sean. I'm just thinking out loud. But regardless of what was going on in her head at the time, if she's guilty, I'll prove it. And that's one scenario you can take to the bank."

DANTZLER DROVE HOME, his thoughts simultaneously rolling down parallel tracks: How best to go after Kelly Hilton for murdering Laura Conley. He had to admit the evidence against Kelly was miles away from getting a conviction in court. If he were being totally honest with himself, he'd acknowledge the evidence was too weak to get Kelly in a courtroom. To make that happen he had to collect more evidence against her.

However, the first thing he had to do was prioritize his investigations. This required him to answer a difficult question: Was trying to clear Mike Conley's name more important than his own safety? The obvious answer would be to take care of himself first and foremost. However, his single goal as a cop had been to catch killers and bring them to justice. This was baked into his DNA. Someone had murdered Laura Conley and was still walking free. This was a fact, one he simply couldn't live with. He was now convinced her killer was Kelly Hilton. Therefore, as he saw it, bringing her to justice had to be his number-one priority.

She belonged behind bars and he aimed to put her there.

Chapter Twenty-Six

"I need your help, Ray," Nikki announced, seconds after entering Ray's house.

"What happened to you being pissed off at me?" Ray asked. He was sitting in a recliner facing the TV. *NCIS* was on the tube. "Last time we spoke you were ready to shoot me. What changed?"

"Like I said, I need you to help me acquire a certain item. This is your chance to get back in good graces with me."

"Does my help involve you killing Jack Dantzler?"

"Yes."

"Not interested, Nikki. Sorry."

"Why not? You tried it."

"Yeah, I did it for you. But it was a mistake. I never should've done it."

"I need a pistol, Ray, and I know you have one. I want to borrow it."

"You're not serious, are you?"

"Deadly."

"My pistol? To kill Jack Dantzler?"

"Yes."

"Let's play this out, Nikki. You kill Dantzler with my forty-five, the gun is registered in my name, you get caught, the gun is traced back to me, I go down for providing you with the weapon used to murder a celebrated ex-cop. So, sure why wouldn't I let you have my gun?"

"I'm not stupid, Ray. The gun will be disposed of ten minutes after Jack Dantzler is dead. Somewhere impossible to find. I'd make sure of that. Besides, if I were caught with the gun—which won't happen—I could always tell the cops I stole it from you. That you didn't know I had taken it. You'd be free and clear."

"Nikki, even if it means you stay pissed off at me forever, I will not help you kill Jack Dantzler," Ray stated. "You want a pistol? Get it from another source. You can't have mine."

"Then that's exactly what I will do," Nikki said.

RAY'S REFUSAL TO help left her with two choices: Purchase a gun from a legitimate dealer, which involved paperwork, a background check and time. Or buy one off the street. Maybe not a legal transaction, but that didn't matter. She had to have a weapon. It was the second option she preferred. And she knew who to contact. Duffy Bryant. Famous NFL linebacker slash mistress beater. A reprehensible human being, but . . .

Taking out her cell phone she dialed his number.

"What can I do for you, pretty lady?" Duffy asked. "Or

are you calling to compliment me for my performance during my TV interview yesterday? I thought it went great."

"Yeah, Duffy, I watched every second of it. You did okay."

"Okay? That's the best you've got. Hell, pretty lady, that's not what I call high praise."

"Your delivery was fine. You came across as sincere and contrite, but your body language sucked. Too stiff, too brittle, like a robot. Or an erect dick. In future interviews loosen up a little. Be more natural. And by the way, my name is Nicole not pretty lady."

"Too stiff, huh? Didn't think of that."

"Well, think about it in the future," Nikki said. "But that's not why I called. I—"

"A dude called yesterday inquiring about you," Duffy interrupted. "Gave me his name, but it eludes me at the moment."

"Jack Dantzler."

"Sounds about right."

"He wanted to know if I was at your house one night last week, right?"

"Yeah, that's what he was asking about."

"Did you tell him I was there?" Nikki asked.

"I told him the truth, that you and the other chick were here." Duffy paused, then said, "Now here's my question for you. Was the dude a cop?"

"Former."

"Why was he asking about you?"

"Someone took a shot at him. He thought I was the shooter. The incident happened while I was at your house. You helped clear me by confirming my alibi."

"How about as appreciation for confirming your alibi

you charge me less for your professional services? Seems like a fair trade-off to me."

"I'll go you one better, Duffy. I need a big favor. You help me with what I'm about to ask you, I'll not charge you a penny."

"What about the money I already paid? You gonna return that?"

"Can't do it, Duffy. But going forward, everything I do for you will be on the house. Promise."

"This favor? Is it legal?"

"Technically, no."

"Is it gonna get me in more trouble? I'm already catching plenty of heat. Can't handle much more."

"No trouble, Duffy. No one will ever know about your involvement."

"Okay, what is it you want?" Duffy asked.

"A weapon," Nikki replied. "Specifically, a pistol."

"There are thousands of places where you can buy a pistol. Why come to me?"

"I need one that's not registered. One that can't be traced back to anyone. Maybe one with the serial number scratched out."

"I have plenty of weapons, but they are all legally registered in my name. Not sure how you expect me to help you."

"You're surrounded by all types of hangers-on, Duffy. I've seen most of them. There aren't many I would classify as saints. Surely one of those guys can get me what I'm asking for."

"Why do you need a pistol?"

"Personal protection."

"I may just be a dumb linebacker who's taken too many blows to my head, but even I know that's a crock of shit."

"Can you help me, Duffy?"

"If I do help, it'll cost you."

"Name your price."

"Three grand."

"Done."

"What caliber pistol you looking for?"

"I'm not picky. Just make sure you get one that's in excellent working order."

"Give me a week," Duffy said. "Call, schedule another meeting at my place. I'll have the weapon when you get here. Bring the three grand. Cash, of course."

"Thanks, Duffy. You're a real prince," Nikki said.

"Yeah, well, just make sure I don't end up like Prince Hamlet. Dead."

"Why, Duffy. An intellectual linebacker? You're a rare species, you know that?"

A WEEK TO get the gun. Two to three weeks for practice.

Nikki considered this, then quickly amended the timeline. No need to practice that long, she concluded. *Doesn't take an expert to shoot someone standing less than five feet away. That's a can't-miss shot.*

Still, though, a couple weeks of practice couldn't hurt. The time spent would be more about getting familiar with the weapon rather than honing in on accuracy. The extra time would also serve a second purpose. It would allow the temperature to cool regarding the search for the person who shot Dantzler. (She was assuming Ray had not left tracks leading back to him, and that he would not be caught.)

For Nikki, the challenge facing her was how and where to get Dantzler alone, especially now that he knew her true identity. Who her father was. *Where?* she asked herself. His house was the obvious answer. She shouldn't have a problem coming up with an innocent reason to meet. Maybe tell Dantzler she wanted to apologize for lying. Or to ask him questions about her mother's role in finking on her husband. On her father. Either of those reasons ought to be legitimate enough for Dantzler to agree to a meeting.

What happened next she had played out a hundred times in her head. Her own personal movie.

Once inside the house, talk for a few minutes, get Dantzler comfortable, perhaps let him fix drinks, then take out the pistol, look him straight in his eyes and pull the trigger.

Jack Dantzler would be dead.

Just like that.

And Tommy Doyle's dream would then be reality.

Chapter Twenty-Seven

Having decided to go after Laura Conley's killer first meant Dantzler had to put together a plan. This didn't take long. Interviews were the key, beginning with Robert Hilton, followed by Leah Wallin, then concluding with Marianne Lofton. By the time those talks had ended, hopefully he would be better prepared to know for certain who killed Laura and why.

Dantzler was sitting on his deck, Pernod and orange juice in hand, pondering how best to approach Robert Hilton for a second time. Interviewing him could be tricky. Dantzler needed to gather more information without letting Robert know all the facts, namely that Kelly, his ex-wife, was now the prime suspect in Laura Conley's murder. At some point Robert would find out, but unless Dantzler blundered during the interview that bit of information should come later.

But was keeping this information a secret from Robert

really so important? Dantzler wondered. Maybe letting Robert know would be a plus. Could be Robert hated Kelly and would love nothing better than to learn she was a cold-blooded murderer. If so, he might be more inclined to reveal pertinent information. On the flip side, however, maybe Robert and Kelly had patched up their differences and continued to share information with each other. In that case, should Robert learn Kelly was a suspect, he might alert her to what was happening, thus giving her time to lawyer up, create a better alibi, or, worst case, take flight. A third reason for keeping Robert in the dark? What if he played a role in Laura's death? Unlikely, yes, but a possibility not to be dismissed.

Dantzler checked the time on his cell phone. Nine-forty. Only eight-forty in St. Louis. A good time to phone Robert. Collecting his thoughts, mentally arranging his questions, he punched in Robert's number and waited. Robert answered after several rings.

"Detective Dantzler? Anything wrong?" Robert asked, concern in his voice.

"Jack, remember? And no, nothing is wrong," Dantzler replied. "Just have some follow-up questions I'd like to run by you. Can you spare a few minutes?"

"Of course. But I don't know what else I can tell you now that I didn't share with you the first time we spoke. I've kinda been out of the Lexington loop for several weeks now. But go ahead. What questions do you have?"

"You told me you're a hunter, right?"

"Deer and elk only. Deer in Kentucky, elk in Wyoming."

"So, as a hunter you have rifles?"

"One rifle. A Remington two-eighty."

"Any pistols or hand guns?" Dantzler said.

"No, I have no need or desire for them," Robert said. "Can't kill deer or elk with a pistol. Why the questions about guns?"

Tricky. A question Dantzler had to carefully dance around. His answer better be a good one, even if it wasn't necessarily true. A better tactic, he decided, was to do what he hated, which meant answering a question with a question.

"Robert, do you know anyone who owns several pistols?"

"Yeah, Kent Lofton. From what I hear he has an arsenal of weapons. Of all sizes, types and calibers."

"How do you know this? I thought you said the two of you aren't friends."

"We aren't; I can't stand the bastard. How do I know? Because Marianne got Kelly involved in shooting. *Hooked* on shooting is more accurate. Marianne was quick to inform Kelly that Kent has plenty of guns to choose from. Since we don't own any pistols, Kelly used one Marianne loaned to her."

"Loaned? For what purpose?"

"Target shooting. They usually went to the indoor shooting range three, four times a week. Always stayed a couple of hours. Kelly quickly became obsessed with that nonsense."

Dantzler said, "Kelly and Marianne are close friends?"

"Yeah, after they bonded over guns," Robert said. "Shocked the shit out of me. Up until then Kelly had no use for Marianne. And she hated guns."

"When did this bonding happen?"

"Maybe three months before Kelly and I split up."

"How did it happen? I mean, I'm having a hard time picturing those two as pals."

"By accident, actually. At your Tennis Center. Kelly overheard Marianne bragging about what an accurate shot she was with a pistol. Kelly mentioned she'd never fired a pistol. Said she was scared of guns. Marianne said Kelly didn't know what she was missing, that if she ever did it once, she would love it. Said it was almost better than sex. Then Marianne invited Kelly to accompany her to the firing range. Kelly went, did some shooting and that was the start of it. They became a regular gun-happy duo. Bonnie and Bonnie."

"What caliber pistol did Kelly use?"

"Don't have a clue."

"Did Kelly ever bring one of those pistols home?"

"Not when we were still together. After we split, I can't say."

"Let me untangle this, Robert," Dantzler said. "Your wife, who you knew was having an affair, was spending three or four days a week at a gun range? Didn't that worry you?"

"My affair with Laura had ended by that time," Robert said. "Listen, Jack, I really need to go. I'm meeting a lady for drinks. Not sure how long she will wait if I'm late."

"No problem, Robert. Thanks for speaking with me. If I come up with more questions in the future I'll be in touch. Good luck with your lady friend," Dantzler said, ending the call.

Robert had given one piece of surprising—and valuable —information: Kelly Hilton was no stranger when it came to using a pistol. While this revelation didn't solidify Dantzler's belief that Kelly murdered Laura Conley, it did strengthen the case against her. The noose was beginning to tighten around Kelly Lynn Hilton's neck.

Dantzler smiled.

Time for a second drink and another phone call.

WITH A TWO-HOUR TIME difference between Lexington and Mountain Daylight Time—it was only eight-twenty in Denver—Dantzler decided to call Leah Wallin, Laura Conley's lifelong friend. He'd intended to ask Robert if he was familiar with Leah, but chose not to. Any information he gathered would come from Leah.

After going into the kitchen and making another drink, he went back to the deck, sat, picked up his phone and placed the call. When a man answered, Dantzler quickly identified himself.

"Jack Dantzler? Lexington? What business do you have with my wife?" the man said, sounding more suspicious than inquisitive.

"I would like to ask her a few questions about Laura Conley," Dantzler said. "I understand they were close friends."

Silence while the man apparently transferred the phone to Leah. Dantzler wondered why the husband had answered his wife's phone. Was she indisposed at the time, or was he the jealous, overbearing type? Dantzler got his answer when she took the phone.

"Sorry I didn't answer," Leah said. "I was in the kitchen putting dishes and silverware away. That was Steve, my husband. He said you wanted to talk about Laura and your name is Jack Dantzler. Is that correct?"

"Correct, on both counts, Leah. I'm working for Mike Conley. He has hired me to investigate the case. To try and find Laura's killer."

"Most people are convinced Mike is guilty of murdering Laura. Because of her affair with Robert Hilton. I don't happen to be one of those people."

"We'll explore that in a moment. But first, tell me about your relationship with Laura."

"We met when my family moved to Longview Drive. This was in eighty-one; I was three at the time. We lived two doors down from the Lewis family. That's Laura's name. Laura Renee Lewis. We clicked from the first moment we met. An instant friendship, you could say. It was a great neighborhood back then. Lots of kids, boys and girls, and we all did everything together. Play ball, swim, go bowling, ride our bikes, fight . . . it was a joyous time. Laura and I were born three months apart—I'm the oldest—so we were almost like twins. We went to Lafayette High School, we both graduated from the University of Kentucky, which is where I met Steve. He was in law school at the time. Steve and I eventually married and he got a terrific job with a law firm in Denver. Even after we moved, Laura and I never stopped communicating, mostly by letters and phone calls, with the occasional text message thrown in. I loved Laura and I miss her every second of every day."

"When was the last time you saw Laura?"

"At Christmas, when I flew in to visit my mom. I stayed three days."

"Was Laura still having her affair with Robert?"

"Yes. But I pleaded with her to end it, which she soon did."

"I came across your name when I was going through Laura's things. Found a stack of letters you'd sent her."

"That answers a question I was going to ask," Leah said. "How you found out about me."

"In your last letter to Laura, you warned her to end the affair with Robert," Dantzler said, "because KL could be dangerous. Who is KL?"

"Kelly Lynn Hilton."

"How do you know Kelly is dangerous?"

"Because I've witnessed things she has done. Heard about others. Listen, anytime she feels slighted or mistreated or cheated, her only goal is revenge. You dis her even in the most-insignificant way you'd better be prepared to experience some retribution. She does not forgive, forget or turn the other cheek. Those concepts are alien to her."

"Tell me about some of the things you've witnessed."

"Where to begin? Kelly was two years behind me and Laura in school, but we all had a few classes together. And we were all cheerleaders. Go Generals! On one occasion, Kelly set a girl's hair on fire because the girl made a complimentary comment to a guy Kelly was interested in. Of course, Kelly claimed it was an accident, but none of us believed her. She did it to send a message that it wasn't wise to show interest in her guy. A kind of hands-off message. Another time Kelly bit a guy who accused her of cheating off his exam paper. He turned her in, she got a failing grade. The bite drew blood. Kelly did receive a three-day suspension for that. There were other incidents, but I'm sure you get the picture. Kelly Lynn Hilton is not a woman to offend."

"Back to your earlier comment about not believing Mike killed Laura," Dantzler said. "Who do you think did kill her?"

"Kelly," Leah stated without hesitation.

"What would be her motive? Laura's affair with Robert had ended prior to the murder. He had moved to St. Louis by then."

"You think that would matter to Kelly? No way. Laura had stolen a possession Kelly considered strictly hers. In Kelly's eyes, anyway. In her demented brain, she had been slighted, disrespected, cheated. Those are grievances that call for revenge. For retaliation. So that's what she did. She eliminated the source of her grievance."

"Do you know Marianne Lofton?"

"Never heard of her. Why do you ask?"

"Kelly has recently become a gun enthusiast. Goes to the shooting range three or four times a week. Shoots with a pistol. Marianne Lofton is the person who got Kelly involved in shooting."

"Laura was killed by a pistol, wasn't she?" Leah asked.

"A thirty-eight," Dantzler replied.

"Well, any doubts I may have had that Kelly murdered Laura have just been erased by that bit of news. Is Kelly going to be arrested?"

"Not unless I can come up with more evidence, which I plan to do."

"When you do, and when she is arrested, please let me know. I'll hop the first plane to Lexington, go straight to the jail and tell Kelly I hope she burns in hell for all eternity."

A Book of Revelation girl, Dantzler thought, but said, "Come on, Leah, tell me how you *really* feel about Kelly Hilton."

ALL IN ALL A PRODUCTIVE EVENING, Dantzler concluded, as he finished off the last drops of Pernod and orange juice. His talks with Robert and Leah had yielded good results; Robert for alerting Dantzler to Kelly's recent love affair with shooting, Leah for information about Kelly's violence and thirst for revenge.

None of what he'd learned sealed the deal that Kelly killed Laura, but it did convince him he wasn't on a wild goose chase. That he was headed in the right direction. It also further strengthened his belief that Mike Conley was innocent.

Now all he had to do was prove it.

His thoughts immediately shifted to his next target—Marianne Lofton. Getting with her again would likely present a serious challenge. Considering how elusive—and reluctant—she had been the first time around, he could only imagine how difficult it might be to pin her down a second time. He had to acknowledge his relationship with Marianne and Kent Lofton was about as bad as it could possibly be. But this really didn't make any difference to him. He needed to speak with Marianne and he would, whether she liked it or not.

But exactly what information did he expect to get from Marianne? he asked himself. What did she have to offer that might be helpful? A couple things came to mind. She could give him some idea about how proficient Kelly was as a shooter. Even more important, what caliber weapons Kelly and Marianne normally used. Marianne might even reveal if Kelly had purchased a pistol of her own. If he could get those questions cleared up, his talk with Marianne would be a success.

But that talk, if it happened, would have to take place at another time. He was done for the day. One more Pernod and orange juice, another hour on the deck listening to his nightly chorus serenade him, then hit the sack.

A good night's sleep beckoned.

Chapter Twenty-Eight

Dantzler's sleep turned out to be anything but good. A pair of disturbing dreams infiltrated his usually quiet nocturnal landscape. The kind of dreams that tend to linger well into the next day. Those not easily dismissed or erased.

In the first dream, a woman stands facing away from him. When she turns, he realizes it's Kelly Hilton. She holds a pint of Guinness in one hand and a pistol in the other hand. Grinning, she offers him the Guinness. As Dantzler reaches out to accept it, she points the pistol at him, squeezes the trigger and . . . he wakes up.

Thinking about it later, he lamented the fact he reached for the Guinness while ignoring the pistol. Guinness is good, true, getting shot not so good.

The second dream was murky, like watching a slightly-out-of-focus movie. In this one, he is walking across the Tennis Center parking area, stops and bends down to pick up an empty cigarette pack. As he leans over, he notices a blurry figure aiming a rifle at him from a vacant building across the street. Scooping up the trash, he hears the crack of a rifle shot and . . . he wakes up.

Upon waking and dissecting the second dream, he suspected Kent Lofton was the shooter. But after further reflection, seeds of doubt began to take root. The figure he saw holding the rifle was smaller, leading him to believe the shooter was a woman. Kelly Hilton? Marianne Lofton? Nikki Doyle? All viable possibilities, but he couldn't say for sure.

But as he got out of bed, a familiar question quickly came to mind:

Who says Lucifer can't be a female?

FEELING SLUGGISH AND WORN OUT, he took a long, hot shower, hoping to wash away the lingering stink of those dreams. It didn't work. Their dark presence stayed with him as he dressed, left his house, got in his car and headed for Nicholasville Road.

He had to accept this as one of those times when the unreal overwhelmed the real.

ENTERING IHOP for the traditional weekly breakfast with David Bloom and Sean Montgomery, he was startled to see Amy Countzler sitting at the table. He shouldn't have been surprised; Bloom and Sean, both of whom adored Amy, had often hinted at inviting her to join them. Now that they had, the trio was a quartet for the first time since Erin Collins,

Dantzler's former girlfriend, relocated to Manhattan last year.

Seeing the look on Dantzler's face, Amy said, "Sean asked me to join you guys this morning. Hope it's okay with you."

"It's nice having you with us, Amy," Dantzler said, sitting next to her. "Just proves Sean is more intelligent than he looks."

"Don't downplay my intelligence, Jack," Sean said. "After all, I am the third smartest man at this table. Number three ain't too shabby."

"My apologies, Einstein," Dantzler commented.

The waitress came, took their orders and left. When she was gone, most of the conversation was between Bloom and Amy. Bloom kept peppering Amy with questions about how she was holding up now that she had so many irons in the fire. Amy shrugged it off, saying she was perfectly fine. For her part, Amy began asking Bloom for his insights into several psychological disorders she found fascinating. Sean listened to their banter, appearing to be trapped somewhere between bored and curious. It was always a mystery when it came to what Sean was thinking.

Showing no interest at all in their conversation, Dantzler remained quiet, staring off into the distance. After a while Sean picked up on Dantzler's moody silence.

"What's up with you, Jack?" Sean asked. "Something's troubling you. I can tell from that glum look on your face."

"To be honest, Sean, I'm disappointed in Jake and Vee's investigation of the Laura Conley homicide," Dantzler said. His statement ended the chat between Bloom and Amy. They were now all ears. "They made the oldest mistake detectives can make when working an investigation. They gave up too soon."

"Meaning they didn't uncover all the evidence?"

"It's worse than that, Sean. They failed to *look* for all the evidence."

Bloom said, "Maybe they think all the evidence has been collected. That's possible, isn't it?"

"In this instance, no," Dantzler flatly stated. "Jake and Vee could've done more. A lot more. They are superb investigators, equal to or better than I was, yet they bought into the notion Mike Conley was guilty. They followed the herd, not the evidence. Had they dug deeper, conducted more interviews with other potential suspects, they would have arrived at the same conclusion I have: someone other than Mike murdered Laura Conley."

"Two things, Jack," Sean said. "First, a correction. Jake and Vee, though excellent detectives, aren't in your class. You're just being kind to say that. Second, from what I just heard you say, I take it you know who killed Laura. Am I right?"

"Yeah, Sean, I'm fairly certain I know her killer. And let me assure you Jake and Vee, at whatever level you rate them, would have come to the same conclusion if they had put forth more effort. The evidence was there for them to find if they had only looked for it."

"Who did kill Laura?" Amy asked, as their food was being delivered. "Let me guess. Kent Lofton."

"I can't reveal the name, Amy. Not until I'm one-hundred percent certain. But no, it's not Kent Lofton."

They ate in silence, gloom having replaced levity among the foursome. This was the polar opposite of their many past get-togethers. Normally there was non-stop chatter.

Dantzler ate his omelet, hash brown potatoes and toast without enjoying it. His focus was elsewhere.

Finally, Sean broke the silence, asking Dantzler, "How are you going to deal with Jake and Vee?"

Handing his empty plate to the waitress, Dantzler said, "When I'm sure I have the right person I'll turn everything over to Jake and Vee. They can take it from there."

"They'll be devastated knowing they failed in the eyes of their hero," Bloom interjected. "That they let you down. You'd better be prepared to deal with that."

"What will you say to them?" Sean asked.

"The truth, that they screwed up. I'm not about to sugar coat it. They performed a lousy, unprofessional investigation. As a result a killer could've gone free. They have to acknowledge their mistake, own it and vow to never let it happen again. I'll assure them they are talented, gifted detectives who made a mistake, something that happens to all of us. But I will also tell them the important thing is not to dwell on the past. That their objective is to make certain to do better in the future."

"End on a positive note," Bloom said. "Smart."

THREE SETS of tennis (he crushed one of Kentucky's top-ranked high school players) and thirty minutes on the stationary bike did little to shake Dantzler's dark mood. It clung to him like an extra layer of skin. He showered, dressed and headed up to his office, intent on getting to the bottom of what was troubling him.

One of his dreams was responsible, this much he knew for sure. The one where he sees a shadowy figure aiming a rifle at him. But it was more than the dream. Something else was bothering him. But what? he kept asking himself. The answer was agonizingly close, but slightly beyond his grasp. Just then, as though a heavenly light suddenly shown down, it came to him: The dream wasn't troubling him; rather, it was a question that begged for a response:

Did Kelly act alone while murdering Laura Conley or did she have help from Marianne Lofton?

Were Bonnie and Bonnie the newest murdering couple? Dantzler wondered.

DANTZLER LEFT his office at two-thirty, went to the lounge area and bought a Pepsi Max. He'd remained at the Tennis Center for the purpose of speaking with Marianne Lofton. Recently, she had been showing up around three o'clock, five days a week, usually to either play tennis or to workout, staying close to two hours with each visit. Dantzler hoped to catch her before she went downstairs.

Realizing Marianne would be reluctant to answer more questions, Dantzler decided to take a different approach, one almost certain to succeed—play to Marianne's ego. Praise her, make her the center of attention and the odds were good she would be more than happy to engage in a conversation.

Dantzler was in his office when he saw Marianne walk past the door. She carried her equipment bag, meaning tennis was on her agenda today. Dantzler hopped up and went to the door when he saw her stroll by.

"Hey, Marianne, got a second?" he said.

Stopping, looking over her shoulder, she said, "To

answer more of your shitty questions? Or listen to you chastise me for what I'm wearing? Hell no, asshole, I have no time for you."

"Peace, Marianne. I come bearing praise, not questions. Only want to say I heard you are a superb shot with a pistol. Simply wanted to compliment you, that's all."

Now interested, Marianne did a one-eighty, took several steps toward Dantzler. "Oh yeah, where did you hear that?"

"From Wendell at the indoor gun range."

This was true. Yesterday afternoon, prior to phoning Robert Hilton and Leah Wallin, Dantzler had visited the gun range, where he spoke with Wendell, one of the managers. Wendell was quick to confirm Marianne's shooting skills. *"That damn lady could shoot the buffalo off an old nickel rolling across the floor."* Wendell had this to say about Kelly Hilton: *"Good shot, once she overcame her fear of guns."*

Dantzler left with the understanding Wendell was definitely impressed with both women.

"Why were you at the shooting range?" Marianne inquired.

"Checking to see if it's a good place for me to shoot," Dantzler said. "Since leaving the police force I haven't done as much shooting as I should. I need to get in some practice." A lie: If he wanted to practice shooting he'd go to the Law Enforcement Firing Range on Airport Road.

"Wendell's a good guy." Marianne was now extremely interested. "Exactly what did he say about me?"

"Something about how you could shoot the buffalo off a nickel rolling across the floor."

"He said that?"

"Wouldn't lie to you, Marianne."

"Well, he wasn't exaggerating." A slight pause, then, "Did he say anything about Kelly Hilton?"

Dantzler understood this as Marianne's way of verifying the veracity of what he was saying. Was he being truthful or was he lying?

"Wendell said Kelly became an excellent shot once she managed to get past her fear of guns," Dantzler said.

"He didn't say Kelly is a better shot than me, did he?" Marianne asked, her ego in need of reinforcement.

"No, he made it clear you are the superior shot. Let me ask you, Marianne. Do you use a specific weapon at the range? I mean, is there one you prefer above all others?"

"All depends on which gun I happen to take with me on a particular day. I've used a twenty-two, a thirty-eight and a forty-five. I'm equally good with all of them. Once I took a forty-four Magnum, but Wendell refused to let me use it. Said it was overkill. He was probably right. It was too much gun."

"What about Kelly? Which gun does she use? Not the forty-four Magnum, I hope."

"A twenty-two at the beginning, because it's smaller, easier to handle. Lately, she's been using a thirty-eight. An old one I gave her. It's still in mint condition, though. I take good care of my weapons."

Kelly has a thirty-eight. Laura. Conley was shot with a thirty-eight. One more nail in Kelly's coffin.

"Didn't mean to hold you up this long, Marianne," Dantzler said. "Just wanted to pay you a compliment. Go, play tennis, have fun."

"Am I dressed appropriately?" Marianne said, turning snarky once again.

"You look fine."

"Well, hallelujah."

Dantzler smiled as he watched her sashay down the stairs. It had been an enlightening conversation. Finding out Kelly Hilton had permanent possession of a thirty-eight was like striking gold. And he had Marianne Lofton to thank for leading him to the treasure. Actually, to be more accurate, it was Marianne's ego he had to thank.

YESTERDAY AT THE SHOOTING RANGE, had Dantzler stayed around for another hour he would have crossed paths with a familiar face:

Nikki Doyle.

She came to the range seven nights a week, always at nine, and practiced shooting until the place closed at eleven. Initially, her pistol, a Glock 19, was difficult to get used to. But thanks to constant practice this changed over time. Now the gun was easy to handle, almost like it was part of her hand. She had come to love the gun. Vowed to never part with it. Told Ray she wouldn't object to being buried with it in her hand. Ray scoffed at that notion.

Nikki loved it for a second reason—Dantzler also used a Glock. She wasn't sure which model Dantzler used, but in a perfect world it would be a Glock 19, just like hers.

How poetic would it be if Jack Dantzler were shot by the same type of weapon he normally used?

That would be like winning the lottery not once but twice.

Chapter Twenty-Nine

At ten the next morning, Dantzler entered the indoor shooting range for the purpose of speaking once again with Wendell Dalton, one of the managers. The place was virtually empty, only two men shooting at the time. Wendell was behind the counter when Dantzler stepped inside. Seeing Dantzler, Wendell grinned and waved.

Wendell Dalton had to be in his thirties, stood about five-eight, weighed maybe one-eighty, had short, thick legs, massive arms and virtually no neck. He resembled a tree stump, or perhaps a former wrestler. Dantzler had no doubt Wendell was a strong man.

"Back again, huh?" Wendell said, as Dantzler moved closer to the counter. "Mr. Dunlap, or Mr. Dunleavy, or . . ."

"Dantzler," Dantzler corrected.

"Yeah, Dantzler, my bad. I'm terrible when it comes to names. Damn lucky I can remember my own."

"I've been called worse, Wendell. Name's Jack. That should be easy to remember."

"Jack Dantzler? Sure. You were once a cop, am I right?"

"Homicide, twenty-seven years."

"Man, how did I not recognize you? You once arrested a guy I know. You remember Oscar Young?"

"Hard to forget Oscar," Dantzler said, chuckling. "He's doing life at Eddyville. How do you know Oscar?"

"We were in the same grade at school," Wendell recalled. "That is, until he dropped out. Or got booted out. I'm not sure which, but one day he was gone for good. This was in ninth grade. Oscar was one of the dumbest humans I've ever met. Always breaking the rules, always getting caught. It was like he had 'Here I am, I'm guilty' tattooed on his forehead. I once told him he should go straight, because he wasn't intelligent enough to be a successful criminal. But heck, the poor bastard didn't have much of a chance, not with an old man like he was cursed with. The whole bunch of Youngs were raised to be criminals. Sad, really."

"Couldn't agree with you more, Wendell." Dantzler looked around. "Do you have a place where we can speak in private? An office, maybe?"

"Sure, follow me." Wendell came out from behind the counter and led Dantzler down a narrow hallway to the office. After turning on the lights, Wendell moved to the small desk, sat and indicated for Dantzler to take one of two visitors chairs. "What is it you want to talk about?" he asked.

"I'm here to seek a favor, Wendell," Dantzler said, after taking a seat. "But it comes with a stipulation. If you agree to help, you have to give your word you won't tell a soul. Not your wife, not your priest . . . no one. It has to stay strictly between us. Can you make that promise?"

"Well, I'm not married anymore, and I'm not Catholic,

so wife and priest don't come into play. And I never break my oath once I've given it. My word is my bond. So yeah, you can trust me. What is the favor you're seeking?"

"Are you expecting Marianne Lofton and Kelly Hilton to show up this afternoon?"

"Can't make any promise they will, but I'd be very surprised if they didn't. They've become hard-core regulars."

"When they get here, make sure Kelly is using the thirty-eight she normally shoots with. If she is, don't say anything or make a big deal of it. Act natural. Let her follow her standard routine. Once she's finished shooting, give her and Marianne time to leave, then retrieve two or three of her slugs. Can you do that?"

"Not a problem."

"You have to be one-hundred percent sure they came from Kelly's weapon."

"Again, not a problem," Wendell reiterated. "I'll reserve one of the lanes, won't let anyone use it before she gets here. That's the one I'll assign her. Once she and Marianne are finished shooting, and I'm positive they have gone, I'll go get the slugs."

"Once you have the slugs, seal them in an envelope or a plastic bag, then give me a call at this number." Dantzler took out one of his business cards and handed it to Wendell. "I'll come back here and get them from you."

"Unless you're in a great hurry to have them, perhaps I can save you a trip. I go to the bank every afternoon around one. Give me your address and I'll be more than happy to drop them off. I can be there by twelve-thirty."

"Sure you don't mind?"

"Not at all."

"Okay. Do you know where the Tennis Center is located?"

"Yeah, I drive by there all the time."

"Bring them to the Tennis Center. To my office. That's where I'll be."

"Count on it," Wendell said. "But . . . can you give me a hint what this is all about? Why you need the slugs?"

"Since you've agreed to help, and you've given your word to keep this between the two of us, you deserve to know the details. I've been hired by a man who was recently tried for murdering his wife. He was acquitted, but everyone is absolutely convinced he's guilty. My goal is to find the real killer. To prove my client is innocent. The victim was shot with a thirty-eight. I happen to believe the gun used to commit the murder belongs to Kelly. It's the one she uses when she comes here. Once you've retrieved the slugs and given them to me, I'll pay a visit to the ballistics expert and ask him to match them against the slug used in the homicide I'm investigating. Unless I'm badly mistaken, the slugs from Kelly's gun will be a match."

"You're telling me Kelly Hilton is a murderer?"

"If they do match, it has to be Kelly. Unless someone else used her weapon, which I doubt."

"Damn, that's hard to believe," Wendell said. "I mean, Kelly doesn't look like a killer. On the other hand, Marianne strikes me as a woman who wouldn't hesitate to pull the trigger."

Dantzler stood, said, "I'll expect you around twelve-thirty tomorrow, Wendell. If you run into any problems, you have my number. And once again, this has to be a secret between you and me. No one else can know."

"You have my word," Wendell said, opening the door.

"Know what's really weird? All of a sudden we're having more and more female shooters sign up. Used to be we didn't have hardly any women here. Boy, has that changed. Can't blame them, really, with all the violence in the world. All the asshole men who think it's perfectly okay to beat up women. Being capable with a gun gives women some sense of security, I suppose."

"Are most women accurate shooters?"

"Ah, I'd say the majority are only average. Some are better than others, as you'd expect. However, we have three ladies who are deadly shots. Well, two, actually. Kelly Hilton is only slightly above average. But the other two? Marianne Lofton and a woman named Nikki? They are superior to most men."

"Nikki Doyle?" Dantzler asked, surprised to utter that name.

"Yeah. You know her?" Wendell asked.

Certain facts Wendell didn't need to know. "Not personally. I know she owns a public relations firm here in town. Does she come here often?"

"Every night at nine, regular as the sunrise, stays until we close. Fires hundreds of rounds, uses a Glock 13. I mean, she burns through them. And man, is she intense. It's like she's killing someone with every shot."

"Maybe she is," Dantzler said, shaking Wendell's hand. "Catch you tomorrow, Wendell."

A MIXED BLESSING, that's how Dantzler felt about his visit to the shooting range. There was good news (Wendell agreed to retrieve the slugs from Kelly's thirty-eight) and disturbing news (Nikki Doyle was practicing to become the next Wild Bill Hickok).

What was he to make of that? He couldn't say, but his gut was telling him it couldn't be good.

Putting thoughts about Nikki on the back burner, Dantzler drove straight to the Tennis Center, went to his office, sat at his desk and placed a call to John Ireland, Sean's cop buddy from the Miami area.

"Detective John Ireland. How can I be of assistance?" John answered.

"Detective, this is Jack Dantzler, Sean Montgomery's friend from Lexington," Dantzler said. "We spoke not long ago, remember?"

"Of course I remember. Haven't got dementia just yet. What's up, Jack? Still interested in Marianne Blackstone?"

"Interested, yes, but that's not the reason for my call. You have a few minutes to talk?"

"Yeah, what's on your mind?"

"I need help with the case I'm working. I'm thinking you're the man for the job."

"Help? If possible, sure, I'll do what I can."

"Tomorrow afternoon I'm going to mail a package to you. I'll send it Express Mail, so you should have it in two days. The contents could end up helping both of us."

"I'm intrigued. What are you sending me?"

"Two thirty-eight slugs from a pistol once owned by Marianne Lofton. Or Blackstone. I'd like to know if they match the bullet that killed Marianne's first husband."

"What if it does? That won't change anything. The death was ruled accidental, remember? Besides, we know the bullet came from a thirty-eight owned by Richie Blackstone, her husband. I'm not sure what you're looking for. And how does this factor into the case you're working?"

"I believe the gun's current owner is responsible for killing my client's wife," Dantzler said. "Her name is Kelly Hilton. But I need more proof. Hopefully, I'll get that proof once my people run a ballistics test comparing the new slugs with the one that killed Laura Conley. I will get the slugs from the firing range where Kelly practices shooting. If I'm right and they match, that should seal the case for me."

"Okay, but I'm still unclear why you need my help."

"Do you continue to suspect Marianne of murdering her first husband?"

"I think she pulled the trigger, yeah."

"If the slugs I send you match the one that killed Richie Blackstone, that gives me more leverage when I interview Marianne," Dantzler explained.

"Why interview her? You don't suspect Marianne of killing your client's wife, do you?" John asked.

"No, but she was having an affair with my client. This means she did have a connection to the murder victim. I'd say that gives me a solid reason to question her again. When I do, if I fib a little, toss in some bluff about the matching bullets and what happened in Palm Beach, perhaps I can get her to admit murdering Richie Blackstone."

"From what I remember about her, I doubt she'll squeal. She was a block of ice when we brought her in for questioning."

"Trust me, John, she hasn't thawed out one ice cube since you questioned her."

"Send the slugs to me, I'll have my guy do a test. Maybe we'll find a magic bullet like the one that went through Kennedy, shattered several bones in Connelly, only to be miraculously found in pristine condition. I'll gladly take magic if it helps bring Marianne to justice."

"Marianne, or her current husband. I haven't completely ruled out Kent Lofton."

"I'd be pleased to have either one. Or both," John said. "No killer should go free."

"My sentiments, exactly," Dantzler said. "Be on the lookout for that package. Let me know what you learn."

"Soon as I know, you'll know. Next time you see Sean, tell him I said hello."

"That will be tonight. We're meeting for dinner. Sean doesn't know it yet, but he's picking up the tab."

"You'll need plenty of magic for that to happen, Jack."

DANTZLER DISCONNECTED, then immediately phoned Eric Gamble, the police chief. When Eric answered, Dantzler asked if they could meet in the next hour or so. Eric agreed, and after a brief discussion about where, they decided on the main library, located only a few blocks from the police station.

Eric, more handsome than Denzel Washington (and a classier dresser than Denzel) had been Dantzler's partner for more than ten years. Dantzler loved the kid. So when Richard Bird retired as police chief, Dantzler was a strong advocate for hiring Eric. Naturally, there was resistance, primarily from veteran cops (and many politicians), most of whom felt Eric was too young and too inexperienced for the job. But in the end, Eric got the job, thus making him the first Black to hold that position. Most would agree he'd done outstanding work since taking the reins.

Dantzler realized what he was about to ask Eric bumped up against standard operating procedure. Gave it the middle finger, to be more precise. Eric would have every right to deny Dantzler's request, and if he did, Dantzler wouldn't put up a fight. He had no desire to butt heads with Eric. However, that being said, Dantzler felt compelled to make his request. His professional detective's bones demanded it. He had always held firm to the belief that what you start, you finish. He saw no reason to alter his philosophy at this point.

"Good to see you, Jack," Eric said, shaking Dantzler's hand. They were on the second level, sitting at a table next to the wall. "We haven't really talked since Erin left. I was sorry to see her go. I'm sure you were too."

"Yeah, it's been tough," Dantzler admitted. "But I couldn't blame her for leaving. She landed a prestigious job."

"That's not surprising. She's a talented, brainy lady. S.D.N.Y. is lucky to have her."

Thinking *enough with the chit-chat,* Dantzler said, "Eric, my reason for meeting is to make you aware that I'm ninety-nine percent certain I have identified Laura Conley's killer. If all goes as I expect it to, I'll be one-hundred percent sure in two days. Kelly Hilton murdered Laura Conley."

"Ah, man, you know what this is, don't you, Jack?"

"Good news you hate to hear."

"Exactly. Good news that a killer will finally be brought to justice, bad news that my two best investigators blew it." Eric rubbed his eyes, a grim look on his face. "What did Jake and Vee miss?"

"It's not so much what they missed; it's that they didn't dig deep enough to find the truth. They gave up too soon."

"Hate to admit it, but I might belong in that camp with them."

"What's that supposed to mean?"

"Unlike everyone on this planet I was never convinced Mike Conley killed Laura. Truthfully, I thought the guy was innocent. From the very beginning I had my eye on Kelly as the shooter. I looked at other potential suspects, but I kept coming back to her. Jake and Vee were adamant that Mike committed the murder, so I let them run with it. I kept quiet, didn't share my thoughts with them. That was my mistake. I should have insisted they take a harder look at Kelly. Bottom line: I failed them."

"Come on, Eric, they're experienced professionals. They should've taken a harder look in *all* directions. As professionals, they didn't need to be told to do that by you or anyone else."

"Still . . ." Eric said, letting his thoughts drift away.

"You know why I wanted to meet? What I'm about to ask you?"

"You're seeking my permission to allow you to close the case before handing it over to Jake and Vee, right?"

Nodding, Dantzler said, "I want to see it through to the end. To finish what I started."

"How soon can you wrap it up?"

"Two days, three, tops."

"You don't have the authority to arrest her."

"When it gets to that point, I'll make sure Jake and Vee are there to slap the cuffs on and read Kelly her rights." Dantzler reached across the table and touched Eric's arm. "If you're uncomfortable with this, Eric, if you think I'm overstepping the boundaries, don't be afraid to say no. You won't hurt my feelings. Believe me, I'll understand. I mean, let's be real here. I *am* overstepping the boundaries."

"Anyone else I would say no," Eric said. "But you've earned the right to some special treatment. So, you have my blessing."

"When to inform Jake and Vee, that will be your call, Eric."

"Probably better if I tell them sooner rather than later. Either way, I can't imagine they'll be very happy. But the truth is, they don't have much room to put up a fight. Not after I remind them of their less-than-sterling investigation."

"Thanks, Eric," Dantzler said, getting up from his chair. "The second I know for sure Kelly is guilty, I'll be on the phone to Jake and Vee."

"I appreciate you running this by me first," Eric said, standing. "For showing me professional courtesy. That means the world to me."

"Never thought of proceeding without your blessing. You're like my kid brother, Eric. A man can't mistreat his brother, can he?"

"Tell that to Abel."

"*Touche*, Brother."

Chapter Thirty

Wendell Dalton showed up at the Tennis Center thirty minutes early, a man on a mission, eager to see justice served. Dantzler liked Wendell, sizing him up as a decent guy, a humble man who never lost contact with his better angels. Dantzler regretted there weren't more Wendell Daltons in the world.

Dantzler was sitting in the Tennis Center lounge drinking a Diet Pepsi when Wendell came in. Breathing hard, face flush with excitement, Wendell handed Dantzler a plastic bag containing three slugs.

"I know you only asked for two, but I brought an extra one just in case," Wendell said. "You know, on the off-chance one of them is too damaged to test. Was that okay?"

"Not only okay, Wendell, it was a wise decision," Dantzler said, holding up the bag and studying the slugs. "Can't say for sure, but they look good. I'm sure at least one of these will work. Thank you for doing this. You've really helped me out."

"Happy to do it. But I gotta be honest, Mr. Dantzler. I'm kinda hoping you're wrong about Kelly being a murderer. She's always been nice to me. But if she is guilty, well, she should go down for it, regardless of how she treated me."

"We should have an answer later this afternoon."

"You really believe she's guilty, don't you, Mr. Dantzler?"

"Yes, I do. And all my friends call me Jack." Dantzler tossed his empty cup into the trash. "Wendell, you look like a man who lifts weights on a regular basis. Do you?"

Wendell nodded, said, "Until last week I lifted every night. But Johnny Simms, the night manager, had to go out of town for a death in the family. With him gone, I've been holding down the fort from open to close. Haven't had time to do much lifting. Johnny should be back Sunday. Then I can get back to my regular routine."

"We have a terrific workout room downstairs, with lots of up-to-date equipment, including plenty of weights. Go downstairs, check it out. If you like what you see, I'll give you a free one-year membership to the Tennis Center. That means you can come here anytime between seven a.m. and one a.m. and workout."

"That sounds cool," Wendell said, looking at the time on his cell phone. "I've got time. Thanks, Jack."

Dantzler went behind the counter, found a notepad and a pen. "I'll be gone when you've finished looking around," he said. "If you're interested, write down your name, home address, Social Security number and phone number on this pad and leave it next to the cash register. I'll take care of everything when I get back. You're free to come here anytime after tomorrow."

Grinning ear to ear, Wendell shook Dantzler's hand,

thanked him once again, then hurried for the stairs. Dantzler was out the door and on the way to his car before Wendell reached the exercise room.

Dantzler's next stop—a meeting with Rudy Crawford, ballistics expert extraordinaire. And hopefully, solve at least one mystery.

IT TOOK LESS than an hour for Rudy Crawford to complete the ballistics test. The results confirmed Dantzler's suspicions. The bullet that killed Laura Conley was a match to the bullet from the firing range. Both came for the thirty-eight now owned by Kelly Hilton, the weapon she used to commit the murder.

This knowledge presented Dantzler with a pair of options—wait until he heard back from John Ireland before confronting Kelly or immediately question her. It didn't take long for him to make his decision. Although he strongly believed Marianne Lofton used that same thirty-eight to murder her first husband, bringing her to justice had to come later. At this moment, his goal was to present Kelly with certain facts and get her to admit killing Laura Conley.

Dantzler caught a break when he saw Kelly and three women enter the Tennis Center later that afternoon. Obviously, a doubles match was scheduled. This was ideal for Dantzler. He would wait until Kelly's match concluded, follow her home, then hit her with the evidence.

Three hours later, Dantzler was parked on the opposite side of the street and one block down from Kelly's house. He'd watched her say goodbye to her tennis friends, get in her car and drive out of the parking area. Once she was a safe distance away, he began tailing her, careful to stay far enough behind that she didn't notice his car. She made a quick stop at Total Wine, then drove straight home. Dantzler was in no rush to confront her. He would give her time to shower, put on fresh clothes, pour a glass of wine and get relaxed. When he felt she was cozy and comfortable, he exited his car, crossed the street, went onto the porch and rang the doorbell.

"I have nothing to say to you, Detective Dantzler," Kelly said, opening the door maybe five inches.

Dantzler considered correcting her, but decided not to. If Kelly thought he was still a detective, she might be more inclined to answer his questions. Authority can be intimidating.

"Actually, you have a lot to say, Kelly," Dantzler noted. "Mind if we talk inside?"

"Talk about what? My ex? Nothing else to say about that cheating bastard."

"Let me in and I won't mention Robert. You have my word."

"You'll have to be brief." Kelly held up her glass of wine. "I'm meeting friends for a drink in an hour."

Dantzler judged this to be a lie but he let it pass without offering a challenge.

She led Dantzler to the kitchen. He waited until she was seated then he scooted back a chair and sat down. Kelly didn't appear to be nervous or suspicious. *Good*, Dantzler thought. *Let's see if she's still this composed fifteen minutes from now.*

Taking a sip of white wine, Kelly said, "Mike Conley murdered Laura. Everyone knows that. Why the jury failed to convict him, I'll never understand."

"Had the verdict gone the other way, the jury would

have convicted an innocent man," Dantzler said. "Mike didn't kill Laura, and I can prove it."

"If Mike didn't kill her, who did?"

"I'm looking at Laura's killer."

"Seriously? You think I killed Laura? That's absurd. The cops questioned me and dismissed me as a suspect. Maybe you haven't heard, but I had an airtight alibi when Laura was killed."

"Two phone calls made from your house? The second one at nine-forty? Plus, you were alone at the time. Not what I'd classify as an airtight alibi."

"Then you aren't familiar with the facts of the case. Laura was killed between nine-thirty and ten. I was on the phone during that time. A person can't be in two places at the same time."

"Let me correct you on the facts, Kelly. According to the coroner, Laura died sometime between ten-thirty and eleven. That's well after your second phone call. You live no more than twenty minutes from the Conleys. Therefore, you had ample time to manufacture an alibi, then drive to Laura's house and kill her."

"You're living in dreamland, Detective," Kelly said. "And dreams aren't proof."

Dantzler reached into his coat pocket, took out the plastic bag, lifted it up and said, "But these aren't dreams."

"What are those? Two pebbles? How are they proof of anything?"

Dantzler dug into the bag and removed one of the slugs. "This was retrieved from the firing range after you finished shooting yesterday afternoon." He then took out the second slug. "This one was the bullet that killed Laura Conley. I borrowed it from the police. (A fib: He had no authority to remove anything from evidence storage. But Kelly wasn't aware of that regulation.) Both bullets are a match to your thirty-eight. The gun you used to murder Laura Conley."

"How do I know those are real? That you aren't making up shit?"

"Stop denying it, Kelly," Dantzler said. "Ballistics aren't like people. They don't lie. These two little pebbles, as you referred to them, have sealed your fate. It's time for you to own up to what you did."

"I did not do what you are accusing me of."

"No need to keep denying it. Unfortunately, Kelly, this is one of those times when the truth won't set you free. It will land you in prison."

"I want to make a deal," Kelly said, tearing up, her cloak of invincibility now shattered. "I'll give you information about another murder if you agree to the deal."

"I don't have the authority to make deals, Kelly. That's up to the district attorney."

Kelly's eyes widened. "That's right, you aren't a detective anymore. You have no authority to question me about anything."

Dantzler picked up his cell phone and typed a message. "You're absolutely correct, Kelly," he stated, placing his phone on the table. "But I just sent a message to Jake Thomas. He and his partner Vee Jefferson will be here within the next fifteen minutes. They do have the authority to question you."

"I'll tell them everything you say is bullshit. That I have no idea what you are talking about."

"Two reasons why that won't work," Dantzler said, holding up the plastic bag. "First, these slugs are real, they are a match to your weapon and to the bullet that killed

Laura. Second, do you really believe I would question you without bringing a tape recorder?"

Removing the small device from his shirt pocket, he continued, "What you need to do is start being truthful, beginning with why you killed Laura."

"Not until I have a deal in place. You advise the detectives to speak with the district attorney. If I get that deal, I will tell everything I know about that other murder I mentioned."

"What? That Marianne Lofton murdered her first husband? Is that what you're willing to share with me? Sorry, Kelly, I already know all about that."

Stunned, Kelly mumbled, "How'd you know?"

"The bullet that killed Richie Blackstone came from your thirty-eight." (Technically, another lie, since he hadn't received confirmation from John Ireland concerning the status of that bullet.) "Marianne previously owned that weapon. It only makes sense she was the shooter. And like I told you, ballistics don't lie, Kelly."

"Yeah, Marianne did kill her first husband. For his money, of course."

"Did Marianne admit this to you?"

"No, Kent told me. One night when he'd had too much to drink he started coming on to me. He said if I'd sleep with him he would let me in on a big secret. I . . . well, that's how I found out."

"Was Kent involved?"

"No. He barely knew Marianne at the time."

The front door opened and Jake and Vee came inside.

"Back here, guys," Dantzler said. Then when they were in the kitchen, "Kelly Lynn Hilton murdered Laura Conley. It's all on this tape."

"Stand up," Vee ordered. "Kelly Lynn Hilton, you are under arrest for suspicion of murdering Laura Conley. You have the right to . . ."

Jake took the recorder from Dantzler as Vee put the cuffs on Kelly. "We let you down, Jack," Jake said. "We should've been better."

"Amen," Vee said.

"We all make mistakes, guys," Dantzler said. "Just vow to do better in the future."

"Roger that," Jake said, adding, "won't happen a second time."

"Amen, again," Vee echoed.

Dantzler turned to Kelly, and said, "You and Laura hated each other. Why did she let you in the house?"

"A gun pointed at your face is very persuasive."

"Why did you murder Laura?"

"The arrogant cunt broke up my marriage," Kelly said, venom in her voice. "You think I was going to let that slide? Not in a million years."

"The affair had ended before you killed Laura."

"If Robert told you that, he's lying. They were still going at it like two cats in heat. No, the affair ended when I ended Laura."

"But you divorced Robert."

"So . . ."

"I don't think cold-blooded murder is a solution to any problem, Kelly."

"Oh, well, different strokes, right?"

JOHN IRELAND PHONED at ten-thirty to let Dantzler know the results of the ballistics test conducted in Palm Beach. Once again, Dantzler wasn't surprised by the outcome. The bullet was a match to the thirty-eight that once belonged to Marianne Lofton. This was the final nail in her coffin. Marianne murdered Richie Blackstone and the evidence proved it. Like her pal Kelly, Marianne was looking at a lengthy period of dark years behind prison bars.

"Do you want me to make a call and pass along this information to my detectives and have them arrest her?" Dantzler asked. "Or would you prefer we hold off until you get here?"

"Oh, hell no, don't wait," John replied. "The sooner she's in custody, the better I'll sleep at night. I don't want to give her any chance to flee. With her money, if she gets wind we're coming for her, this time tomorrow she'll be living on a beach in some remote country. I'll catch a flight to Lexington tomorrow. Then I will sit down and have a little chat with Miss Blackstone-Lofton."

"I'll text Jake Thomas, have him bring her in first thing tomorrow morning. Text me your arrival time; I'll have Sean pick you up at the airport."

"Look forward to seeing you, Jack. Don't you just love days like this, when everything goes right for the good guys? Makes this job seem worthwhile, doesn't it?"

"Putting away murderers is always worthwhile."

But you are right, John. Today was an especially good day.

Chapter Thirty-One

Mike Conley was so thrilled to finally be completely exonerated from murdering his wife (a lengthy article in yesterday's *Herald-Leader* informed the reading public of his innocence) that he wrote Dantzler a check for fifty-thousand dollars.

Dantzler took the check, glanced at it and immediately ripped it in half.

"Listen, Jack, I realize no amount of money is adequate repayment for what you've done for me, and perhaps I can come up with more in the future, but at the present time fifty-thousand is really all I can spare," Mike said, sounding apologetic.

"The amount is more than adequate, Mike," Dantzler said. "But I want you to write two checks, one to me for thirty-five thousand and a second one to Wendell Dalton for fifteen-thousand."

"I'm not familiar with Wendell Dalton. Why am I giving him money?"

"Because without his involvement you would still be living under a cloud of suspicion. He helped me, and for his assistance he should be compensated."

Mike began writing the new check for Dantzler without further comment.

"Were you surprised to learn it was Kelly who murdered Laura?" Dantzler asked.

"Honestly, yes, I was," Mike stated, head down, still writing. "In hindsight, I probably shouldn't have been surprised given what was going on between Laura and Robert Hilton. But I never once considered Kelly a suspect. She had what I assumed was a solid alibi. Hell, *everyone* assumed it. That's why she was never on my radar."

"Her phony alibi worked," Dantzler said, taking the check from Mike. "Until it didn't."

"Is Kelly currently in jail?"

"Yes. She is scheduled to be arraigned tomorrow morning. Her attorney will ask for bail, which, if granted, will be so high I doubt she can afford it. I can't imagine Robert going out of his way to help her."

"I certainly wouldn't if I were him."

"Have you heard from Laura's family since the truth finally came out?"

"Not directly, no. But their attorney sent a text informing me the civil suit has been dropped. I'm hoping her family will eventually reach out to me. That would be nice. Before Laura was murdered I got along very well with her family. But it's up to them. I will not make the first move."

Mike carefully tore out the second check and handed it to Dantzler. "I heard from two former employees this morning who resigned after I was charged with murder.

They both wanted their old jobs back. I didn't hesitate to tell them, yes, your desk is waiting for you."

"You're much more forgiving than I'd be. I would've told them both to take a hike."

"It's not about forgiveness, Jack, it's about talent. They are both exceptionally gifted young men. Hate to admit it, but business has slipped considerably since all this nonsense began. Having those two guys with me again means we can get back to creating the high-quality products that we're known for. What our customers expect from us."

Dantzler stood, said, "Thanks for the checks, Mike. I'm just thankful everything worked out for the best."

"No, Jack, thank you," Mike said, standing and offering his hand to Dantzler. "You've given everything back to me —my name, my reputation, my business. I'll forever be in your debt."

A soft rain was coming down when Dantzler left Mike's building. Sprinting to his car, he got in, started the motor and drove out of the parking lot. His next stop was the firing range.

Time to play Santa Claus.

WENDELL DALTON WAS in the process of cleaning a pistol when Dantzler entered the firing range. Wendell picked up the cleaning rod and was about to insert it into the barrel when he noticed Dantzler. Putting the rod down, he used a cloth rag to wipe oil from his hands. He waved for Dantzler to join him.

"Have something for you, Wendell," Dantzler said,

holding up the check. "A well-earned, well-deserved reward."

Wendell took the check, looked at the amount and blurted out, "Fifteen-thousand dollars? Wow. Is this for real?"

"It's signed, isn't it?"

"But this is way too much. I didn't do enough to deserve fifteen grand. No way."

"Don't undervalue your contribution, Wendell. You helped clear an innocent man's name and you helped put away a murderer. That's a good day's work by any standard of judgment. Besides, you were my partner and my partners don't work for peanuts. You earned every penny."

"Man, I simply can't believe this. Fifteen-thousand dollars? Thanks, Jack."

"I'm the one who should be thanking you," Dantzler said. Then: "Changing the subject. Did you get your membership card to the Tennis Center?"

"I did, yes. The pretty lady had it ready for me yesterday morning," Wendell said, still staring at the check. "I think her name is Amy."

"Amy Countzler, yeah. Have you worked out yet?"

"Haven't had time. But that will change when Johnny gets back Sunday. Once things return to normal around here, I'll be there every night. You can count on it."

"Look forward to seeing you." Dantzler started to walk away, stopped and turned back around. "Has Nikki Doyle continued to show up?"

"Yep. Nine o'clock, stays until we close," Wendell said. "Goes through two, three boxes of ammo each night."

"Interesting. Do me a favor, Wendell. Don't mention that I was asking about her, okay?"

"Hey, man, I'll be more silent than a corpse."

BEING INVOLVED in a press conference was never Dantzler's thing. He usually avoided them the way a person avoids a poisonous snake in the woods. The usual suspects—the mayor, district attorney, various city council members—hogged most of the TV time before eventually handing it over to the ones who did the actual hard work. Dantzler had no time for such *mishegoss*.

A press conference was held the morning after Marianne Lofton was arrested. During the briefing it was announce that "local detectives" had solved two murders, a recent one in Lexington and one that occurred more than a decade ago in Florida. Dantzler wasn't mentioned, nor was John Ireland or anyone else from the Palm Beach Police Department. Dantzler didn't care that his name was omitted, but it did bother him that neither Jake Thomas nor Vee Jefferson were recognized for their work.

As usual, Mayor Elizabeth Anderson did most of the gabbing, taking up the first twenty or so minutes. She was followed by district attorney Pamela Lundy. Thankfully, she limited her remarks to approximately five minutes. When the media were finally given the opportunity to ask questions about the two homicides, the mayor and D.A. were savvy enough to let Eric Gamble take over. Eric, like Dantzler, and unlike his predecessor, Richard Bird, had no love for these dog-and-pony shows. He answered each question honestly but without elaboration. *Just the facts, Ma'am*. Dantzler smiled while watching this circus unfold, knowing how uncomfortable Eric was, and how he couldn't wait until the circus shut down.

In related news, Kelly Hilton managed to secure the services of a well-respected—and expensive—defense attorney, leading Dantzler to suspect someone (Robert?) was helping her out financially. The attorney had already given a preview of his defense strategy, arguing that Kelly had been tape recorded without having given her consent. Naturally, he avoided any mention of the thirty-eight Kelly used to commit the murder, or that the bullet was a match to the one that killed Laura Conley.

Surprisingly, Marianne Lofton didn't fight being sent back to Palm Beach to face the charge of murdering Richie Blackstone. Virtually everyone expected her to fight it tooth and nail, certain she'd be willing to spend as much money as necessary to remain in Lexington for as long as possible. But she fooled everyone by putting up no argument at all. There were several theories why, with perhaps the best coming from John Ireland.

"Because Marianne knows that's where the cameras and the spotlights will be."

Dantzler tended to agree with John.

So did Amy Countzler, who said, "A highly publicized murder trial is exactly what that vain bitch lives for. The more sensational, the better she'll like it."

Dantzler also tended to agree with Amy.

Chapter Thirty-Two

With the Laura Conley case behind him, Dantzler could now turn his full attention to identifying the individual who shot and wounded him. He wasn't sure who tried to end his life, but he knew the one person who could supply the answer: Nikki Doyle. She was aware that Dantzler's life had been spared by a stroke of luck when he bent down to pick up that empty cigarette pack. Whoever shared that detail with her had to be the shooter.

But was he acting in haste by dismissing Nikki as the shooter? This was a possibility that continued to nag at him. Maybe she knew about the cigarette pack because she *witnessed* Dantzler bending down and picking it up. Another question nagged at him—was Nikki's alibi legit? Duffy Bryant, the NFL star, said Nikki was at his house at the time of the shooting. However, Dantzler had never followed up by examining the security tapes that supposedly prove Nikki was in Cincinnati. Had Duffy lied for Nikki? Dantzler doubted he had. Why present an alibi that could so easily be disproved if it wasn't true? Dumb as he might be, Duffy was too smart to take such an unnecessary gamble for a woman he hardly knew.

Okay, so Nikki wasn't the shooter. But she definitely did know who was.

RAY DOYLE.

Tommy's brother.

Could he have been the person who fired that shot?

Only one way to find out. Pay him a visit and ask him.

Several factors led Dantzler to cast Ray in the role of shooter. First: As Tommy's older sibling, perhaps Ray made the decision to get the revenge denied to his late brother. Second: Ray was a former Marine who had seen combat in Iraq. This meant he knew how to handle a weapon. Third: Being related to Nikki, Ray, had he taken the shot, would have no qualms about informing Nikki of the cigarette pack incident. That's how she found out about it.

On the drive to Ray's farm, Dantzler formulated a plan for how to approach Ray, a plan that involved telling an outright lie. At some point in their conversation, he would hit Ray with the falsehood, then gauge his reaction, which, Dantzler felt, would likely go one of three ways: Ray would deny it with a straight face; he would deny it but a tell would expose his lie; or he would order Dantzler to get the hell out of his house.

Dantzler was betting the get-the-hell-out option would prevail.

Calling Ray's place a farm was a real stretch, Dantzler quickly assessed. Maybe it had been a farm in the past, but not anymore. The area was dominated by a nice-size two-story wooden house and a barn now surrounded by several fenced-in sections overrun with weeds and tall grass. Those two structures were the last remnants of what may have been a working farm years ago. But Dantzler saw no indication any crops were being grown. There were no animals milling around, nor was there a single piece of farm equipment anywhere in sight. Whatever Ray did for a living, farming wasn't it.

Dantzler parked behind a truck, got out of his vehicle and headed for the house. Passing the truck, he noticed the requisite rifle rack across the back window. He also noticed the rifle was missing. This caused Dantzler to wonder if the absent weapon was the one Ray used in his assassination attempt.

As Dantzler crossed the yard and stepped onto the porch, Ray opened the screen door. Ray was dressed in faded jeans, a black T-shirt and dusty boots. His silver hair was tied in a ponytail. Dantzler was immediately struck by Ray's resemblance to Tommy. They definitely looked more like twins than simply brothers. Dantzler also detected a slight resemblance to Nikki, especially around Ray's eyes. Both had eyes that registered suspicion, wariness and distrust. Definitely all members of the same clan, Dantzler concluded.

"You're a long way from town," Ray stated. "You lost?"

"Like to talk, if you can spare a few minutes," Dantzler said.

"Sure, follow me." Ray led the way to the kitchen. "Want a cold Budweiser? That's what I'm drinking."

"No, thanks."

"Talk here or in the living room?"

"Here's fine."

"Have a seat."

Dantzler pulled back a chair and sat. Ray did the same.

"Talk about what?" Ray asked.

"Why you took a shot at me," Dantzler replied.

"What gives you the idea I took a shot at you?"

"Logic."

"Afraid you've lost me, Dantzler. Logic? Explain what you mean."

"Happy to oblige. Tommy scammed his way out of prison for one reason—to get revenge against me. His death ended that dream. So, being Tommy's older brother, you took it upon yourself to see it through to the end. To complete the mission."

Ray took a long swig of beer, said, "Logic, huh?"

"Also, Nikki knew I survived the shooting because I bent over to pick up a cigarette pack. Only the actual shooter could have shared that detail with her. Had to be someone close to Nikki. Like you."

"Nice theory, but do you have any proof?"

Time for the big lie. Nodding, Dantzler said, "A clean fingerprint was found in the abandoned building directly across the street from the Tennis Center. On the second floor, where the shooter was when he fired that shot. The print was a match to you, Ray."

Ray snickered, said, "That's the best you've got, Dantzler? That's your ace in the hole? I would've expected better from an experienced law enforcement dude like you. We both know that if my fingerprint had actually been found it would be the detectives sitting here questioning me, not an ex-cop. You'll have to do better than that, Dantzler."

Icy under pressure, Dantzler thought. *Score one for Ray.*

"You got me, Ray," Dantzler said, standing. "Yeah, the detectives would be here if they had solid evidence, which, apparently, they don't. Not yet, anyway. You're a cool cookie, Ray, I'll give you credit for that. But you want to know something? Despite your cool demeanor and your clever answer I'm more convinced now than ever that you were the shooter. Just feel it in my gut, you know?"

Shrugging, Ray said, "Conviction without proof is like an ocean without water. Just a bunch of meaningless sand."

"Which only tells me I need to do what it takes to make sure the ocean has plenty of water, wouldn't you say?"

"Good luck with that, Dantzler."

STANDING AT THE DOOR, fresh bottle of Bud in hand, Ray watched Dantzler drive away. When Dantzler's car was out of view, Ray closed the door, went back into the kitchen, sat, picked up his cell phone and keyed in Nikki's number.

"Just had an interesting visit from your favorite ex-detective," Ray said. "Quite the unexpected visit, I might add."

"Jack Dantzler?" Nikki asked.

"In the flesh. And trust me, it was no welfare check. He came asking questions."

"What did he want to know?"

"Was I the one who shot him. Naturally, I denied it. That's when he tried to trick me by using a pathetic lie as a way of getting me to admit taking that shot. A wild fable about my fingerprint having been found in the building where the shot came from. I put the kibosh on that falsehood in about two seconds."

"Did he believe you?"

"Doesn't matter, Nikki." Ray paused, then said, "When your dad and I were kids we had an old mutt we both loved. His name was Luther. Don't ask me who gave him that name, but that's what we called him. Anyway, we would throw a stick as far away as we could, Luther would go fetch it and run it back to us. But when we tried to take it out of his mouth, he refused to let go. Taking the stick away from that crazy dog turned into a real tug of war. Dantzler's like Luther. He's got his teeth into finding the person who shot him and he ain't about to let go. I doubt I've seen the last of him."

"You let me worry about Dantzler. He won't be seeing anyone much longer. I'll make sure of that."

DANTZLER WAS SITTING ALONE in McCarthy's, working on his second pint of Guinness, his thoughts squarely on Ray Doyle. Despite his denial and his failure to fall for the lie, Ray Doyle was the shooter. Dantzler firmly believed this. All he had to do now was prove it.

And he knew where to start.

He checked the time. Nine-twenty. Picking up his drink, he went out the back door to the courtyard, sat at one of the barrels that substituted for tables, took out his cell phone and punched in the number for the shooting range. A squeaky-voice female answered. Dantzler asked to speak with Wendell Dalton. The woman didn't respond; silence ensued for nearly a minute, then Wendell finally answered.

"This is Wendell," he said, sounding slightly out of breath.

"Jack Dantzler, Wendell. Need to ask you for one more favor."

"Name it, you got it, Jack."

"When Nikki Doyle is finished shooting, tell her I called and would like to meet her tonight in McCarthy's Irish Bar. It's located on South Upper, although I'm sure she already knows that. Will you give her that message for me?"

"Be more than happy to, Jack, but there's a big problem. Nikki isn't here. She didn't show up tonight. First time since she started shooting that's she's been a no-show. I doubt she'll show up this late, but if she does, I'll certainly pass along your message."

"You won't see her tonight, Wendell. She has other plans and I'm fairly certain I know what they are."

Dantzler ended the call, sat in the darkness and finished his beer. His thoughts were racing at warp speed, with one thought easily winning the race:

Why didn't I bring my Glock with me?

Chapter Thirty-Three

Reconnaissance time.

Headlights off, Dantzler slowly drove past his house, his eyes scanning the darkness for any sign of Nikki's car. He didn't see one, nor did he expect to. Nikki was clever enough to park some distance away, then hoof it to his house. Once there, gaining entry would pose no problem. She would eventually work her way around back, to the deck, where she would discover the back door was unlocked.

For whatever reason, Dantzler had never felt compelled to lock that door. Perhaps this was a habit that might be worth re-evaluating, he concluded.

Only a single light was on inside the house, the one Dantzler left on in the living room before leaving. One of his cardinal rules was never come home to a dark house. He wasn't sure where this came from, but it went back to long before he became a detective. An incident from his childhood, maybe? He simply didn't know.

Dantzler made one final pass by the house, looking for

any hint Nikki was inside. He saw nothing that indicated she was.

Was Nikki inside? Or was he being paranoid, worrying for no reason, creating a demon when none exist? The rational side of his brain was telling him the idea Nikki was inside the house, weapon drawn, waiting to kill him was absurd. On the face of it, he tended to agree with this assessment. However, his detective's voice screamed otherwise, arguing that to be vigilant was not only wise, it could mean the difference between life and death. This had always been his thinking and he wasn't about to change now.

He drove around the corner and parked on the street that ran parallel to his street. Before exiting his car, he silenced his cell phone; sound at the wrong time could prove fatal. That small-but-important task taken care of, he got out of the car, walked behind the house next to his, then made his way around the edge of the lake that bumped up against his backyard. He immediately realized one fact: His presence had no impact on the birds, crickets and frogs; they simply ignored him while continuing to make their nightly music.

Dantzler had no idea where Nikki might be located (if, indeed, she was even in the house), but he suspected she was somewhere in the living room, her gun aimed at the front door, expecting him to enter there. This was what he *hoped* was the case. If she was on the deck, or standing in the kitchen, he was a dead man.

Quickly crossing the yard, he made it to the steps leading to the deck. They were constructed of wood and were solid and silent. Going up them without being heard was the least of his worries. However, if Nikki was on the deck when he opened the door, well, it would be bang . . .

game, set, match. Still, he had no other alternative. To retrieve his Glock meant getting inside the house. Nikki's location was out of his control.

If Nikki was inside.

Dantzler slowly opened the door, waited several seconds, and hearing no sounds or sensing her presence, he began to crawl snake-like onto the deck. Moving to his left, he came to an opening that led to the hallway. He looked to his right, hoping some light from the living room illuminated the hallway. It didn't; a wall blocked the light, transforming the hallway into a dark, forbidding tunnel no rational individual would be eager to enter.

Undeterred, Dantzler slithered across the hall and into his bedroom, when, suddenly, everything went darker than dark. What little ambient light there had been was now gone. Apparently driven by fear, or perhaps as a way to increase her advantage, Nikki turned off the living room light, plunging the house into total darkness.

This was informative on two fronts for Dantzler—he now knew for sure Nikki was in the house, and that she had just committed a monumental strategic blunder. She had, in effect, yielded her clear advantage to him. This was Dantzler's home turf, he was familiar with every inch of the place, and this knowledge provided him with the upper hand.

He now had no doubt about the eventual outcome.

He would survive this deadly one-on-one match-up.

That is, unless he committed a blunder of his own.

At that moment a voice cracked through the darkness, shattering the silence.

"I know you're in here, Jack," Nikki said. "Can't see you, but I feel your presence. Have bad news for you, Jack. You are going to die tonight. Ray had his chance and blew it. I won't fail."

Ray fired that shot, Dantzler said to himself. *Another mystery solved.*

Dantzler crawled across the room, pulled himself up to a sitting position, his back against the bed, taking time to regulate his breathing. After waiting until his breathing returned to normal, he carefully open a drawer on the table next to his bed, reached in and removed his Glock. Switching the safety off, he stood, stretched the kinks out of his legs and went to the door. He looked first to his right, then to his left, seeing nothing but darkness in either direction.

Keeping his back against the wall, moving to his left, he eased down the hallway until he reached an open door on his right. Through the opening was the living room. Still unsure where Nikki was located, or in which direction she was facing, a tantalizing question confronted him: What's my best move at this point?

Just then, modern technology provided the answer.

Nikki's cell phone buzzed and lit up.

Bad break for Nikki.

Good break for Dantzler.

Good because it let Dantzler know two things for certain—where she was standing, and she was facing toward the deck.

Meaning her back was to him.

Raising his Glock, easing around the corner, he stepped into the living room. "Drop your weapon, Nikki. It's all over."

Ignoring his command, Nikki turned and fired at Dantzler. He heard/felt the bullet whiz past his left ear, missing his head by fewer than three inches before traveling on and smashing into the wall behind him.

Another close call, he thought. *How many does one man get in his lifetime? An existential question to ponder at a more opportune time.*

Dantzler responded by returning fire, squeezing off two quick shots, unsure if either one hits its target. After all, with Nikki's cell phone once again silent and dark, he had essentially aimed at where she had once been standing. If she had moved he likely missed with both shots.

But he hadn't missed. This became apparent only seconds after he fired. Three sounds happening almost simultaneously erased any doubts about the accuracy of his shots: Nikki screamed, her weapon hit the wooden floor and she tumbled over.

Taking no chances, Dantzler ducked behind a chair before turning on the lights. When the room lit up, the scene before him assuaged any lingering fears he might have had. Nikki was on the floor, groaning, having been struck by a bullet just below her left collar bone. The wound was bleeding profusely, requiring immediate attention if she were to survive.

Dantzler stood, quickly crossed the room, bent down and picked up her Glock. After removing the clip and ejecting the bullet from the chamber, he tossed the weapon onto the sofa. Kneeling, he examined the wound, which was, he could tell, a through and through. Nikki, like Dantzler, had missed being killed by a stroke of good fortune. Three inches lower and her heart would have received a direct hit.

Dantzler hurried to the bathroom, grabbed two towels, came back into the living room, took hold of her neck, gently lifted her left shoulder and put one of the towels between the exit wound and the floor. Next, he took the second towel and placed it on the entry wound. Taking her right hand, placing it on the towel, he said, "Keep the pressure on. You're losing a lot of blood. We need to minimize the loss."

"Am I going to die?" Nikki asked, tears running down the side of her face. "Be honest, Jack. Don't bullshit a bullshitter."

"No way, Nikki," Dantzler replied. "I'm not about to let that happen. You're gonna live, and then you're gonna spend the rest of your life in prison. You have my word on that."

Dantzler took out his cell phone, turned it on, waited until it powered up, then placed the call to nine-one-one. He gave the dispatcher his name and address, then informed her what had just happened. He concluded by telling her to send an ambulance and to alert the police.

"Keep applying the pressure, Nikki," Dantzler said, after ending the call. "And try to breathe normal. Help will soon be here."

"A fucking empty cigarette pack. You are one lucky bastard, Dantzler," Nikki managed to say before passing out.

Dantzler took over applying pressure to her wound, silently waiting until help arrived.

And thankful to still be alive.

Nikki was right . . . he was a lucky man.

Chapter Thirty-Four

Vee Jefferson walked into McCarthy's Irish Bar on South Upper Street for the first time in her life. She was on a mission to find Jack Dantzler. It didn't take her long to spot him. Straight ahead, he was sharing a table with Sean Montgomery, David Bloom, and to her surprise, Eric Gamble, the police chief and her first cousin.

Sean did a double-take when he saw Vee striding toward their table. Standing, he said, "Am I hallucinating, or is the lovely Miss Vee Jefferson about to grace this motley crew with her beauty and intelligence?"

"Sit down, Sean, and try not to make a spectacle of yourself," Vee said with mock seriousness. "I know that's a challenge for you, but if you try hard you can manage it. Just requires a little effort, that's all."

"Ah, Vee, how dull my life would be if you didn't continually bust my balls?"

Vee ignored the remark, pointed at the drinks in front of Dantzler and Sean, and said, "Guinness, I presume?"

"Nectar of the gods," Dantzler replied. "Much superior to the scotch and soda Bloom is having. As for your cousin, he claims to still be on duty, hence he is sticking with straight water on the rocks."

Vee glanced at her wrist watch. "Technically, the Boss is off-duty. But I happen to know Eric, like me, has never touched a drop of alcohol in his life. So, him drinking water is par for the course."

"Have a seat, join us," Bloom stated. "At this table, your presence would up the beauty and intellectual levels by a minimum of fifty percent."

"Would love to, Doc," Vee said. "But I don't have the time. I'm here to deliver a message to Jack."

"Message? Who from?" Dantzler asked.

"Your lady friend, Nikki Doyle."

"When did you speak with Nikki?"

"I just came from the hospital. Thought I'd pay her a visit, see how she's doing."

"How is she doing?" Eric asked.

"Improving. The doctor says if all goes well she will be released to us next week."

Dantzler said, "What's the message she wanted you to give me?"

"She requested to meet with you," Vee said.

"Did she say why?"

"No. Just that she wanted to speak with you. I'll probably see her again tomorrow. What should I tell her?"

Dantzler was silent for a moment before answering. "Tell her no thanks. Tell her I'll see her in court."

"Nikki Doyle will never set foot inside of a courtroom, Jack," Sean stated. "She'll cop to the first plea that comes her way. You should visit her. See what's on her mind."

"Think I'll pass, Sean," Dantzler said. "As for Nikki taking a plea, that's not gonna happen."

"Why not?"

"She has nothing to bargain with. Tell these guys why, Vee."

"Nikki wouldn't roll over on Ray," Vee noted. "The case against him was weak to begin with; all the D.A. had was Jack's word Nikki told him Ray was the shooter. Nikki now swears she never made that statement to Jack. Because of that, the D.A. had to cut Ray loose, claiming she didn't have enough evidence to charge him with attempted murder."

Eric said, "We're going to keep working that case, Jack. If there is even a shred of evidence against Ray, we'll find it. Right, Vee?"

"Absolutely," Vee said.

Sean said, "If Nikki gets hit with a lengthy prison sentence she might have a change of heart. Maybe conclude Ray's just not worth it. A woman like her isn't going to enjoy prison life very much. The surroundings don't exactly mesh with her lifestyle."

"What prison life might do is harden her resolve to kill you, Jack," Bloom said. "You know, to make Tommy's dream come true."

Dantzler shrugged, said, "So, what are you saying, Bloom? That I should spend my life worrying about hypotheticals? Ain't gonna happen. If Nikki wants to send someone to take me out, so be it. I'll deal with it when—if—it happens. That's for another day, another time. As for right now, how about another round of drinks? Sure you won't join us, Vee?"

"Already stayed longer than I should," Vee said. "Guys, I'm outta here. Drink responsibly. DUIs can be expensive."

"Not to fear, Vee. That's why we keep Eric around, to serve as our designated driver," Sean said. Then after Vee was gone, "Man, if only I were twenty years younger."

"Like you would have a shot," Bloom said. "Sean, she is so far out of your league you wouldn't have a snowball's chance in hell of getting with Vee."

"You're probably right, Doc. But we all know I do possess mucho charm. If I really lay it on thick, I might win her over."

"Drink your Guinness and stop dreaming, Sean," Dantzler said. "This is the real world, not Hollywood. Regardless of your age, Vee wouldn't give you a second look."

"Damn, that's harsh, Jack." Sean took a long pull of Guinness, said, "Harsh, but true."

"Welcome back to planet Earth, Sean."

SITTING ON HIS DECK, glass of scotch and soda (his third) in hand, Dantzler replayed in his head the events that had transpired during the past few weeks. All things considered, and factoring his role in what had occurred, the overall outcome was better than expected. Not counting, of course, the lone exception—he'd been shot. That was, he admitted, a bummer.

But, overall, he had no complaints.

Mike Conley's name had been cleared, his reputation restored. Two women were awaiting trial for murder—Kelly Hilton in Lexington, Marianne Lofton in Palm Beach. Both were sure to be found guilty, barring any plea deals their smooth-tongue attorneys are able to pull off. Either way, Kelly and Marianne are looking at lengthy prison sentences.

Same went for Nikki Doyle. Her guilt was unquestioned, well beyond any degree of reasonable doubt. Although she lied to keep Ray out of jail, her attempt to murder Dantzler, along with the wound she received during an exchange of gunfire, were facts that could not be successfully denied, disputed or explained, regardless of how clever the smooth-tongue legal eagle she hired might be.

Nikki Doyle was in possession of a one-way ticket to the slammer.

As for Ray Doyle, he was in the clear unless new evidence could be uncovered (Dantzler had his doubts), or Nikki had a change of heart and flipped on Ray (Dantzler definitely didn't believe this would happen). Didn't matter to Dantzler. He wasn't going to waste a minute worrying about Ray Doyle.

Dantzler's thoughts were interrupted when his cell phone began to buzz. He checked the number, which he didn't recognize. Normally, he ignored such late-night calls, but for some unknown reason (three drinks, perhaps?), he elected to answer. Upon hearing the caller's voice, he realized he'd made an ill-advised decision.

Nikki Doyle.

"No need for this call, Nikki," Dantzler stated.

"That's a rather shabby way to greet an old friend," Nikki responded. "Way out of line for a man of your character."

"Cut the bullshit, Nikki. What do you want?"

"For one thing, to ask why you haven't visited me at the hospital. To check on my well-being. That displays a lack of concern, a lack of compassion. You're better than that, Jack."

"I repeat . . . what do you want?"

"To let you know your word doesn't count for very much. Remember what you told me? That I would spend the rest of my life in prison? I'm afraid you badly overshot the mark on that prediction. See, Jack, my lawyer worked out a deal with the district attorney. In exchange for my guilty plea, and for eliminating the need for a costly trial, I agreed to a sentence of ten to twenty years. My guess is, with good behavior I won't have to serve even the minimum. And we both know I'm a good girl."

"You rolled on Ray, right?"

"Never. Ray's a good guy. Let him live in peace."

"Answer this for me, Nikki," Dantzler said. "Was all this worth the heavy price you're going to pay? Fulfilling your dad's dream of getting revenge against me? Don't you recognize that as an insane mission?"

"Insane to you, maybe, not to me."

"Knowing what you're facing, do you have any regrets?"

"Just one. That I didn't kill you."

"You know, Nikki, a wise old man once told me there was no reason why Lucifer couldn't be a female. After meeting you, I have to say he was right. You are one evil bitch."

Dantzler ended the call, put his phone down, picked up his drink and finished it. Leaning back in his chair, he closed his eyes, smiled and listened as the birds, crickets and frogs continued making their comforting night music.

He was sound asleep in two minutes.

Acknowledgments

Thanks to the McCarthy's gang, which includes Roger "Roddy" O'Byrne, Peter Kiely, Bobby O'Byrne, Oisin Kiely, Edwin Kiely, Liza Hendley Betz, Barry Donworth, Joe Bryant, Nick Shinners, Annie Lubicky, Roberto "Mike" Mendez, Sean Sutton, Jimmy Ryan, Greg Clark and Heliodoro Reyes.

Thanks (again) to my solid band of readers for their continued support and encouragement. This list includes, but is not limited to, Julie Watson, Sarah Small, Wanda Underwood, Jake Small, Kendall Phelan, Keitha Vincent, Chris Boggs, Scott Boggs, Christina Young, Suzanne Slinker, Denny Slinker, Bonnie Vincent, Jim Vincent, Jimmie Nell Jenkins, Karen Gentry, Bill Gentry, Erin Tomasic and John Tomasic. Also, family members Richard Iler, Clara Louise Iler and Sally Polan. From the old days, Coach Ralph Evitts, Barbara Lile Powell, Deborah Vincent Eaves, Hugh Sweatt, Charlotte Vincent, Mary Jane Wormer and Ralph Paxton.

As always, thanks to Frank Hall for bringing me into the Hydra family, and to Tony Acree, who somehow manages to juggle multiple tasks while keeping the Hydra Publications and Enigma House Press ships rolling smoothly along. Lastly, to Marilyn, may her memory be a blessing.

Author Bio

Tom Wallace is the award-winning author of eleven previous Jack Dantzler mysteries, including: *Pit of Vipers, 88, The Journal, Heroes For Ghosts, Murder by Suicide, The Poker Game, The Fire of Heaven, The List, Gnosis, The Devil's Racket* and *What Matters Blood*. He also wrote, *Heirs of Cain, Divine Rebel* and *Bloody Sundae*.

His novel, *Gnosis*, won the prestigious Claymore Award at the Killer Nashville Writers Conference, and *The Devil's Racket* captured the Mystery Writers top award. *Murder by Suicide* was an Amazon best-seller.

Tom, a former sportswriter, has written several successful sports-related books, including *The Kentucky Basketball Encyclopedia, So You Think You're a Kentucky Wildcats Basketball Fan?, Inside/Outside: A Behind the Scenes Look at Kentucky Basketball* and *Golden Glory: The History of Central City Basketball*.

While sports editor for the Henderson *Gleaner*, Tom was twice honored by the Kentucky Press Association for writing the Best Sports Story in Kentucky.

Tom is a Vietnam vet who currently lives in Lexington, Kentucky.

Made in the USA
Columbia, SC
28 January 2025